FINDING APRIL

RON BURROWS

Chalk Stream Books

Ron Burrows asserts his moral right to be identified as the author of this book.

Published in partnership with Chalk Stream Books

www.chalkstreambooks.com

Printed and bound in the UK.

Dedication

For my family and friends

Illustrations

By Alice Mawdsley
alicemawdsley.com

Chapter 1

**Backworth Colliery, Northumberland
October 1935**

At sixteen years old, Benjamin Hardy was blessed with the sort of adolescent good looks that would mature with age into handsomeness – an intelligent face, a strong jawline, dark brown wavy hair, and chestnut-coloured eyes. At five foot eleven, he was also inches taller than most other boys in his street and had the sturdy build of someone they'd never mess with. He'd left school in 1933, just after his fourteenth birthday, then the school-leaving age in England. In Backworth, the Northumberland coal mining village where he'd done his growing up, all the boys who'd left school with him then had gone straight into the colliery. But not him. Being a coal miner for the rest of his life didn't fit the mental image that young Benjamin Hardy had conjured of his future self.

He wanted to be the sort of chap who wore a clean shirt every day and did interesting things; the sort of chap who had an occupation that was (a) stimulating, (b) would expand his horizons, and (c) would lead to a fulfilling life. Perhaps it was too much to expect at a time when so many men were unemployed, but that didn't stop him dreaming. He knew he had it in him to do better than his father and all the other men in his street who came home grubby and black-faced every day. He also knew that his girlfriend, April Palmer, hoped that he would make something more of himself too. He and April had been sweethearts since their latter days at school, and, like any young man besotted by a woman, he wanted to impress her and win her admiration. So, when she had wrinkled her nose at the idea of him working underground, he had taken notice; and her higher hopes and ambitions for him had also encouraged him to follow his heart.

In the two years since he'd left school, therefore, he'd tried desperately to find other employment that would give him the opportunity to learn and progress. He'd knocked on the doors of a dozen local businesses and factories as far as his cycling legs would carry him to enquire about trainee positions and apprenticeships; he'd visited every 'Jobs Vacant' board in his locality again and again; and he'd explored every other possible avenue he could think of. Yet the only work he could get was menial and casual – like being a gofer for a local tradesman or doing odd jobs here and there that no one else would do. As hard as he'd tried, moreover, he still wasn't able to bring home enough money to pay his keep. So, in the end, paternal pressure had prevailed, and he had to concede that his bid to strike out on a different path in life had failed. For generations, the Hardy men had been coal miners, his father had told him, sternly. 'It's what we Hardys do,' he'd said. So now, it seemed, it was what Ben would have to do too.

Ben's father, Levi Hardy, was a good, hard-working coal miner of few words who bore the burdens of his life without resentment or complaint. He had the gaunt face and sallow complexion of a labouring man employed in a subterranean profession and the yellow fingers of a heavy smoker. He'd joined the Backworth Colliery Company as a pit boy straight from school but had volunteered for the Northumberland Fusiliers when the last war broke out. Having survived the trenches of the Somme as a corporal rifleman, he'd gone back to the colliery after the Armistice and had worked there ever since. He was a hewer now and earning top pay – one of the men who worked directly at the coal face hewing out the coal. With a tall and wiry frame, powerful shoulders and strong arms, he could have passed for a middleweight boxer.

As the day of Ben's first descent approached, Levi had taken his young son aside to tell him what to expect. 'You'll be starting as a putter,' he'd explained. 'Working right behind me and the other hewers at the coal face. Your job will be to shift the coal that we cut out and send it on its way to the lift shaft. We work as a team on a piecework basis, which means we only get paid for the coal we produce. So, you'll have to work fast, OK!' Levi stuck out his jaw to emphasise his point. 'If you let too much of the stuff pile up behind us, it'll slow us down, and then we all lose money. Understood? But don't worry, lad, you'll be shown what to do and you won't be alone.' Ben had listened attentively but could not conceal his rising apprehension as his first day approached. He'd heard stories from his old school friends about how filthy, claustrophobic, and backbreaking the work was. The whole thing sounded very frightening. He wondered if he'd be up to it.

'Look Ben,' said Levi, seeing the look of consternation on his son's face and not wanting to frighten him off, 'it's not difficult work! You just have to put your back into it. Work hard and you'll soon be earning a good, steady wage, and when you marry that girl of yours, you'll get a colliery house and free coal with it! That won't be so bad, will it?' He smiled encouragingly. Ben was not so sure, but by then he had accepted his fate, at least for the time being, consoling himself that he'd have money in his pocket and not have to drop his gaze when he passed his former schoolmates in the street. Backworth was a close-knit community of miners whose dangerous work created a sense of manly pride and comradeship amongst its membership. If you weren't one of them, you didn't seem to count for much.

As dawn's light crept under the curtains of Ben's bedroom window that first morning, Ben raised himself from his pillow and quietly turned back his bedclothes. His twelve-year-old brother, Frank, was still asleep in the adjacent bed and Ben didn't want to wake him. The two boys shared the back-bedroom of the terraced cottage in Walkworth Street provided rent-free by the Colliery when their parents had married. Ben could already hear his mother pottering in the kitchen below, preparing breakfast. She'd also be filling the break tins that would get her two men through the day.

Kneeling up on his bed, Ben pulled the curtains apart and propped his elbows on the windowsill to look out.

He rubbed the condensation from the windowpane with his pyjama sleeve and saw at once that it was black with coal dust. He'd be in for a scolding if his mother spotted it. She'd told him off before for this, but he smiled at the thought – a ticking off from her amounted to no more than a cuff around his ears and a few cross words – which usually ended with her ruffling his hair and an indulgent smile. He loved his Ma and liked to pull her leg and make her laugh, which she didn't seem to do that often. At five foot two, she was petite and nice-looking, but had so little flesh on her frame that Ben sometimes worried that she'd break if he squeezed her too hard. What she might lack in physical presence, however, was made up by her indefatigable spirit. She was a determined little lady, obsessive about her house-cleaning and the whiteness of her laundry, although she must have known that she was fighting a losing battle with so much coal dust in the air.

The windowpane through which Ben now peered revealed a scene that had greeted him every morning in all the years he could remember. To anyone not used to it, it would have been a depressing sight – a coal-blackened landscape of slag heaps, shunting tracks, and industrial detritus, with coal dust and smoke swirling about it on the wind. Ben had grown up with all that and took it all for granted. It was his world and all he'd ever known. The pit head itself was surrounded by a cluster of oddly proportioned buildings housing machinery of one sort or another. A tall steel latticework gantry sat above them carrying two huge, spoked wheels which spun first one way then the other almost continuously day and night. This was the headgear over which the cables ran from the winding house to the cages in the shaft below that moved men, coal, and equipment between the tunnels and the surface. Ben gazed at them ruefully as they began to spin again. The first gangs of the night shift were probably already on their way up, he thought – which meant that it would soon be his turn to go down.

Next to the gantry, two brick chimneys pumped out great volumes of black smoke from the boilers that raised the steam to power the mine machinery – the winding motors, the coal washing and grading machines, the conveyors and so on. The graded coal was stored in two huge hoppers straddling lines of empty wagons ready to be filled. Several saddle-tank engines were in attendance nearby with steam already up. Like sheepdogs, they'd soon be marshalling the wagons into sidings, and later haul them off to the Tyne and Wear where the coastal coalers waited.

Watching from his bedroom window, Ben had always been fascinated by these little engines as they puffed about so busily. It was as if they had minds of their own. He was still watching them dreamily as the pithead whistle piped up. A continuous wailing tone signalled an accident at the pit, a time when wives and loved ones rushed to the pithead gate and waited in dread. The intermittent blasts that morning, however, signalled the change-over of the shifts, and this time the whistle was calling Ben too.

A creak on the landing floorboards told Ben that his father was already up and about – he'd probably already done his daily chores and would be getting ready to go. Then came his quiet knock on the bedroom door followed by his muffled voice:

'Ben lad, you up?'

'Just getting up, da.' Ben called back. 'Be down in a minute.

'Then look sharp, lad! Your ma's got your breakfast ready.

Leaving his brother still fast asleep, Ben dressed himself quickly and went downstairs to join his father at the table.

Susannah Hardy fussed about the kitchen as her two men tucked into a breakfast of porridge and home-baked bread, thickly spread with beef dripping from the Sunday roast. It was the sort of substantial meal she knew her husband needed when he faced a hard day's work of manual labour. This morning, she was making sure that her son was as well fed too. But she hardly spoke as she flitted about her domain in her pinafore, glancing at her son from time to time with an anxious look upon her face. This was the morning that she had dreaded; the morning that her first son would join her husband underground. Her men would soon be setting out across the back fence and over the shunting tracks on the short-cut to the pithead. From her kitchen window, she'd watched Levi go off that way almost every working day – his canvas satchel on his shoulder, his kneeling pads strapped around his knees, and his favourite old cap upon his head. Sometimes, he'd meet up with other miners from their street and they'd chatter and laugh together as they ambled towards the lift shaft and the cage that would take them untold hundreds of feet underground. Like all the wives and all the mothers in all the cottages in her street, Susannah knew that a coal mine was a dangerous place to work. She tried not to dwell upon it, but it worried her. Some of the men she'd grown up with had lost their lives or limbs in those deep tunnels. Now that the day had come when her son would face those dangers too, she could not help but be afraid for him.

Chapter 2

Benjamin Hardy's family lived in one of the four long terraces of brick-built, slate-roofed cottages constructed by the Backwoth Colliery Company in the late eighteen-hundreds for miners and their families. As well as these uninspiring terraces, the village of Backworth also included some individual older houses, and a school, a bank, a cobbler, a post office, a chapel and a church, and a Co-op and a hardware store. On the southern edge of the village stood the former Backworth Hall, a large Georgian-style grand house with several acres of parkland, purchased by the Colliery and remodelled as a miners' sports and recreation club – a calculated investment by the Colliery directors in their workers' health, welfare, and productive working lives. The row in which Levi Hardy and his family lived backed directly onto the unattractive mining landscape already described, but the nearby allotments provided a small oasis of relief – and some winter vegetables and summer fruit. The miners' cottages were all identical: two rooms up and two rooms down, a lean-to scullery, an outside lavatory, a coal shed, a tiny patch of grass (which Susannah called her garden), and a walled yard where the dustbin, the tin bath, and the washing tub and mangle were usually kept.

The village was located about three miles north of the city of Newcastle-upon-Tyne and about the same distance west of Whitley Bay and the North Sea coast. There were regular bus and train services southwards to the nearby city and northwards to Morpeth Alnmouth, and Berwick-on-Tweed. The surrounding countryside was largely made up of woods and arable and pastoral farmland owned, like most land in the area, by the Duke of Northumberland – who also made a great deal of revenue by way of royalties from the black gold extracted in the tunnels deep below. From the top of the highest ground in that gently undulating landscape, it was possible to catch glimpses of the North Sea.

———

At the end of Ben's first day underground – the day that had started with the dismal view through his smeary bedroom window – he was walked home by his father and a fellow mine worker, a near neighbour in Ben's street. They walked amongst hundreds of other miners who'd poured like a torrent through the pit gate when the whistle had signalled the end of their shifts. At changeover times like these, the streets were full of drably dressed men going home in crumpled jackets and baggy trousers. Levi's normal route home would have been to retrace his morning short-cut across the railway tracks. That day, however, needing to buy tobacco at the Co-op, he led his two companions via the village centre. They walked three abreast along the lane in that direction, with Ben sandwiched between the two veterans as if to stop him running off to sea, an idea that had crossed his mind more than once during the day. His body was still recovering from the sheer intensity of his labours. The work had been more exhausting than he'd expected. His hands were sore, his muscles ached, his phlegm and nostrils were black, and when he blinked, his eyelids felt like sandpaper. His mind was still reeling from the experience.

The coal face where Ben had been put to work that day, was at least half a mile from the bottom of the lift shaft in which he'd made his first dizzying descent. Before any of the men did any work at all, therefore, they'd had to walk in single file along dank, dark tunnels. In the dim light of their helmet-mounted safety lamps, the silent column had constantly to duck and weave to skirt the props and low timbers. The further they penetrated, the narrower and lower the tunnel became, forcing the men eventually to walk bent-backed as they approached the coal face to be worked that day.

Ben's first task had been to clear the pile of rubble left by the previous shift. He'd been teamed up with a fellow new boy for that, and once they'd finished, the pair had spent the rest of the day shovelling and shifting coal. Their job had been to clear what had been cut out by the hewers and move it on its way using little cast-iron wagons (called tubs) for transport. A putter from a coal face further down the tunnel had been sent back to show the new boys what to do, which he'd done with some impatience, no doubt anxious about his own team's productivity. He'd had to shout above the constant din of mine machinery and the thud and scrape of axes and shovels echoing in the tunnel. 'And put your backs into it! The more you move, the more you'll earn,' he'd added, as he'd left them to get on with it.

In one of the few breaks taken for a swig of cold tea from their tins, Ben's fellow new boy introduced himself as Tim Wainwright. Only fourteen years old, he was small and puny. His father was a senior administrator in the colliery office, and his influence had secured his son's employment at the mine. Like Ben, young Tim had been pressed into mine work to earn his keep. But the lad was clearly not very strong, nor was he very happy, and strain and consternation had creased his brow the whole day.

It was rough and tough work for which Ben's young body was not prepared, and the day turned into a frantic race to keep the coal moving fast enough to stop the hewers from complaining. If the coal piled up too much, it got in the way and slowed them down, which earned the two new boys harsh rebukes. The tubs ran on narrow-gauge tracks that passed behind them., and once filled, had to be pushed a good fifty yards to where they could be hooked on to the loop that would drag them to the lift shaft. Tim and Ben had worked together, but even working their hearts out, they were only just able to shift the coal fast enough. One of the hewers shouted sarcastically that a lame pit pony could do better. To which another added: 'Ah, but these young nippers come fully fed and watered and don't need mucking out!' The comment was met with a wry grin from Ben, but it didn't help his morale.

Waiting at the hook-on point, the checker made a tally of the tubs arriving from the different coal faces to determine what each shift would be paid. He showed the boys how to hook the tubs on and send them on their way to the lift shaft. But as they disappeared, empty tubs returned, which then had to be pushed all the way back – where the shovelling would start all over again! When they finally put their shovels down at the end of the day, both new boys looked completely shell-shocked.

Ben's first day had been eight hours of gruelling, blistering labour, but his hard work had obviously been noticed. 'Good on you, boy,' said one of hewers, as tools were stacked away. 'You've earned a pint at the Welfare tonight,' another said, 'if you can lift it!' he laughed.

Ben knew and respected these men, so their praise counted. His father flashed him an encouraging grin too as he straightened his bent frame and wiped his black hands on a dirty rag. For a moment, the acknowledgement raised Ben's flagging spirits, but he recognised these compliments for their purpose, which was to encourage him to do the same again tomorrow (and again and again!). If he were not careful, he might find himself boxed in by his own desire to please his elders and impress his peers. An inner voice made him wary; he understood the power of peer pressure and was determined to resist it. He'd already made up his mind.

Though he'd worked hard all day, Ben's thoughts had been in full rebellion throughout. Working in dim light, breathing coal-dust laden air, Ben's chest ached, and his eyes were sore. His ears still rang from the incessant clattering and scraping of pickaxes and shovels. The work had been in tight, claustrophobic spaces with water dripping on his back through the fissures above his head, and his boots had quickly become sodden. As the coalface was driven forward foot by foot, moreover, the earth above had settled, and the timbers had creaked under the shifting weight. More props and timbers had been manhandled into place by the carpenters, but while the hewers had worked on apparently regardless, Ben and Tim sometimes found themselves cowering in fear of a cave-in at any moment.

All day, Ben had watched the men around him working so hard and uncomplainingly and had marvelled at their fortitude. He recognised, however, that he was neither built of the same stuff physically, nor would he be able mentally to accept the sheer tedium of the work long-term. He accepted that he'd have to bear it for a while, but from that first day he resolved that it would not be for long. As he walked home that day, sandwiched between his two veteran companions, he had to struggle to stop himself blurting all his feelings out. He had found the whole experience a sort of purgatory.

He was sure also that young Tim Wainwright had felt the same. The boy would return the following day and the day after and the day after that, and he would always try his hardest; but he was simply not strong enough and it was clear that he would not last. Within the month, he would be working topside in the admin office with his father, a job for which he was patently better suited. During those few weeks of working together, however, the support that Ben had given his young companion had built a friendship. It was a friendship that Ben would nurture. Some instinct told him that having a friend working in administration might come in handy later on.

Chapter 3

April and Ben

As the three men turned a corner on their round-about route home, Ben caught sight of April and her sister in the distance. Still so far away, they were unlikely to have spotted him amongst so many other home-coming miners on the street, but he shuddered at the thought of being recognised as they came closer.

April was the last person in the world he'd want to see him looking as he did. Until today, inconsequential as his earlier work had been, he'd at least been able to pretend that he was doing better for himself, just as he'd set out to do. His present appearance, however, would make his failure obvious in that respect. If he'd been less coy about stripping off in the pit-head baths and exposing his adolescent private parts to all and sundry, he might have cleaned himself up a bit. But having not been brave enough to do so, his face was so smeared with coal dust and sweat, his hair so matted and disordered, and his clothes so grimy and dishevelled that even his mother might pass him by without recognising him. His only hope now was that April might not recognise him either.

———————

No one would describe April Palmer as stunningly beautiful. She didn't have the sensual lips, the lustrous hair, and the sultry eyes that might have labelled her like that; but there was a certain prettiness about her features that Ben found captivating. He loved her clear blue eyes and rosy cheeks and the way she wore her fair, wavy hair. Tall and slender, she was a good physical match for him too. It was her poise, however, and her gentleness and quiet self-assurance that had drawn Ben to her at the beginning and made her so attractive to him now. Ben had fallen for April the first time he had set his eyes on her when she first took her seat in the senior classroom at the parish school. For Ben, it had been love at first sight, and it hadn't taken him long to make his liking for her known – which to his delight was soon reciprocated. Their relationship had matured as time had gone by. At first, Ben's father had dismissed his son's infatuation as puppy love – it seemed to irritate him that his son should be so preoccupied with a girl when other more manly pursuits should better fill his time. But Ben's feelings for April ran much deeper than his father understood, and it was not long after the couple had started to walk out together more regularly that Ben came to think (secretly in his young heart) that April was the girl that he would like to marry.

Schooling for most youngsters finished when they reached the age of fourteen in those days. The school term in which that birthday fell marked the end of state-funded education and the start of work, with not a huge amount of learning crammed into those young heads save the three 'R's and some random snippets of history and geography. But, while Ben's formal education had come to an end at that young age, April's had continued. Her father, the owner of a petrol station and automobile repair business on the eastern outskirts of the village, was well off enough to send his two daughters to an independent girls' school in Newcastle to improve their prospects for employment. The school was a short daily commute by train from Backworth station, and April was now in her final year there preparing for her school certificate. Her sister, Susan, two years her senior, was already employed as a clerical assistant at the Backworth branch of the National Provincial Bank and April had set her heart on joining her. The two sisters were bubbly, flirtatious, and gregarious – amongst the brightest buttons in Backworth's button box. They never failed to draw admiring glances when they walked out together in their Sunday frocks.

Ben had been flattered and amazed to have won the attachment of such a lovely girl as April. Young as they were, the pair had become devoted to each other. They'd meet on summer evenings and at weekends to walk out together across the fields or along the grassy banks of the little burn that wound above the village heading for the sea. When the air was warm and the ground dry, they'd find themselves a secluded spot to sit together and talk – about anything and nothing – and sometimes just quietly contemplate the slowly moving water with hardly a word passing between them for minutes on end. The physical side to their relationship was proper and restrained – the private intimacies that took place in leafy glades beside the babbling brook, would not have shocked her parents

– at least not too much. He and she simply enjoyed the closeness of each other's company. It had seemed to Ben that they were made for each other.

With April's move to her new school, however, things had begun to change. As the months had passed, each was developing a sense that their lives might be leading in different directions. She was mixing with her independent school friends socially – other young people with backgrounds like her own, with fathers in business or the professions. These people were not at all like Ben, an odd-jobbing miner's son living in a miner's cottage in the drab colliery terraces behind the railway sidings – a young man apparently with no prospects other than a grubby life of toil. Ben would sometimes meet these new friends of April's when in her company, and he immediately felt awkward. They spoke a different language, used words that Ben didn't understand, and had ambitions set on careers and salaries than were outside his comprehension. Before long, even the conversation between the pair had changed too – became less easy, less spontaneous – and Ben began to feel that he had better watch his p's and q's. Educationally, his progress had stalled since he'd left school, while she was moving on. In the company of these friends of hers he felt his lack of learning keenly, soon resorting to any excuse to avoid meeting them. In his tender young heart, April was still the love of his life, but somehow it felt as if he were being slowly left behind – and that their relationship was no longer as secure as he once thought.

When Ben had been so taken by surprise at the sight of April and her sister on his walk home from the mine after his first day underground, his first instinct had been to hide himself, using his two companions as cover. Hoping to pass by unnoticed on the opposite pavement, he kept his head down and flicked only occasional glances in her direction. She looked so prim and neat in her school uniform with her straw boater sitting jauntily on the back of her head, and she had that confident air about her that young girls often seem to acquire when they know they are attractive. Ben found the sight of her entrancing. It was the way she walked so uprightly and so elegantly, the bounce of her wavy hair, and her lovely, bonny, animated face that Ben found so mesmerizing. Such bewitching femininity must have triggered a sudden rush of signals across the neural networks of Ben's brain, for his heart literally skipped a beat at the sight of her. Still watching, he saw her hand rise to her lips as if something had amused her. It must surely have been a response to something that her sister had said, but in Ben's young and insecure mind, he thought they must be laughing at him – looking like a chimney sweep! He dragged his eyes away, feeling hurt and embarrassed. If the earth beneath his feet could have opened up and swallowed him at that moment, he would have considered it a blessing.

But he could not keep his eyes away for long. As the two sisters came closer, he threw them another glance, this time unavoidably catching April's eyes just as she caught his. Her sister was looking across at him too, and both were smiling affectionately now. This time, he could not tear his eyes away, for he saw that he had been recognised. He felt his cheeks grow hot – though neither of the girls could possibly have seen his blush under all the muck on his face. Ben's father must have noticed the girls' glances and his son's shrinking reaction to them, for he nudged him to recapture his attention. The two older men had been talking about football all this time, but Ben had not been tuning in. He reacted to his father's nudge with a start, feigning interest for a second or two, but then glanced back across the street. April's eyes were still upon him as the two girls drew opposite, her face more serious now. She threw him a little wave and a knowing, sympathetic smile as if she understood his discomfiture. Her gesture signalled her fondness for him and gave him hope that she might still be his. Yet, for all that, he could not shake off a deep sense of unease that in his present state and with his present prospects he would lose her.

His father's husky voice interrupted his thoughts. 'You did well today, our Ben,' said his father as the threesome walked on. 'So don't be put off. I probably felt a bit like you when I first started,' he added, wrapping an arm around his son's shoulders. 'It's tough work, I know, but you'll get used to it, believe me. And, like I said, you'll earn yourself a colliery house of your own and good money too. So, stick with it, son. It'll get easier, just you see. And it'll be good for us to be working together as a team, won't it? Father and son, eh?'

Ben nodded absently, while noticing out of the corner of his eye that April and her sister had already turned the corner at the end of the street, and thus disappearing from his view. Her father's garage, with its petrol pumps and workshop, was on Springfield Road, the main road eastwards out of the village on the way to Whitley Bay. Ben had an urge to run after her but knew it would make things worse. Besides, his father's eyes were still upon him, waiting for a response.

'Looking forward to it, Dad,' he replied with as much conviction as he could muster; but in his heart, he contemplated the next descent into the depths with dread. His feelings must have shown on his face because he saw his two companions exchanging glances as they crossed the street towards their respective front doors. The two men's expressions were revealing: Ben's father's look signalled: 'the boy'll get used to it; just give him time.' But his neighbour returned his companion's glance with a derisive smirk that said: 'He'll bloody well have to, poor sod!'

Chapter 4

One day underground followed another while Ben threw himself doggedly into his work, not wanting to let his father or his workmates down. His pride also demanded that he daily demonstrate strength, willingness, and endeavour to earn respect and position within his gang. Whatever his secret ambitions, he was determined not to risk losing face amongst his elders and his peers. The days turned into weeks and the weeks into months, and despite the initial shock, he became hardened to his labour and grew in stature amongst his fellows. Indeed, he might even admit to a quiet sense of satisfaction at the end of each day to see the product of his shift's work trundling along the railway tracks towards the docks. He and these new comrades of his had slaved all day to produce the glistening black rock that fuelled the nation – it was hard and dirty work without glory or acclaim, done out of sight and taken for granted. It seemed to Ben that so long as the population had enough coal to keep their houses warm, their streets lit, and enough coal to keep the generators turning, nobody much cared about the miners. It was a case of 'out of sight, out of mind'. Ben sensed nevertheless that the miners themselves knew how important their work was, and they were fiercely proud of it. There was a nobleness in such work, Ben thought; and despite himself, he came to feel strangely honoured to be accepted as one of them, to join them 'down the Welfare' of an evening, to listen to their stories and to join in the singing of their songs. It was this very sense that he was being drawn yet further in by the strengthening bonds of comradeship and mutual dependency, however, that also reinforced his instinct that he must not allow himself to be drawn in too much.

Yet Ben's rebellious thoughts were tempered by an underlying sense of insecurity. To strike out on a different path posed uncertainty and risk – the risk of leaving the fold, of not being 'one of us', the uncertainty of securing the yet undefined new way of life he sought. It would have been excusable for him to abandon his ambitions and instead to make the best of what he had, but for his own sake he knew that he must still try to move on as soon the chance to do so came. The longer he left it, the more difficult a move would become. He was obsessed with the thought of working in the daylight and the fresh air and being free to spread his wings, but he could not imagine what form this alternative life might take. Only in his dreams would he shake off the shackles that restrained him and break free of the relentless and unchanging tasks that confined him.

Perhaps he also coveted a life that used his brain rather than his brawn. After all, there must certainly be easier ways to earn a living than shovelling coal and pushing coal tubs around! He knew he lacked learning, but he had a sharp wit and a hunger to better himself. All he needed was the opportunity to put these assets to work. If he was honest with himself, he also wanted to elevate himself in April's eyes – to set himself apart and above the potential rivals that he now had in her better-educated social circles. It might take time to find the new path that would achieve this goal, but the drive to do it was strong. In time, he would come to realise how fundamental the drive to win back April's admiration had been in setting the course of his future life.

It was the early summer of the following year that he finally decided to act. On one of his days off, with savings from his pay in his pocket, he took the train into Newcastle, a thirty-minute stopping train directly to the centre of the city. Ben's father and mother had taken him and his brother there once on a summer holiday outing when they were younger. They had crossed the Tyne on the ferry to Gateshead where there was a street market and a visiting fair with swings and penny-rides in the shadow of the Tyne bridge. It had been sunny that day, full of new and colourful experiences, and his eyes had been opened to the wider and more exciting world that lay outside his village.

The memory of that family outing was still in his mind as he got off the train in Newcastle's Central Station and followed signposts towards the dockside, thinking that that might be a good place to start his search. He walked along side-streets of tall, terraced houses with window boxes and cast-iron railings until he got to a main thoroughfare, where walls were plastered with colourful posters advertising Colman's Mustard and Craven "A" cork-tipped cigarettes. The pavements there were crowded and noisy – full of people striding one way or the other with such apparently serious purpose, like a tidal flow in full flood. But here and there along the pavement, like islands in the stream, small gatherings of men stood about with hands in pockets looking glum. His route took him past flat-capped street-traders who bellowed from their stalls and women in flowery hats selling things from baskets. There was so much activity and hustle and bustle that Ben's eyes and ears could hardly take it all in. In those days, horse-drawn omnibuses still clattered on the cobbles, but there were few. The steel wheels of electric trolleybuses were also rumbling and squealing on rails that ran along the same routes, while spluttering automobiles and horse-drawn carriages dodged and wove in a fight for space. Ben took his life in his hands just to cross the street. It was smelly too. The unwholesome stench of horse dung and the fumes of gasoline exhausts and hot lubricating oil formed a pungent mixture that brought a handkerchief to his nose. He knew straight away that city life was not for him.

Eventually, he came to the dockside just up-river from the great iron arch of the Tyne Bridge. It was the first time that he had been out of Backworth alone and he felt like a real adventurer. Here, along the quay, there were more men standing about, all dressed in grubby jackets and baggy trousers, wearing shirts without collars and flat caps as if the attire were some sort of motley uniform. He wandered along the waterfront looking at the coastal and fishing vessels loading and unloading, wondering if the life of a seaman would suit him. The clear skies and fresh air of the open seas were suddenly appealing after months labouring in dark and suffocating tunnels with tons of earth above his head. On impulse, he approached a couple of men standing by the gangplank of one such vessel, a dirty coaster with black smoke rising from its funnel, its derricks busy swinging loads from the dockside into its hold.

'Excuse me, sir,' he asked, tentatively interrupting the two men's conversation. 'Can I ask you how someone like me might go about finding regular work at sea?'

The two men fell silent mid-breath and gave Ben a baffled look. 'Well now, lad, what work d'you do now to earn a living?' The man's response had a slightly mocking tone.

'Backworth Colliery,' Ben replied. 'I'm a putter and general worker – shovelling coal most of the time, but don't much like it.'

'Well, my advice would be to stick to it, lad,' said the man. 'You're lucky to have a job at all. It's hard enough to get any permanent work these days and you'll certainly get no work around here. You saw them men standing about along the quay, didn't you?' he added, nodding his head in that direction. 'What d'you think they're doing? Waiting for, their ship to come in?' The man's derisiveness stung Ben's fragile pride and made him feel a little foolish. He heard the two men laughing as he walked away with his hands thrust firmly into his pockets.

Wandering further down the quay, Ben tried a few more times to engage with likely-looking officers on the decks of moored vessels, but he soon came to realise that he was deluding himself. As things would turn out, it was just as well that he didn't sign up for a life at sea, because it would never have suited him, and a better opportunity was anyway just about to present itself.

He left the waterside feeling despondent. Back on the busy main street, he now realised that all those little groups of men he had seen standing about earlier must be looking for work too. Unemployment in the area was clearly high, and in finding a new way to earn a living there would be a lot of competition. It had been his father's influence with the mine foreman, after all, that had got him his job at the colliery when other hopefulls were still queuing at the pit head gate. It now dawned on him that the steady work and the steady income of a miner would be difficult to match. Reality was dawning and he began to wonder if he should be grateful for the work he had and just put up with it.

Halfway along Northumberland Street, taking what he thought must be a short cut in the direction of the railway station, he turned down a narrow side-street. The street looked quiet and interesting, with several little shops and small business premises dotted amongst the tall, terraced houses on both sides, some with grand steps, pillars, and porches. It was a relief, suddenly, to find himself not pressed by the pedestrian surge and traffic commotion of the main thoroughfare that had raised his pulse. He slowed his pace to allow himself some time to look into the shop windows.

He passed a small hardware shop, and then a baker's with cakes and current buns on display. Seeing such delights, he suddenly felt hungry and bought himself a Chelsea swirl, then continued along the street eating the confection, tearing the soft, current-dotted dough from the sugar-crusted coil bit by bit, while gazing idly into more shop windows along the way. In one of them, a second-hand bookshop, a poster displaying the image of an aircraft caught his eye. On closer scrutiny, he saw the poster to be an old pastel-coloured recruitment poster for the then newly formed Royal Air Force. There were others of the same vintage, their edges a little dog-eared, their colours faded by the sun. These old posters must have been a forgotten backdrop for some previous book display.

Below the words: 'JOIN THE ROYAL AIR FORCE' written in bold letters, was a depiction of a biplane of some unidentifiable type. It was an amateurishly painted scene of an attack against a German submarine, which was already on fire apparently as a result of the airborne attack. Under the picture, were the words: 'AND MAKE A DIRECT HIT', below which, in a sepia panel, framed by art-nouveau-style swirls, the script read:

AGE 18 to 50 YEARS. Rate of pay 1/6 to 12/- per day.

IF YOU JOIN THE ROYAL AIR FORCE VOLUNTARILY,
YOU CANNOT BE TRANSFERRED TO THE ARMY
OR THE NAVY WITHOUT YOUR CONSENT.

The message on the poster was certainly way out of date, Ben realised, but he'd heard recently on the wireless that recruitment to the armed forces was back in full swing – apparently in response to German re-armament. He'd noticed headlines to this effect plastered all over the newsstands as he'd passed them at the station. 'RAF TO BE TREBLED IN SIZE' said one. 'YOUR COUNTRY NEEDS YOU – AGAIN!' said another. But it had not occurred to him before that such a career might be open to the likes of him. After all, he had no qualifications to speak of and had not done particularly well at school, except perhaps in drawing, sport, and arithmetic, a combination unlikely to equip him to pass any service entrance tests. On the other hand, he reasoned, if the RAF was so desperate to sign-up new recruits, even someone like himself might be accepted. To have come across this poster must be more than mere coincidence, Ben thought, and he wondered if some higher power was guiding him. A rush of adolescent enthusiasm was now surging in his veins for it seemed that the RAF might be the very thing for him. He'd got a taste for mechanics by helping April's father in his motor repair workshop, and the idea of working on aeroplanes and engines suddenly seemed very appealing. Had he not stumbled upon a RAF recruitment office a short while later, however, his ardour might have cooled, but spotting its frontage enthused him more, and he immediately went inside. A WAAF corporal stood behind the counter. Ben would have liked to talk to her, but she seemed rather overwhelmed by a queue of other young men making enquiries too. Too impatient to wait his turn, Ben simply picked up some pamphlets and an application form and left to catch his train. If he liked what he read later, he thought to himself, he would return another day.

By the time he got home that afternoon, more sober reasoning had taken hold, and it had planted several reservations in his mind. The foremost of these, being frank with himself, was a reluctance to put too much distance between him and his beloved April, whose feelings for himself he still hoped to enliven in one way or another. It was no good finding a new way of life with better prospects and status that would impress her, he reasoned, if it took him too far away or for too long. He already felt insecure in his relationship and thus feared what might occur in his absence, especially when there was evidently some serious competition about for her affections. Not wanting to put too fine a point on it, it was the green hand of jealousy that now took hold of his thoughts, and it was quite debilitating. He therefore hid the RAF forms under his socks and underwear in his drawer while he mulled things over.

Chapter 5

Several more months were to pass while Benjamin Hardy did his mulling over. Meanwhile, he continued to endure his toil in the Backworth tunnels hour by hour and day by day throughout that dark winter while closing his mind to any disaffection with his lot and taking his pleasures where he could. Money in his pocket, respect on the streets, and camaraderie at the Welfare club were great mollifiers of his ambitions.

It was during this time, that April gained her School Certificate and secured employment at the Backworth branch of the National Provincial Bank as a trainee counter clerk where her sister already worked. Over the years of their relationship, Ben had visited April's home on Springfield Road regularly, where he enjoyed assisting her father, Jack (Ben called him 'Mr P'), in his workshop and serving at the petrol pumps from time to time. A down-to-earth practical man, Mr P must have slept in his overalls, Ben thought, because he never saw him wearing anything else. Ben had taken a great interest in the many marques of motor vehicles that came through Mr P's hands for maintenance and repair – indeed they intrigued and fascinated him – and Mr P had been quick to rope him in as his part-time (and unpaid) assistant. It was a mutually beneficial relationship as it would turn out: Ben was Jack's willing and handy helper, and in return he was taught a few things about engines and vehicle maintenance that would soon prove very useful. The two men also got on very well together.

Meanwhile, things between April and Ben also seemed to tick along quite happily – meeting regularly, enjoying private moments together, and so on – but as time passed, he began to feel that their relationship was stagnating – that it was not developing in the way he thought it should if, as he still hoped, perhaps naïvely, it might be leading to an eventual union. Ben also sensed a growing reticence on April's part that suggested that she might be feeling the same way, but he hesitated to confront her with his thoughts and thus let things drift for fear that he may not like the outcome if he did. While she was evidently blossoming in her new role as a bank counter clerk, often speaking about her work and her new colleagues with enthusiasm, Ben found himself with nothing to talk about that had not been talked about before. The silences that fell between them now were more to do with awkwardness than the peace of mutual contentment that they had hitherto enjoyed. The fateful day of reckoning was soon to come, and it was she who brought things to a head.

One Saturday, as had become a regular week-end routine, the pair had taken tea together with her mother in their kitchen. Mrs Palmer (Ben called her Mrs P) was a straight-talking woman who did the company's books, ran the home, and kept chickens in the small orchard at the rear of their home. She had taken a shine to her second daughter's young boyfriend from the start and repaid the time he spent relieving her in serving at the petrol pumps with tomato sandwiches and home-made cake for tea. Over the years of Ben's acquaintance with the Palmer family, he had come to feel as if their house was his second home.

When the time came for him to leave that Saturday, April accompanied him to the end of her road. It had become a bit of a ritual for her to do so, but on this occasion, she seemed preoccupied. Indeed, a lengthening and awkward silence developed between them as they walked, which was mercifully broken by the shrill whistle and metallic rumble of a steam locomotive as it approached the road crossing ahead. A wizened old man in overalls, carrying a red flag, emerged from his roadside kiosk and ambled into the road to prevent the couple from proceeding as the engine neared. The pair halted obediently and waited as a hissing shunting engine chuffed slowly across the road hauling a dozen loaded coal wagons, each of them emblazoned in the bright red colours of the Backworth Colliery Company, the company who paid Ben's wages. It was a welcome distraction, but as the last of the wagons passed and the rumbling died away, he became aware that April was not ready to move on and had instead turned her face towards him, taking his hand as she did so. It was as if she was steeling herself to speak, and he knew instinctively that she was about to venture onto that dangerous ground that he himself had feared to tread.

'Ben?' she uttered tentatively, fixing him steadily with her bright blue eyes, 'I've been wondering if perhaps it might do us both good to have a rest from each other for a while?' She paused, possibly waiting for a response that Ben was too afraid to offer. 'You know, to give ourselves some breathing space to take stock,' she continued, hesitatingly, 'now that we have set ourselves upon our different paths in life – me at the bank and you as a miner, I mean…to give ourselves some time to adjust. Things are so very different now, aren't they?'

The intensity of her gaze didn't falter, and she squeezed his hand tightly. Her meaning was clear. This was the break that Ben had feared, and while he had half-anticipated that it might come, his heart sank and his mouth went dry on hearing it articulated.

He wanted to protest but thought it better not to. 'I know, sweetheart,' he said, after a reflective pause. 'Perhaps you're right. Perhaps we do need a little time apart. Things haven't been quite right between us for a while, have they? A break might do us good.'

He searched April's face, looking for some hope in her expression that the break she was proposing was not final, but he saw only resolution in the firmness of her lips. The moment of their parting had come. Ben had seen April with her new friends and colleagues from the bank in conversations full of laughter and quick wit and knew that he could never compete. His mind went back a few weeks to the time he had waited for her after work one afternoon and she had introduced him to one of her colleagues as he and she had left the bank together. The two of them had seemed so at ease in each other's company as they walked towards him, neither yet aware that he was there. April's companion was a tall, good-looking fellow, with smoothed-down dark hair and a neat centre-parting. He wore a grey suit, horn-rimmed spectacles, and looked just as Ben expected a bank clerk might look – not that he had ever been inside a bank to see one. Even from where he stood watching, Ben had instantly taken a dislike to the man.

'Oh, Ben!' April was both surprised and flustered as she came upon him, her glance shifting between the two men as a little wrinkle of consternation furrowed her brow.

'Ben, er, this is one of my colleagues,' she said breathlessly, her cheeks turning a little red as her companion moved a little closer to her side. 'Robert,' she said, 'this is Ben... the old friend I told you about. We used to be at school together...remember?' She hesitated and looked a little lost for words. Robert raised an enquiring eyebrow.

Ben thrust out his hand. 'Ben Hardy,' he said, announcing himself and wanting to fill the sudden hiatus. But his offer was viewed dispassionately and then declined, and Ben understood why when he saw how grimy his hands were.

'So, this is your miner friend, April,' said Robert in such a condescending tone that it made Ben want to hit him with the hand that had just been rejected.

April shifted on her feet, switching her gaze uncertainly from one man to the other. But then she grabbed Ben by his arm and led him swiftly away, calling a hasty farewell to her erstwhile companion over her shoulder, and leaving him standing on the pavement looking bemused.

The memory of that uncomfortable encounter had hung in Ben's mind ever since. And now, while still standing together at the railway crossing as April's proposal for a break sank in, his suspicion that this Robert fellow had charmed his way into April's affections now seemed confirmed. If this were true, he knew he could not possibly compete. There was no way in his current occupation that he could provide April with a life that would match that offered by a salaried man. Strangely, he was able to remain calm as these thoughts swirled around his head. In his heart he knew that he had lost April, and he would not demean himself by protesting. No words of his could fill the gap that had at that moment opened between them.

Besides, he must preserve some dignity and not descend into pique or angry recriminations, which he knew would only make things worse. If he could not retain her love, then at least he would retain her respect. 'It's that Robert chap, isn't it?' Ben asked quietly, letting go of her hand, already convinced that that was the truth of the matter.

April sighed and shook her head gently. 'It's not like that, Ben,' she insisted, almost too adamantly. 'Robert and I work together, that's all. I'm fond of him and we get on well together. But that's as far as it goes.' In that moment, April was no longer the girlfriend that he had grown up with, the young woman that he had loved ever since he was capable of such feelings. She had become a stranger. Ben searched her eyes for the truth in what she had said but could not find it. 'Look Ben,' she went on, 'you and I have had such good times together and I really want us to remain friends – best friends even.' She seemed earnest, but it wasn't very convincing. 'I…I just need some time to think things over,' she went on. 'So much has changed, hasn't it,' she added, her eyes pleading for understanding, 'and I…I just need to be sure…about us, I mean. So, please…please give me some time.' She frowned as if struggling to find the right words. 'We can still see each other, and you can still come and help my dad in the workshop if you want to.' Her voice hardened now. 'But we'll just be friends, Ben… good friends, I hope, but nothing more. Maybe after a break we'll get back together?' She paused for breath then brightened and added quickly: 'Maybe you'll find someone else? I'd understand if you did…I really would! Someone better than me?' With this attempt at levity, she smiled stiffly, and raised herself on her tiptoes to kiss him lightly on his cheek.

April's words did nothing to soften Ben's sense of rejection – each sentence that April had uttered had struck home like an arrow to his breast. He pulled away from her gently and found himself acting out some half-remembered part from a sixpenny movie – stiff upper lip and all that – though his heart felt as if it had been torn in two. 'I'll always love you, April,' he said steadily, resisting a hopeless urge to take her in his arms to prevent her from going. 'I know I don't look much of a prospect as I am. You've moved on and I haven't, have I? I know that. I've been aware of it happening…of you slipping away, I mean; but I couldn't seem to do anything about it. Perhaps one day …?' Ben's voice faltered and it took a moment or two for him to regain his composure. 'Just remember that I love you, April, and always will.' And with those last words, he took her hands in his and squeezed them gently, then turned and walked away, leaving her standing at the crossing.

With welling eyes, April looked forlorn as the distance between the couple widened, wondering if what had just happened was real and final. Meanwhile Ben strode on at a determined pace, keeping his gaze steadfastly ahead while April stood watching him go. She opened her mouth and took a quick breath as if to call out to the retreating figure, but then clenched her lips together tightly. While the pain of parting was acute, she was sure, for her own sake, that she had made the right decision. She must look forward now rather than back.

The old man at the crossing had by this time returned to his kiosk with his red flag to await the next train, but his view of the young couple had not been obstructed, and he had watched them thoughtfully as they had stood together talking. Although he could not possibly have heard what had passed between the two, he had interpreted their interaction for what it was, remembering an unrequited love of his own. He felt for the young man as he strode off so determinedly, his gaze fixed so steadfastly ahead, and he felt the young man's pain as if it were his own. He had observed the young woman's changing expression too as she stood at the crossing watching her friend go. He had seen her eyes redden and her lips part, and he had willed her to do what he guessed she really wanted to do and call him back. The young pair seemed so clearly right for each other. But then the young woman closed her lips and sagged visibly where she stood.

And the old man looked on sadly as she turned and slowly walked away.

Chapter 6

That night, thinking things over, Ben's heartache turned into resolve. He must now act decisively to change the course of his life or risk missing his chance. Doing so was as much for his own self-respect as to show all those around him that he was capable of more than the life that others had assigned to him. April had severed their relationship because he was going nowhere, metaphorically as well as literally. In the life currently laid out before him – the mining life of his father and all the other men in his street – he would never be able to offer a future that would satisfy a woman not content simply to be a miner's wife, to devote herself to cooking and cleaning for him and bearing his children, with no life of her own. He thought about his mother's role in his family home and that of his late lamented grandmother, both worn down by a life of drudgery and toil. Much as he had loved them both, theirs were lives of subservience – free spirits tamed and imprisoned by domesticity and a sense of duty to their men. He saw only weary resignation in their eyes and would not want any woman of his to endure such a life. April must have seen this too, he realised, and he knew that she was right to want more.

The following day, a Sunday, Benjamin Hardy woke early, impatient to move things forward and commit himself to his new resolution before he wavered again. His brother, Frank, stirred as Ben swung his legs out of bed and sat for a moment looking around their little room, wondering if he'd miss it when he left home to join the RAF. There was now no doubt in his mind that this was what he must do. Not for one second did he acknowledge the possibility that he might fail to be accepted. The hurt of April's gentle push-off had spurred him, and nothing now would cool his resolve.

Four years Ben's junior, Frank seemed to live in a world of his own. He was a soft-hearted boy with dreamy eyes, not likely to win any prizes in his class except perhaps for attendance, and not known either for his initiative or quick-thinking. The two brothers had absolutely nothing in common, but Ben had always looked out for Frank as older brothers should, and he included him in the street games with his peers despite the difference in their ages. Ben wanted to tell his brother what he now intended, partly to declare his decision and thus fix it in place but also to prepare his brother for it, worrying that by leaving home, he would be leaving Frank without a big brother to protect him. His young brother seemed not to have made friends of his own, often trailing around in Ben's wake, sometimes even becoming irritating in his persistence. He needed to grow up and become more self-sufficient, Ben thought, and he persuaded himself that his going would be the catalyst for this. It might be a hard lesson, but Ben was sure it would be good for him.

'Are you awake, Frankie boy?' Ben whispered.

Frank yawned audibly. 'Yes,' he drawled.

'Can I tell you something serious?'

Frank sat up in bed and rubbed the sleepers from his eyes. 'What?' he asked slowly, his brow furrowing.

'Promise not to tell a soul?'

'Cross my heart,' Frank said, looking at his brother in wide-eyed expectation as if some cataclysmic revelations were about to be made.

Ben took a breath and told his brother of his plan, knowing that by revealing his intentions, there would be no going back without loss of face. He had to be an example for his little brother and not be seen to vacillate. 'I've decided to join the RAF, Frankie – if they'll take me, that is,' he said. 'I don't want to be a miner all my life – and the Air Force is recruiting in a big way now so there's a good chance that they'll take me.' He told his brother about his visit to the recruitment office in Newcastle and the application form he now intended to complete. He spoke no word of April and his parting from her. Frank, he thought, was far too young to understand the effect that the females of the species can have on a man. Ben had often been ribbed by his brother for his mooning over April and was in no mood to bare his soul now. 'And when I'm gone, Frankie, you'll have to step up and take my place and help Ma around the house. No more lazing about. You'll have to pull your weight. Understand?'

'OK, big brother,' Frank agreed, with a readiness that was not entirely convincing. Frank sat with furrowed brow for a few moments, as the consequences of Ben's declaration sank in. Then, suddenly brightening, he added: 'So, I'll get this room all to myself when you've gone,' his face breaking into a broad grin. 'Then I really do hope you get in, Ben!' he said, laughing. 'Actually Ben,' he went on after another thoughtful pause, his voice becoming more serious now, 'I don't really like the idea of working underground either and I've been wondering what else I could do. It's not long now before I leave school – only a couple of years. Maybe the Air Force would take me too?'

'Hmmm. Maybe,' replied Ben in as positive a tone that he could muster, while worrying that his young brother may not have the drive and determination to turn such fancies into action.

Thus was Ben's intention to join the RAF made firm, and, swearing Frank again to secrecy, he quietly resolved to strike while the iron was hot and act that very day.

A few days earlier, Ben's parents had signed up for a family Sunday outing to Whitley Bay in a charabanc organised by the miners' welfare club. Ben had, of course, been expected to join his parents and brother but now absented himself as gracefully as he could, though not without their disappointment. He explained apologetically that he had promised Mr P some help in his workshop with an engine change – a short-notice and urgent two-man job for a wealthy motorcar owner, he'd said. He'd be paid for doing it, he said, lying through his teeth, adding this latter point of detail to lend the untruthful commitment some extra credence. His excuse was reluctantly accepted by his parents, but his mother's sideways glance as the threesome had departed, told him that she must have suspected that he was up to something.

No sooner had the front door closed behind them, Ben rushed upstairs to his bedroom and took out the application form hidden in his drawer. Settling himself at once to completing it in his neatest hand, he knew well by now that there is no one better at singing one's praises than oneself. Thus, with immodest yet plausible embellishment, he wrote of his scholastic and sporting prowess, of his motor maintenance skills (newly learned in Mr P's workshop), and of his childhood ambition (as he described it) to join the RAF. He also made a small amendment to the date of his birth to elevate his age to eighteen just in case. In doing so, he abandoned his fate to the guiding hand of providence without a single pang of conscience. Ben hoped that the RAF's need for recruits in a time of potential national mobilisation would override the normal diligence of their selection processes.

To set all this in a historical context in relation to German rearmament and expansionism, Adolf Hitler had by then already formed his Wehrmacht and had sent them into the Rhineland, thus ignoring the terms of the treaty signed in Versailles at the end of the last war. He had also pledged support to Spain's republican General Franco, signed a treaty of friendship with the Italian dictator, Mussolini, and was poised to form an alliance with Japan. A cooperative pact with Russia would soon follow and might already have been mooted in diplomatic circles. It was understandable, therefore, that the British government would be nervous about the new German chancellor's territorial ambitions despite the strong lobby for restraint and accommodation.

Chapter 7

Given the heightening state of national anxiety, a subject of frequent commentary on the wireless and seen emblazoned on every street-corner newsstand, Ben was not surprised to receive an invitation to be interviewed by the RAF only two weeks later. He was astonished, nevertheless, at the cursory nature of the procedure when he came to it – which was probably just as well. The written references that he'd attached to his application must have done the trick, he thought. He'd persuaded 'Mr' Tim Wainwright, writing on misappropriated BCC letterhead and masquerading as Ben's employer, and Mr Jack Palmer, writing as proprietor and 'chief engineer' of the 'Backworth Automobile Company', to endorse his application and speak of him in suitably positive terms. The high volume of applications must have relegated the usual vetting diligence, he thought, just as he had hoped. Indeed, thousands of applications had been received from across the north-east, many undoubtedly from the ranks of the unemployed and probably including some of those that Ben had seen standing about on the streets and docks in Newcastle.

When he arrived for his interview at the City Hall, he found himself swept inside by a jostling crowd of other eager men, mainly young and dressed like him in their Sunday best. There was a lot of noise and confusion as upwards of one hundred and fifty of them assembled on the auditorium floor. The hubbub died when a warrant officer wearing his number ones walked onto an elevated stage. A brief welcome followed, after which a supporting cast of sergeants provided a short overview of the RAF's many different roles and training opportunities. On this occasion, training for a range of specific trades was being offered to attract young recruits, including aircraft and engine mechanics, transport drivers, administrative and medical orderlies, and specialists in the armament, wireless, photographic, and navigation equipment trades. Questions were invited but no one seemed brave enough to raise a hand. The assembly was then instructed to arrange itself into queues according to the first letters of the attendees' surnames, labels for which had been placed around the walls printed in large, black capital letters.

Chaos set in very quickly in the ensuing melee, some individuals almost coming to blows with others in the rush to be first in their respective queues. Several young men were even sent sprawling in the contra-flow that followed, with those making for letters N to R encountering an equally forceful torrent who'd set their sights on letters A to D. Realising that things were getting out of hand the warrant officer rapped a tabletop with his swagger stick. 'Gentlemen, please!' he implored loudly, bringing those who had been too quickly off the starting blocks to a screeching halt. 'This is not an excuse-me in the village hall,' he said, glaring under raised eyebrows as quiet fell. 'A little more decorum if you please! Now, without pushing or shoving, gentlemen, please go quietly to your line.' More confusion and chatter followed nevertheless in the scramble for places, but Ben, luckily already on the right side of the hall, managed to be one of the first in his line.

Seated at a trestle table under the label H, with only one or two men in front of him, Ben's interviewing panel comprised a flight-sergeant, a sergeant, and an airman admin clerk. With the prospect of a long day ahead and a likely desire to be done with it quickly, the business of the trio was conducted at a brisk pace.

'Name?' asked the flight-sergeant brusquely when it was Ben's turn to step forward.

'Hardy,' he answered.

'Hardy, sir!' the sergeant retorted, with emphasis on the 'sir!'

'Hardy, sir!' Ben repeated stiffly, with the same stress.

'First name?'

'Benjamin, sir'

The airman admin clerk leafed through his pile of application forms and handed the one labelled with Ben's name to the sergeant, who scanned the form quickly before passing it to the flight-sergeant with a nod.

'It says here, Hardy,' said the flight-sergeant, after flicking his eyes across Ben's carefully written pages, 'that you have worked as a motor mechanic and did well at school?'

'Yes, sir,' Ben lied.

'And that you've wanted to join the RAF since childhood?'

'Yes, sir!' replied Ben, digging himself more deeply into deceit.

The senior NCO sat back in his chair, folded his arms, and looked Ben straight in the eye. 'Then you'd better tell me why, lad,' he said.

'Well, er,' Ben uttered, caught by surprise. 'Er, to serve my country, sir?' Ben offered naively, thinking that this might be the required answer and only then realising that serving his country was exactly what this was all about.

'God's gift, eh?' muttered the sergeant, a sarcastic smirk skewing his face.

Enthused by the earlier briefing on the range of training opportunities being offered to young entrants, it was at this point that Ben realised that speaking from the heart might serve him better. Having rubbed shoulders with so many bright-eyed and excited young men who seemed so eager to take advantage of these opportunities, he now realised how sought-after and prized they were. Until that very day, joining the RAF had represented merely a means of escape from his present lot, but now it felt more like a treasure chest of opportunities had been opened before him with such tantalising jewels lying within his grasp. Here was his chance to change the course of his life for ever. Fate, fortune, and a bit of enterprise had dealt him a lucky hand and brought him to this place on this day. He now knew that this was what he wanted to do more than anything else in the world and he could not let this chance slip carelessly through his fingers. He took a breath and let his heart speak. His words tumbled out in a sort of stream, full of earnestness and self-knowledge.

'Sir,' he started, 'I admit that I knocked about a bit after leaving school, trying to find my way,' he said honestly, meeting his interviewers' eyes. 'I picked up odd jobs here and there to start with and then I worked underground at the colliery for a couple of years because there didn't seem to be much else that I could do. But that wasn't very satisfying, sir. I wanted more out of life, and I knew that I could do better for myself. Then I started helping out in a local motor garage, part-time – working with the owner.

I liked working with him, sir – he taught me a lot – and I liked working with engines too. I only did the basic stuff, of course – filters, spark plugs, oil changes and so on, but I also helped him with some of the more complicated things, like carburettor adjustments and valve and piston changes. Then I saw a recruitment poster for the RAF When I came to Newcastle one day, and it got me thinking that joining up might be just the thing for me.'

Ben paused a moment, reflecting on the words that had just spilled from his lips in a torrent, thinking that they had just about summed up his feelings (plus or minus a detail or two), so he then concluded: 'It's occurred to me that you'll probably need a lot more mechanics and engineers now, and if there's an opportunity to train as one, I think I could become quite good at it.' He sat back, thinking that he'd said enough, then added a belated 'Sir.'

The flight-sergeant looked at the sergeant and raised an eyebrow.

The sergeant returned his superior's glance with a satisfied nod.

'Right, young man,' said the flight-sergeant, bringing his rubber stamp down on Ben's application form firmly. 'That'll do. So far so good, I'd say. We like to see some enthusiasm in our young men, and, if not much else, you seem to have plenty of that!' he said, exchanging a grin with his companion. He handed Ben a slip of paper. 'Take this across to that desk over there,' he said, pointing across the hall.

'So far so good, indeed!' thought Ben.

The 'desk over there' turned out to belong to the clerk administering candidates' medical examinations, which appeared to be taking place in several open-fronted cubicles separated by curtains that offered hardly any privacy at all. Candidates in various stages of undress right down to their underpants were being subjected to tests of one sort or another, surrounded by odd-looking contraptions and men in white coats. Ben watched with interest, wondering if he might have some unknown defect or affliction that would be discovered and be his downfall. He had noticed men leaving the hall with downcast faces after the first interview stage, and more leaving after the medical stage in front of him right now. He did not want to follow them. The number of men in the hall seemed to be diminishing rapidly and the level of chatter seemed noticeably more subdued. He waited about half-an-hour in this queue before being ushered into a cubicle where, stripped of his clothing down to his underclothes, he was prodded, poked, measured and weighed. Eyesight and hearing were also tested, and the inside of his mouth and teeth were inspected so closely that the examiner must have been a horse trader in his spare time. Ben's ability to stand on one foot and count backwards in sevens from a hundred also seemed for some reason to be important. At last, it seemed that Ben must have passed muster, for having submitted himself to all these indignities, he was invited to head over to the final desk.

Behind this desk, sat the warrant officer who had given the introductory address to the candidates on arrival. Ben's papers must have arrived before him, for the clerk was able to find them in his pile straight away. The warrant officer gave Ben the once over as he took the sheaf of papers from his corporal. 'Now, let's see...' he muttered. Ben was left standing as the WO ran his eyes over the several pages and attachments of his application. 'Well, Mr Hardy,' he said at last, raising his eyebrows, 'impressive references! How much did you have to pay for these?' he smirked. Fortunately, his question was meant to be rhetorical for he didn't wait for an answer. The WO flipped back to the front page of Ben's application form, examined it closely, then sat back and looked Ben square in the face. 'Just turned eighteen, eh?' he said, eyeing Ben up and down again, this time more critically. The quizzical look suggested that Ben might have been found out.

'Er, yes, sir,' he asserted, brazenly.

'Hmmm,' uttered the WO, raising only a single eyebrow this time. 'Well, it's a bit of good luck for you that the minimum entry age for technical apprentices is sixteen now, isn't it! Eighteen's the minimum for officer cadet entry and they're not who we're looking for today. Anyway, I don't think you're quite ready for a commission yet, Hardy, are you?' He dropped his eyes to Ben's application form again, sighed audibly, shook his head slowly from side to side, then fixed the candidate with a piercing look.

Ben felt his face flush. Disaster! He'd lied about his age; his references were probably suspect; and this warrant officer was no fool. Ben sagged, thinking that this would be the end of the line for him, but then his interviewer took up his pen and scribbled his initials on the form.

'Alright young man,' he said with a tight smile. 'You'll do! Full marks for initiative. So, what should I put here for the real year of your birth, Hardy? It's not 1917, is it?'

'No sir,' Ben admitted, shifting his feet awkwardly. '1918, sir,' he said, sheepishly. 'Probably a slip of the pen, sir.' He offered glibly but regretted it instantly as the WO threw him a withering look.

The officer made the correction. 'You're not the first, Hardy,' he said. 'We'll let it go this time, but truth's a virtue, remember.' He threw Ben one or two more questions about his background and his ambitions (which were answered with more respect for the truth) until at last the warrant officer seemed satisfied. 'By the way, does your father know about this?' he added finally, almost as an afterthought.

Ben was not expecting the question and so must have hesitated just a second or so too long.

'Thought not,' the WO said, folding his arms across his chest as he leaned back in his chair. 'Then you'd better tell him, hadn't you!' he added, becoming somewhat sober faced. 'You'll get a letter within the next few weeks explaining the terms of your engagement and where and when to report. If you haven't changed your mind by then, sign it and return it, and follow the instructions. We'll complete the rest of the process next time we see you.'

'Yes, sir', Ben replied brightly, grinning like the Cheshire cat as he rose to leave.

'Oh, and Hardy.'

'Yes sir,' Ben answered, turning back.

'Get your hair cut before you arrive, there's a good lad.'

Chapter 8

Reflecting on the course of his life in his later years, Ben would see it as comprising several quite distinct episodes. The first of these, the period most recently described, ended with his acceptance into the Royal Air Force. All that had gone before – his school days and his growing up, his first jobs and his time working underground, his first love, April, and the wound of love's first arrow – all of this was at once buried by the sheer intensity of what was to come next.

When Ben told his father of his intentions, the old miner looked at Ben blankly as if he hadn't understood what had been said. He'd been caught half asleep in his armchair in the front room and Ben had simply blurted it all out without much of a preamble. A newspaper lay open at the sports page on his father's lap while a roll-your-own smouldered in the ashtray at his side. It took the miner a moment or two to register Ben's words. He sat up, letting the newspaper drop to the floor as he reached for the smouldering cigarette and stubbed it out. He looked up at Ben and frowned.

'What's that you say, lad?'

'I said I'm going to join the RAF, Da,' Ben repeated, seating himself on the edge of the armchair opposite his father's while steeling himself for an argument with a patriarchal figure not known to be a push-over. Levi Hardy seemed at first puzzled, and then a little piqued that his son had gone ahead with something so important as joining the armed services without talking to him first. He searched Ben's face for a moment then nodded gravely, perhaps realising that at nearly eighteen, Ben must make his own decisions now.

'I knew something was going on in that mind of yours,' he said, eventually. 'I've been watching you these last few months. Your whole manner seemed to have changed – you've been brighter somehow. So, I guessed you must be up to something.'

'Sorry not to have told you before, Da,' Ben said. 'But I wasn't sure myself until now. In fact, I've only just sent back the acceptance form. They've offered me a technical apprenticeship, Da!' Ben was almost bubbling over with excitement at the training course that he'd been offered. 'Fact is Da, I've hated working underground ever since I started. Plain and simple. I really admire what all you men do…and I've tried hard to pull my weight and be one of you even though I knew I wouldn't be able to bear it for long. But it's just not for me, Da. I'm certain of that now. I can't stand the dark and the dust and the constant hard physical labour. I'm just not built for it!'

Levi was quite clearly disappointed with his son's news, but the slight nod of his head indicated that he accepted and understood. 'I know son,' he said, resignedly. 'You've worked hard, and I'm pleased and proud of you for that. But I've always known that you could do better for yourself, even though I'd hoped you'd settle down eventually. You've got a better brain than me, and more ambition than I ever had. But I'll miss you, Ben. We've worked well together, haven't we? And it's been good to have you working with me – father and son and all that.'

Ben was visibly buoyed to have his father's acceptance. If not enthusiastic, he was at least being supportive. Levi was a strict father, perhaps sometimes a bit heavy-handed in the past, but he was a steady man and a reliable breadwinner. He'd kept a roof over their heads, food on the table, and coal in the hearth; and the family had never really wanted for anything. Ben really did admire him for that and so to have his acceptance was important. The pair chatted quietly for a while longer – Ben telling his father how he'd gone about his application, about his interviews in Newcastle, and how excited he now felt at the prospect of his new career.

'Well, I'm sure you're doing the right thing, son,' said Levi eventually. 'Don't know what your Mam'll think, though! She'll be upset about your going, especially with the bloody Germans arming up again. It wasn't much fun the first-time round, you know.' A shadow passed across his face as these last words were spoken. Levi Hardy, a lance corporal in the last war – said to be the war To end all wars – was worried that there might be another. He'd not want his son to go through what he'd endured in the trenches of northern France, and it must have occurred to him that by joining up, Ben might now be putting himself in that same danger's way. Perhaps he also feared for himself and Susannah – that they might lose a son, like many of his older comrades had lost sons in the last war. Perhaps he was also reflecting on his own life, maybe even envying his son's greater freedom to choose a different pathway when he himself had had no choice at all? Ben suspected that all such thoughts must be going through his father's head, but he would never really know. Levi Hardy had never bared his soul, and Ben had never known him well enough to fathom it.

'You know we'll miss you when you're gone, son,' Levi said at last, looking at his son as if seeing him in a new light. 'And promise me that you'll not do anything rash like volunteering for aircrew or anything stupid like that, won't you?'

At that very moment, with suspiciously impeccable timing, Ben's mother came in carrying a tray to lay the table for tea. She was in the habit of wearing rather drab ankle-length dresses when at home, but she'd brightened her appearance that day with an apron decorated with colourful flowers. A diminutive figure of little more than five feet tall and slender to the point of skinniness, she seemed more fragile in her movements than Ben had noticed before. Her hair, worn short, was prematurely silver for her years, and her skin was so pale that she might never have seen the sun. But her big brown eyes shone from a kindly face that always seemed to carry a hint of humour about the lips, as if concealing some inner self-knowledge that put her at peace with herself.

Ben rather suspected from the way she flashed a glance at him as she came into the room that she'd been listening to the two men's conversation from the kitchen. She touched Ben's shoulder lightly and smiled at him as she passed him on her way back. Her eyes told him that she approved of his decision too. She well knew the risks that miners faced – the regiments of gravestones in St Alban's churchyard at nearby Earsdon were testaments to that. Perhaps she hoped that in seeking a different path for himself, her son might avoid the choked-up lungs and arthritic limbs that cursed her husband and her late lamented father and father-in-law – afflictions that had taken too many of her neighbours sooner than their proper time. She probably knew that there would have been no way of stopping her son from following his dream anyway, and with her light touch on Ben's shoulder, she had given him her blessing. Like him, perhaps she too had convinced herself that war was far from inevitable; surely, the Germans would have learned their lesson from the last one, wouldn't they?

Chapter 9

On Parade at RAF Halton

After another visit to the Newcastle recruitment office, and some more interviews and form-filling, as forewarned in the letter he'd received, Ben was formally attested into the service. From that moment on, he was officially a junior airman entrant, and posted with a month's notice to the No 1 Technical Training School at Royal Air Force Halton, near Wendover in Buckinghamshire. With a service-style short haircut and dressed in his rough, 'Hairy Mary' woollen air force blue uniform, he started his course in July 1937. He was a few months short of his eighteenth birthday, and yet he was probably one of the oldest in his cohort. He certainly had more experience of life than most of his fellow students with whom he was to be instructed for the next two years.

Ben wasn't a great writer of letters, but he finally got round to putting pen to paper:

RAF Halton
4th October 1937

Dear Ma and Da,

I know I should have written sooner, but I just didn't seem to get the time. Anyway, here I am at last, pretty much settled in after my first two months. I must admit that I felt a bit homesick at first, but now I've made some friends amongst my fellow students it doesn't feel so bad. There are about forty of us in my entry, all sorts of chaps from all over the country and some from abroad too. We're billeted in barrack blocks, about ten of us to a floor, and have to clean and polish it spick and span with beds stripped and folded every day, which you'll be very pleased to hear, Ma, I expect! We have to stand by our beds whilst it's all inspected every morning too, so there's no getting away with anything either. And if something's not up to scratch, we have to do it all over again and get extra duties into the bargain!

We don't ever seem to get much free time either – we work a five-and-a-half-day week with matches on Saturdays and church parades on Sundays. We start the day with breakfast in the NAAFI at 6 o'clock, then, after our block's been inspected, we're timetabled practically every minute of the day from then on. Our first session is usually some drill on the parade ground, marching up and down with rifles! You'd never believe it Ma! – some of the boys don't know their left from right so sometimes it's a shambles and the sergeant shouts all sorts of things at us! I can't write his words down as they're too rude! Then we do some PE in the gym before changing into our overalls and going to the workshops or the classrooms. My time with Mr Palmer at the garage has really come in handy, Da. He taught me quite a lot about engines, but we've started to take them apart and rebuild them now, so I know a lot more. If you ever get a motor car or a motor bike yourself, I'll be able to do the servicing for you! We also get taught about electrics and hydraulics, and even about aircraft construction and repair – and we have a lot of practical work to do too. Our days are so packed that our feet hardly touch the ground, but I'm loving it! I think I'm doing quite well at the practical stuff, but I must admit I'm finding the academics quite hard work. We're doing mathematics, science, and English in the classroom. It's just like being at school but much harder, then there's all the theory on aircraft systems too. I just hope that I'll be able to cope with it – and we've only just started!

In the evenings, most of us go to the NAAFI for tea, then it's back to the block or the library for an hour or two to study. Food's quite good, Ma, and I've tried beer for the first time too, though I can't say I like it much. I quite like shandy though. On Wednesday afternoons, we play football or rugby with a coach who teaches us the rules and about tactics. I've gone for rugby because I'm better at running with the ball rather than kicking it about. I'm either a scrum half or a fly half or a centre three-quarter – it's a lot of fun. And, get this, Ma: there's the annual station dance coming up and we're having some dancing lessons so that we don't make complete idiots of ourselves when the time comes. Can you imagine me on the dance floor, Ma! They're even going to bus some girls in from the local teachers' training college! I'm not a Fred Astair though – not quite yet anyway! I can get an engine to sing a tune but can't dance to one for love nor money!

We've only been allowed to go off camp these last few weekends. We were kept in before to settle us in quicker, but some of those who live nearer to base have started going home on Saturday afternoons when there's nothing on like team games or matches. Most of us stay around to keep up with the homework though. I'm getting on well with all my flight so we have some fun; they're a good bunch of blokes from all over the country – and some of them can even understand Geordie, although I'm having to translate a bit!

I think that I've done the right thing in joining the RAF, Da. It seems to be more about how good you are and how hard you try rather than which school you went to or what sort of accent you've got (which is just as well!). If I fail, it won't be through lack of trying.

Well, I'll sign off now – off for a Saturday night in town with some of the chaps!

Love to you both and to Frankie. Will write again when I can.

Ben

Through all the early months at Halton, Ben tried very hard to put all thoughts of April from his mind. In this he largely succeeded but could not help wondering what she would make of him if she could see him on the parade ground with his rifle or in the workshop in his overalls – just like her father but not so oily! Deep down, his severance from her still hurt, but he also recognised that had she not given him the shove, he might never have left Backworth and might never have joined the RAF. In a way, therefore, he owed his change of tack and his new career prospects to her. He hoped that one day, she might see what he had made of himself and admire him for It. In that way he would have won back her respect even if he may have lost her heart. While he was reconciled that April was lost to him, however, fond memories of his first love and their times together would drift into his mind from time to time; and when he thought of home, she was always there.

As time progressed, Ben adapted to (and indeed enjoyed) his new life, and letters home slowly dwindled to a reprehensible trickle. Even so, his mother still wrote from time to time, thankful for his news and uncomplaining at the paucity of it, her letters relating those all-too familiar events that marked the passage of time in Backworth. From his father, however, the most he ever received was a scribbled postscript to his mother's letters, so it was his mother who was the conduit for family information and news at home. Soon, however, Ben found himself hardly thinking of home at all. He would never have admitted it – certainly not to his parents – but he had mentally moved on, and he had left his village and its people very much behind. The pace of his new life was breathtaking, and so full was he of himself that it never occurred to him that he was missed – and not only by his family.

Every four or five months, Ben's course was granted a week's leave and given a free railway travel warrant. This was a great perk, Ben thought, but he was so much enjoying his new independence and the fellowship of his colleagues that he decided to spend the Christmas of that first year with his friends at Halton instead, which turned out to be a very jolly affair with so many overseas students electing to do the same. But Ben did go home the following easter, by which time he was approaching the completion of his first academic year and feeling rather more confident about his progress.

Arriving at Backworth station dressed in his best number one uniform and forage cap, he felt somehow taller as he walked the familiar route home. Acknowledging the glances of a few faces he recognised along the way with a friendly wave, he became aware that other heads were turning as he passed people on the streets. A military uniform in Backworth in April 1938 was unusual, and the heads he turned buoyed his still adolescent ego. In the ten months that he'd been away, nothing seemed to have changed, and the fond memories of playing in those narrow, dirty streets, warmed his nostalgic heart. The distant whistles from shunting engines, the smoke-blackened house fronts, the grey haze that always seemed to hang heavy in the air, and the skyline of chimneys, gantries, and slag – all this was still his home. Yet he had become a different man entirely.

In the run-up to the end-of-term exams at Halton, Ben had neglected to write ahead to warn his parents of his plan to return home on leave. Guessing that his father would still be at work and his brother still at school, he intended to surprise his mother with his arrival. The front door was locked when he tried to lift the latch, so he went round to enter the back yard by way of the narrow passageway that ran between the houses. His mother was pegging washing to the line as he lifted the squeaky clasp that secured the garden gate. There being not a breath of wind, the limply hanging sheets hid her from his view, except for the shadow of her figure projected by the sunlight shining from behind. She hadn't heard his approach.

'Hello, ma,' Ben said quietly, so as not to frighten her.

Susannah Hardy's head popped out between the sheets with puzzlement written on her face. Ben had taken off his cap, but his short back and sides must have presented an unfamiliar sight. His mother didn't recognise him at first, but then her puzzlement turned to sheer delight as it dawned on her who this uniformed stranger was.

'Oh Ben, Ben!' she cried, putting down her basket and pushing through the sheets to seize her son in her arms, her head only just reaching his breast.

Ben folded his mother in his arms, feeling the lightness of her frame as the familiar fragrances of soap flakes and talcum powder entered his nose. She felt so fragile. 'It's good to be back, Ma. I should have let you know I was on my way. Sorry!'

'No, no,' she protested. 'It's so lovely to see you, our Ben. But what have they done with you, boy?' she said at last, holding him at arm's length. 'You look so thin! They're not feeding you properly! Come on in, I've got just the thing for you!' She took him by the hand and led him into the kitchen. Putting the kettle on the stove, she lit the gas hob with a spill from the fire, and then brought her famous hand-painted cake tin down from the shelf, a tin so beloved for its contents in Susannah's family since time began. She was well known for the density of her fruit cakes – one slice of which could keep a miner going at full throttle all day!

'I still haven't forgiven you for not coming home at Christmas, you know,' she said, giving her wayward son a hurtful look. She cut a large slice of her fruit cake and put it on a plate then slid it towards him as he seated himself at the table. 'Still, you're back now, and that's good enough for me,' said she, as she eased herself into her chair with a heavy sigh. Ben watched her expression contort in obvious discomfort as she did so, and it struck him that her complexion was paler and her face gaunter than he had remembered it. 'Now, sit yourself down, our Ben, and tell me your news.' She seemed to have become almost breathless from her efforts.

'Ma, you don't look well. Are you alright?' Ben looked concerned.

'Never mind about me,' she tutted. 'It's you I want to hear about. Now, tell me! What've you been up to in all these months away?'

Ben did not persist in his enquiry about his mother's wellbeing, which he would come to regret in time, not that he could have done more than sympathise about her condition. Instead, full of manly enthusiasm, he launched into some selected tales of his new RAF life. In the telling, he was able to bring a few smiles to her face, but he drew his storytelling to a close when he ran out of amusing anecdotes, and she looked as if she were tiring. 'So, now it's your turn,' he said brightly, interested to hear the hometown scuttlebutt. 'What's been going on in Backworth whilst I've been away?' He did not expect that much had changed.

She sighed, looked up at the ceiling, and screwed up her lips. Loose strands of her hair fell over her eyes, and she brushed them away. 'Not a lot!' was her eventual answer. 'All much the same as when you left,' she said, shaking her head resignedly. 'Your dad's as good and as bad as he ever was – still spending too much time at the Welfare of an evening – but he keeps the roof over our heads and coal in the hearth, so I can't complain.' Her fond chuckle turned into a bout of coughing that seemed to reach deep into her lungs. When it subsided, she hawked up some phlegm and spat it into a ragged handkerchief that she fished hurriedly from her apron pocket. She waved a hand to dismiss her son's sudden worried look.

'I know your dad was hard on you boys, son, but he's a good man and he'll be pleased to see you. He's on the evening shift, so won't be back 'til late, but Frank will be back soon; he's doing a bit better at school since you left – seems to be taking his schoolwork a bit more seriously these days. But we'll have to see,' she added doubtfully. 'He hasn't got the same get up and go as you had, our Ben.'

The chatting between mother and her number one son continued for a while on other topics – the friends, the neighbours, the Saturday evenings at the Welfare and so on – but the conversation soon began to flag, and Susannah must have read this in Ben's face for she changed the subject.

'Oh, I bumped into Jack Palmer in the Co-op the other day,' she interjected cheerfully. And registering the quick upturn in her son's interest, she continued: 'He said he misses you at the garage, and that he was sorry that April had given you the old heave-ho,' she added, flashing a sly glance at her son. 'She's apparently taken up with some chap he doesn't much like. Seems this man of hers has an aversion to getting oil on his hands!' His mother gave out a derisory snort. 'He said he'd have offered you a job if you'd stayed around and not gone off and joined the Air Force. So, if you ever change your mind, Ben.' She added, with a sideways glance and a hopeful lift of her eyebrows. 'The offer would probably still be there, if you wanted it.'

'A bit too late now, Ma,' Ben answered, feeling a small pang of nostalgia for the life he could have had. He was now certain, however, that such a life would never have been enough for him. A new wind had filled his sails and some instinct told him that he still had a long way to go. Later, on thinking about what his mother had said, he felt slightly irritated that he she could still see him employed as Jack Palmer's garage mechanic. Much as he liked April's father – as a friend rather than an employer – Ben was already adamant that he would prove himself much better than anything Backworth could now offer.

Chapter 10

RAF apprentice technician Benjamin Hardy would stay only a few days in Backworth before returning south to Halton, but much as he had enjoyed his homecoming and being with his family again after so long away, he soon tired of being idle. He spent the evenings with his father at the welfare club and a day riding along the North Sea coastal road on his old bicycle (which he'd extracted from the shed and done up). With money in his pocket, Ben also treated his brother to a bus ride to Whitley Bay, where he bought hot dogs and ice creams on the promenade and rides on the roller coaster and the waltzer at the funfair. But time began to drag after a while, and when his brother and father were not at home, he would go out for walks alone around the village simply to pass the time, engaging with anyone he recognised. Perhaps unsurprisingly, he found that his uniform sometimes even drew him into conversation even with people he didn't know.

If on these perambulations there had been any thought of an encounter with April, he was determined that it should be (or at least appear to be) accidental and not contrived. But then again, why should he avoid her, he wondered? They were supposed still to be friends, and his uniform might impress her, mightn't it? The little flutter in his heart when thinking of her should also have told him that he really wanted to see her. But he must not come too close to the National Provincial Bank! Oh no! He had his pride to preserve. An accidental encounter was one thing, but appearing too keen was quite another. Such were his tortured thoughts. Yet distant glimpses of female figures quickened his heartrate, thinking at first glance that April might be amongst them – only to feel let down when she was not. These reactions should also have told him something about himself, but he was not a man inclined to dwell too deeply on such things. Anyway, he never did have an encounter with April on his meandering walks around Backworth, accidental or otherwise.

Towards the end of his stay, however, Ben made up his mind to call upon Jack Palmer in his workshop. He had resisted the idea of doing so at first, thinking at first that his split with the garage owner's daughter should sever the relationship between the two men too. But that had been a silly and immature notion for which after some further thought he became cross with himself. That April and he were no longer 'a couple', so to speak, was no reason to break off his relationship with her parents. They had been kind to him, and he was very fond of them. Moreover, at the time he planned to call by, April would be at work, he thought. In thinking thus, however, there was probably some tiny corner of his mind in which lurked the hope that he might be wrong.

Jack Palmer's workshop and the Palmer family home lay outside the village on the edge of open countryside, and Ben walked there with a bright afternoon sun warming his back. Blackthorn blossom and pale green leaves gave fresh new colour to the hedgerows and bushes that lined his route. Spring was in the air and in his step, and his heart was suddenly full of the joys of that lovely season. It had been a long time since he had last walked that stretch of road to the Palmers' home, and the prospect made him nervous and excited at the same time. He wondered how he might be received, no longer part of what he had come to think of as his second family.

The double doors of the workshop were wide open when Ben arrived, and he stood at the entrance for a moment to let his eyes adjust to the relative darkness inside. The clanking of metal striking metal drew his attention to a shiny black Humber Snipe four-door saloon raised at its front on wheel ramps. Jack Palmer's oily overall-clad legs sticking out from underneath the vehicle's front axle were instantly recognisable. So was his voice. He seemed to be having trouble with whatever he was doing, for Ben could hear him muttering oaths that cannot politely be repeated here.

'Afternoon Mr P,' Ben called, as he crouched down on his haunches by the Snipe's shiny chrome bumper, 'having trouble?'

The cursing stopped abruptly. 'Who's that?' Mr P's words were muffled by the intervening metalwork.

'It's me, Mr P! Ben! I've come to say hello.' Ben called again.

The overall-clad figure propelled itself out from underneath the vehicle on a low, castor-wheeled trolley. He raised himself awkwardly to his feet with an effort that suggested he spent too long on his back on a cold workshop floor. Shorter than Ben and lean in stature, his dark, short-cropped hair crowned a ruddy and oil-smutted face which broke into a wide grin when he saw who it was standing before him.

'Good heavens, it is you, Ben! I thought I must be mistaken,' Jack exclaimed, gripping his back and wincing as he straightened. 'It's so nice to see you back – and in your uniform too. Very smart, I must say!' he said, taking a step back to give Ben the once over. He took a rag from his overall pocket and wiped his hands, flicking a frustrated glance at the Humber. 'Can't seem to free the damned sump nut,' he said, shaking his head hopelessly. 'Need some penetrating oil, I think.'

'Nice car,' Ben said. 'Yours?'

Jack laughed. 'Belongs to one of the colliery managers – bit too pricy for me, I'm afraid. You back for long?' he asked, his broad, bespectacled face smiling openly. He finished wiping his hands, put the rag back in his pocket, and offered Ben his hand.

Ben took it and shook it firmly. 'No. I'm going back Sunday – day after tomorrow.'

'Good. You've got a bit of time then. Come over here and sit yourself down,' Jack said, and led his young visitor across the floor to a cluttered corner of the workshop where two careworn Thonet chairs sat by a desk piled high with papers and manuals. Mr P called this area his office. 'Now, tell me – how's life in the RAF? And how's the course going?' he asked as the two men seated themselves.

With his usual enthusiasm, Ben told Jack about his time so far at Halton: about the content of his course and how he was enjoying it; about his sport and his rifle drill on the parade ground; and how working in Mr P's workshop had helped set him up for it. 'So, I'm sure it's thanks to you I got in, Mr P; and when I finish the course, if I finish the course, that is,' he added modestly, 'I'll be a qualified aeroengine technician.'

Jack looked impressed. 'If I know you, Ben, you will finish the course, and do very well at it too, I expect.'

Sitting in the relative darkness of the workshop, Ben had his back to the open doors through which the brightness of the afternoon sunshine beamed in, projecting a miniature reflection of the sunny scene outside onto Mr P's glasses and thus hiding his eyes. Ben shifted his seat to remove the dazzle, but as he did so, he noticed a tiny silhouette of a solitary figure appearing in the reflection of the doorway. Some instinct told him who it was, but he resisted the urge to turn around and look. Mr P leant forward to come closer to his visitor. 'It's April. Home early,' he whispered into Ben's ear. 'Talk some sense into her, son.' He squeezed his young visitor's arm as he rose from his chair. 'I'll leave you two to it,' he continued quietly. Then, speaking more loudly so that his daughter could hear: 'I'll get Mrs P to put the kettle on. You'll stay for tea, I hope?'

As the older man departed through a side door that led to the house, Ben stood up and turned around. April stood in the doorway, her hair lit up by the sunshine outside, which also threw her face into shadow so that Ben couldn't quite make out the expression on her face. 'Oh! April!' he said, feigning surprise. 'Hello.' He grinned. 'I'm home for a few days leave. I just thought I'd pop in to say hello to your dad.'

'Not to me too?' she replied, as she walked slowly towards him. 'We're supposed to be friends, aren't we? Yet you went off in a huff, leaving me at that railway crossing last year, and I haven't seen you since. A fine friend you turned out to be!' Her words were critical, but her tone was warm, and her expression was one of mild amusement.

Ben replied stiffly: 'I got the impression that it was all over between us, April,' he said, 'and it's difficult just to be a friend to someone you once loved – and thought once loved you.' He spoke the qualifying codicil more quietly. 'Anyway, I thought it best to stay out of the way.' Ben tried to keep the edge from his voice and probably overcompensated, for his words sounded cool and unfriendly, even in his own ears.

April sighed. 'Oh Ben,' she said softly, coming so close that Ben could feel the warmth of her presence on his face. She reached up and touched his cheek. 'Please don't be like that,' she said. 'I've missed you. You are still very dear to me.'

April's warm tone took Ben quite by surprise and he felt his old feelings for her stirring inside. And seeing in her eyes what he was sure must be affection, he felt his heart swell. Her touch was all it took to pierce the shell that he had constructed to protect himself from further hurt. On an impulse, he took her hand, and could not stop himself from kissing it, just as he used to. He saw her eyes watering as she reciprocated his gesture, pulling his hand to her lips and kissing it too.

'Am I dear enough for you to come out with me tomorrow?' Ben asked with a mischievous smile, giving form to a notion that had come straight into his head without any previous consideration. 'If you've not got someone else to see, that is?' he added quickly, fearing that perhaps he'd been too bold.

She laughed. 'I don't think that there's anything in my diary tomorrow,' she replied. 'Not if you're going to be around. We've a lot to catch up on, you and I, and I want to hear about your new life in the RAF – I love the uniform by the way!'

The pair discussed ideas for spending some time together the following day, eventually settling on a plan to make an outing of it and take the bus to Alnwick.

Ben was flattered and surprised that it had been April who suggested it. It seemed a bit adventurous not to say flirtatious of her to want to spend so much time with him, but Ben found the prospect tantalising and could not resist. Sending his apologies through April to her parents, he politely declined the invitation to stay for tea and left for home soon afterwards.

The following morning was bright and sunny again. It was the start of another perfect Spring day, a day that now held so much promise for Ben as he walked back along Springfield Road towards April's home. The bus stop for the Berwick-on-Tweed bus (calling at Alnwick and other places enroute) was on the main road heading north out of Backworth, close enough for the couple to have walked the distance in thirty minutes. But April's father insisted that he drive the pair there in the Humber Snipe that Ben had admired so much the previous afternoon. The shiny black motor sat gleaming in the sunshine on the garage forecourt when he arrived, where he found Mr P running a soft cloth over its bonnet. 'It'll be a run to give the new clutch a road test,' said he. 'And – er – I've put my tools in the front passenger footwell in case I need to do some tweaking, so you two will have to sit in the back.' Saying this, he flashed a subtle glance at his former unpaid workshop assistant that was unmistakable in its meaning. Ben and April climbed in and seated themselves in the sumptuous comfort of the vehicle's soft leather upholstery, so typical of the Humber marque. The sun had warmed the interior like a glasshouse, and the scents of leather, walnut veneer, and gasoline hanging in the air created a rather heady mixture. Sitting side by side, their arms and shoulders touching in the quiet intimacy of the rear seat, it felt immediately so completely natural to be together again, even so long after the pair had split up. Ben found the touch of his companion electrifying and realised how much he had missed the warmth of her nearness. He had such hopes for the day.

When they arrived at the bus stop, April's father leapt out of his driver's seat and opened the rear door for the two young people to alight as if he were the chauffeur and they, his VIPs. It was clear to Ben that he was encouraging the reunion.

The couple's time in Alnwick, however, was short. The old bus had meandered through the winding Northumberland countryside, grinding its gears and labouring up the hills, and stopping at every village centre enroute. By the time the pair arrived in the Alnwick market square, they would only have a few hours before having to catch the bus back. The priority, therefore, was to set off at a pace in search of refreshment. They soon came across a decent-looking public house in Fenkle Street and found themselves a quiet table at the back of the saloon, each then ordering the dish of the day (steak and kidney pie, peas, and mash) and half a pint of the local ale. It was the first time that they had been able to talk freely and privately because the bus had been packed and conversation between them had been necessarily circumspect and superficial. April was curious to hear about Ben's new career and Ben was keen to impress her.

'There's a big world out there, April,' Ben enthused, 'and I want to see as much of it as I can. Once I've finished my training, I could be posted anywhere in the world – almost literally!' he told her, excitedly. 'The RAF has airfields all over the UK and lots of bases overseas as well – all around the Mediterranean, Arabia and India – even in the Far

East. Just think of it, April, suddenly the world's there for me.' He could have added: '…and for you too if you'd like to come with me!' but something held him back. He would not want to sound presumptuous, and he was not at all sure if April would see such opportunities as exciting a prospect as he did. The arrival of a young waitress carrying two plates of food provided a welcome diversion and Ben hoped that the break might give April some time to think about the direction Ben's talk was heading.

The waitress departed. 'Golly April,' Ben continued in the same effusive tone, 'if I hadn't joined up, I might still be shovelling coal!'

From April's puzzled expression, Ben sensed immediately that she didn't wholeheartedly share Ben's enthusiasm. 'My goodness, Ben. How different things are for you now,' said she, her tone becoming rather flat. 'It all sounds really interesting; but what about RAF bases up here in the North, Ben?' she asked. 'There's that new one we passed on the way up here today near Acklington – perhaps you could get a posting to work there. Wouldn't you want to work nearer to home if you could? Can you choose where to go, or do have to go where you're sent?'

Ben could see straight away where April's thoughts were leading, but he couldn't give her the answer she was probably hoping to hear. He had joined the armed forces and might therefore be sent anywhere once he'd qualified. Like any serviceman deployed in the defence of the nation, he accepted that that was now his duty. Even so, any thought that Britain itself might be drawn into another European war was far from his mind. And war was far from inevitable too despite the German re-armament. Ben was amongst those who thought that diplomacy (some might have labelled it appeasement) would keep the country out of armed conflict. Young and not an avid reader of the newspaper editorials that might have persuaded him otherwise, he still clung to his dream of the travel and adventure that an Air Force life would bring. He had given little thought to actual hostilities breaking out, and even less to any notion that he might find himself on the front line of actual fighting.

'No, April, I'd have to go where I was sent,' he said plainly, 'but that's what I think I'd find so exciting.' His eyes sparkled with naïve enthusiasm. 'It's the sort of life I dreamed of when I was a pit boy. I never thought that such a life would be possible for someone like me. Wouldn't that sort of life appeal to you too if you had the chance, April? Just think of the adventures we could have together!' Ben really had thrown all caution to the wind now. His rash question was tantamount to a proposal, and he knew immediately from April's wrinkled brow that he'd gone too far and too fast.

April studied Ben thoughtfully as he took a long draught of his ale. She said nothing and kept a straight face while she herself took a sip from her glass. 'Oh, I'm not so sure, Ben,' she said eventually. 'It's not quite the sort of life I imagined for myself – living away from home or in a foreign country and all that. I mean, what would I be doing while you went away or when you were at work? I'd have no friends and family near me, would I?' She shrugged her shoulders and smiled haplessly, but then the focus of her eyes dropped to her plate as she deftly guided a small piece of pie onto her fork.

Ben sensed immediately that he had frightened April with all his talk of adventures and postings overseas. While travel was an exciting prospect for him, he could see that the life of a military spouse – tagging along in a husband's footsteps, living in strange and possibly uncomfortable places with no real role to play other than just being a dutiful service wife – might have limited appeal. He must have looked a bit crestfallen, for she added quickly: 'But I'm really, really happy for you, Ben.' And she reached across the table, placed her hand on his and squeezed it gently. 'You've achieved so much. And I'm so proud of you.' But although she smiled fondly, Ben sensed that she had cooled.

With this, Ben felt his old wound reopen and the well-remembered pain of rejection sweep over him all over again. This time, however, it seemed somehow worse, for while he had changed himself for her and seemed to have won her respect, what he could now offer was still not good enough. Only moments before, he had been so confident that he had won April back that he was contemplating a proposal – indeed, he'd practically just implied it. But a shadow had passed across her face. Not long ago, when Ben was a mine worker and she was working at the bank, it had felt as if *he* were being left behind. Now it seemed the other way around. Unable to hide his disappointment, he pulled his hand gently away from hers and sat back, holding her gaze while he attempted to fathom her thoughts. He knew her too well, and so it didn't take him long to understand her feelings. April was a home-loving girl, and she didn't share his lust for travel and adventure. He didn't blame her for that. Indeed, for a few moments, he questioned himself, wondering if he was paying too high a price for his wanderlust. But in the end, he came to realise very sadly that perhaps she was not the right woman for him after all. If she did not want the life that he could offer, and if he would not accept anything less, the outcome was inevitable. He had made his choice, and she, apparently, had made hers.

The pair travelled back to Backworth in an introspective mood, each inwardly examining their own thoughts and positions, each agonising over individual and competing wishes and desires. The mood between them, earlier so sparkling and bubbly, had gone flat. Both had their own very different ambitions for the future, their own very different visions of their future lives, their own very different notions of fulfilment. April sought stability and security, a family, and a home within a stable community she knew and loved. Ben, on the other hand, sought challenge, travel, and adventure, with no thought in his mind of settling down. While he had imagined all these things with her at his side, the two visions, unfortunately for Ben, were completely incompatible.

Ben would look back eventually through the lenses of wiser, older age, and come to know and understand April better in his later years. He would come to comprehend what must have been going through her mind at that moment in the Fenkle Street public house when they had talked about their futures. She was a home-loving girl with deep roots and he had unsettled her with his talk of travelling the world and moving from place to place. How could she possibly be happy with a life so uncertain, so unknown, so itinerant – a life that would take her so far away from all she knew and loved? Ben would come to wonder how he could ever have expected her to find the prospect of being married to him attractive.

Thus, it seemed that love would not conquer all. Neither he nor April was so smitten and starry-eyed that either was prepared to sweep aside material desires and aspirations in pursuit of love. Both had made their choice, yet, as their future lives unfolded, both would often remember that day and wonder if they had made the right one.

When April's father met them with the Humber at the bus stop in Backworth when they arrived back, he greeted Ben with a hopeful lift of his eyebrows. But Ben's downturned lips answered his question better that any words.

Chapter 11

Short Sunderland at RAF Calshot

Benjamin Hardy completed his course at Halton in the middle of 1939. Now about to enter military service in earnest, he faced the distinct prospect of becoming a participant in another war. Only the year before, in the Spring and Autumn of 1938, Hitler and his Wehrmacht had annexed Austria and the German-speaking part of Czechoslovakia. With his assurances that that would be the end of Germany's territorial ambitions, Britain and France had acquiesced to both military occupations. 'Peace in our time' was Mr Chamberlain's announcement on his return from Munich where those assurances had been received. But he had been duped. In the Spring of 1939, Hitler's troops took most of the remaining regions of Czechoslovakia as well. Hitler clearly could not be trusted. And just a few months later, his Wehrmacht would invade Poland and a state of war between Britain and Germany would be declared. Some would say that the writing had been on the wall for a long time; but then hindsight is a wonderful thing.

Ben's first posting as a newly qualified aeroengine mechanic was to RAF Calshot on the southern edge of the New Forest in Hampshire. The airbase was situated at the bottom of Southampton Water on a projecting strip of land that formed a protected bay suitable for the mooring of seaplanes. The RAF couldn't have sent Ben much further away from Northumberland, and it meant that he wouldn't get home for a long time.

Calshot had distinguished itself as the home of the High-Speed Flight that had won the Schneider Trophy three times in the late twenties and early thirties with its Supermarine seaplane designs. Ben arrived there with a fellow Halton 'brat', Bill Green, and the two were paired up as new starters to be supervised by a Sergeant technician until they'd learned the ropes. For reasons that Ben could not remember, Bill Green had acquired the nickname 'Woody' early on in their time at Halton, and the pair had struck up a particular friendship. Like Ben, Woody was a working-class Geordie, so they (almost literally) spoke the same language. If they didn't try especially hard to speak the King's English, few of their compatriots could understand them – which was sometimes an advantage. Woody was an archetypal 'cheeky-chappie', a fast-mover with a quick tongue and a ready eye for the main chance – and an eye for the ladies too. If shorter than Ben by a couple of inches, Woody made up for it in beam. He was a stocky individual with a slightly chubby face and fair hair cropped in the style of a crew cut. While Ben had been a fleet-of-foot centre three-quarter in the Halton rugby fifteen, Woody had been a sturdy prop-forward.

Off-duty, Woody would sometimes drag Ben and other squadron 'techies' along with him on his regular forays into Lymington. Ben enjoyed his friend's company over a beer or two now and then, but as far as chatting up girls in pubs was concerned, he just didn't seem to have the talent or indeed the inclination – which probably made him a bit of a liability when Woody was on the lookout for totty! If Ben had bothered to analyse his feelings more closely, which he rarely did (being a man built more for action than for self-examination), he might have realised that April still occupied a sizeable chunk of his mind and that any girl he met socially was being sub-consciously measured against her. In the months that followed that fateful outing to Alnwick, he'd written to her several times and she to him, and they'd met (mainly in passing) on some of his infrequent trips home. But with no apparent change of heart on either side, it soon became obvious to Ben that he was wasting his time. Painful as it had been for both, each had made a contrary choice in Alnwick. *So, better now to call it a day and get on with the rest of our lives,* Ben thought, *and not invest any more time trying.*

With both Ben and April thinking thus, they had let the correspondence peter out and contact between them to cease. It is often said, however, that one's first love is always remembered fondly, and in the case of Ben and April that would be especially true, for it had been cool reason and ambition that had caused their parting, not a falling out or disaffection. While other loves might come and go in their long lives, therefore, this love would linger on in both their hearts – if only as a precious memory.

There were two operational maritime patrol squadrons resident at Calshot at the time of Ben's arrival, but both were scheduled to be redeployed to bases nearer to sea areas north and west more likely to need wartime patrolling. Ben had been assigned to No 201 Squadron to work on the Saunders Roe A27 'London' flying boats, but he would soon be transferred to the Sunderland sea-plane maintenance unit there when 201 moved away to Sullum Voe in the Shetlands.

The London A27 biplane had an all-metal corrugated hull with fabric covered wing and tail surfaces. It was powered by two Bristol Pegasus radial engines mounted on the upper wing to keep them clear of spray when taking off or landing. The machine was an ungainly looking beast and only about thirty of the type were ever built, probably because of their low cruise speed, limited range, and poor payload capacity. They were also uncomfortable to work on afloat when in choppy conditions or in gusty winds because their light weight made them prone to skittish behaviour and snagging on their mooring lines. When Ben worked high up on the upper wing with his head buried beneath an engine cowling on a windy day, it made him seasick, yet, as he often reflected, the work was still preferable to working in the claustrophobic coal tunnels of Northumberland. He was very glad, nevertheless, when 201 Squadron flew all the Londons away to Shetland and he was transferred to work on Sunderlands instead.

The Short Sunderland flying boat was larger and heavier than the London and had a single high wing and four Pegasus radial engines compared with the London's two. It looked business-like and purposeful with its nose and tail gun turrets, and its side-mounted, forward-facing machine guns for pilot operation. The aircraft was three times the empty weight of the London, could fly faster and further and could carry five times the payload. In its maritime camouflage livery, moreover, it was also a handsome-looking and formidable war machine that rode well on its mooring and was easier than the London to work on.

After several months on the job, having been signed off by his sergeant as proficient on the type, Ben was detailed one day to run some engine tests. This was to clear the aircraft for flight again after some minor rectification work had been carried out on the starboard inboard engine following a rough-running report by the aircrew. The aircraft lay to its moorings in the shallow lagoon in the lee of the airbase where the buildings and hangars provided protection from the prevailing south-westerlies. Ben's task would be simply to go out and run the repaired engine at various RPM and throttle settings up to full power to determine that the reported problem had been corrected. Woody would accompany him to record engine readings during the tests.

High-power engine tests such as this would normally be carried out ashore with the aircraft chocked on beaching wheels and tied down securely to stop it breaking loose and running amok. That morning, however, the hardstanding was already choc-a-block with five other Sunderlands parked ashore and there was not enough space to bring another in. To save a lot of trouble, therefore, it was decided to do the tests afloat. But running the engines at full power on its moorings is likely to rip up the restraining tackle and allow the aircraft to break free and wreak havoc in the confinement of a congested anchorage. Prudence and safety thus dictated that the tests should be carried out in open water with the aircraft free to manoeuvre underway – which would, of course, need a qualified pilot at the helm.

The pilot programmed for the task turned out to be a flight lieutenant by the name of Isherwood, a tall, slim officer in his thirties with a relaxed and easy-going manner. He was standing at the coffee bar chatting with a couple of other aircrew officers as Ben entered the aircrew restroom. 'All ready?' Isherwood enquired, putting down his coffee cup as Ben approached and clearly anticipating Ben's arrival. 'Yes, sir,' replied Ben. 'The tender's on the jetty waiting to take us out. SAC Green will be coming with us to do the recording, so we'll get our stuff and meet you down there.'

The two mechanics collected their headsets, life jackets, and flight test sheets and made their way down to the jetty where the pilot and a flight engineer were waiting. The safety boat lay alongside, its diesel exhaust spluttering softly as its two boatmen singled up the mooring warps readying to slip. Within minutes the four men were climbing onto the lower deck of the waiting Sunderland, a cavernous space with sleeping bunks, a galley, a workshop, and a weapons compartment. The row of portholes running along both sides of its hold made it look more like the inside of a small cargo vessel than a flying machine. Wavelets slapping against the hull reinforced that impression as the aircraft swung and rocked gently in the wind and swell. With all four crew safely aboard, the safety boat backed away and motored to its forward stand-off position, its propwash causing the aircraft to snatch on its mooring chains as it manoeuvred.

'Right, you two, head up to the flight deck and wait for me there,' said the pilot, addressing Ben and Woody first. Then, turning to the flight engineer: 'OK Enge, I'll give you a hand with the turret,' he said. 'Let's head up front.'

The two aircrew made their way forward to the aircraft's nose and slid the front gun turret rearwards on its rails to provide access to the mooring platform. This was the flight engineer's station when arriving at or leaving the anchorage. 'I'll leave you to sort things out down here, Flight,' said Isherwood once the turret had been secured in its retracted position. 'We won't need the drogues today in this light wind, so leave them stowed. Check in on intercom when you're ready and we'll run through the checks for engine start, OK? We'll start the outers first, then when we've warmed them up a bit, we'll slip. I'll give you the word when we're ready.' The engineer nodded his understanding. The captain continued: 'Once we're clear, get the turret back into place as quick as you can then come on up to the flight deck. We'll get the inners going once we're in open water.'

Climbing up to the flight deck, the captain found Ben and Woody admiring the view. With its all-round and over-the-top transparencies, the cockpit resembled the inside of a glass house. From its elevated level, the deck commanded a panoramic view of Calshot Spit, the Solent, and the harbour town of Cowes on the Isle of Wight beyond. In the sunshine, it was a dazzling kaleidoscope of colour. 'Wow!' uttered Ben before he could stop himself. 'You get quite a view from up here, don't you, sir!' he exclaimed.

'And we get paid for it too!' returned to pilot, grinning. 'Anyway chaps, let's get ourselves organised. Corporal, you take the right-hand seat, and you, SAC Green, you can take the navigator's station to do your notetaking,' he said, indicating the chart table that lay directly behind the captain's seat.

'Get yourselves strapped in now gentlemen and put your headsets on please.' With this, he threw a glance at the two technicians as he buckled up his own straps and slipped on his headset to check that both technicians were following his example. The headsets were leather skull caps with telephonic earpieces and a detachable rubber facemask that held a microphone. Ben slipped the cap over his head, secured the chin strap and facemask in place, then plugged the headset jack plug into its socket, immediately hearing the electric hum of the intercom warming up.

'Anyone there?' The captain's voice crackled as he turned towards his front seat companion, indicating with his fingers that Ben should switch on his microphone.

'Loud and clear, sir,' Ben replied, switching on his mike. Woody's breathing could already be heard on the intercom. 'Loud and clear, sir,' he echoed, a few seconds later.

'Engineer here, skipper,' said the flight engineer. 'Bollard safety pin's removed. All set to slip. Ready with the pre-starts when you are.'

The checklist for starting the engines was then read out on a challenge-and-response basis, each item on the list called out as a challenge by the engineer who waited for the correct response from the captain.

'Engine master cocks?' called the flight engineer.

The pilot reached up to a bank of four levers on the console above his head. 'All ON' he replied, pushing all four levers into position.

'Throttles?' called the flight engineer.

The pilot dropped his right hand to the starboard outer throttle lever located below the main instrument panel. 'Starboard outer, one inch open,' came the response, as he inched the lever forward.

'Mixture control?'

'Normal.'

'Propellor controls?'

'All levers fully up.'

'Carburettor air intake?

'Cold'

And so the checklist continued, first starting the starboard outer engine then the port outer. The noise and vibration in the cockpit mounted progressively as first, one then two Pegasus XVIII radial engines were turning over smoothly at fast-idle power.

'Ready to cast off?' called the engineer, as the aircraft surged forward to the mooring buoy under the idle thrust of the two spinning propellors. 'Clear to cast off!' the captain responded.

Through the cockpit windscreen, Ben could see the engineer standing on the turret platform below and watched him as he released the pick-up ropes and cast off the mooring bridles, which fell into the water with a splash. 'All clear, skipper!' the engineer called, as he slid the gun turret back into position. 'Buoy's moving to starboard,' he said. Ben leant forward in his seat to watch the spherical mooring buoy slide along the starboard side of the hull. The captain now gunned the starboard outer engine, slewing the aircraft to port to head out of the anchorage towards the open water. The tender had been holding off as fire guard but now motored ahead to check the manoeuvring area was clear.

'All secure below, Skipper,' said the flight engineer, arriving back on the flight deck somewhat out of breath from his climb. 'OK, Flight, well done,' returned the captain. 'Clear to start the inners when you're ready.' Leaning between the two front seat occupants, the engineer set the levers and switches appropriately and started the two remaining engines. While it was only the starboard inner engine that required testing, the port inner would have to be modulated in parallel to balance the starboard inner's thrust. Without this balancing compensation, the aircraft would become uncontrollable. The outers would only be used for manoeuvring and would otherwise remain at idle power. Aircraft direction on the water was controlled with a combination of rudder and throttle manipulation. The captain took pride in showing Ben how deftly he did this as he navigated the Sunderland along the buoyed channel.

As the aircraft cleared the shelter of the lagoon and rode out into the light swell of the Solent, a light crosswind began to push the Sunderland off its course. Ben watched the pilot's quick reactions on rudder and throttles to correct the drift. He could not help but admire the man's skill; and watching this huge machine ploughing through the choppy water, feeling the swing and heave of the hull under him, his senses assailed by the roar and vibration of the engines, Ben was enthralled.

'Right, Corporal; ready when you are,' spoke the pilot over the intercom, as he ruddered the aircraft to head south-west down the Solent with some coarse legging of his pedals and a bit of dexterous manipulation of the throttles. 'You take control of the starboard inner engine. When you're ready, set up the test points exactly as you need for the schedule. Just tell me what you're doing for each test point, and I'll adjust the opposite engine to keep the aircraft heading in the right direction.' Ben flashed a quick glance at the captain and acknowledged: 'Roger, sir.' He had carried out engine runs before (though never afloat like this) and so knew the procedure. The flight engineer had now strapped himself into the jump seat, positioned directly behind the two front seat occupants. Isherwood flashed him a glance: 'Just keep an eye on the lad, will you,' he said, 'it'll be instructive for him to do this himself. I'll need to keep my eyes ahead... Now, straps tight everyone!' he called.

The tests involved little more than exercising the port inner throttle and pitch levers over their full range. It was not a complicated procedure. 'Ready Woody?' called Ben, glancing over his shoulder to receive a thumbs up from his friend. 'Right sir,' he then said to the pilot. 'Exercising the starboard inner pitch lever now,' he said. And with the captain's acknowledgement, he lifted and depressed the pitch lever a few times, reading out aloud the engine readings for Woody to record. He then returned the lever to the FINE position, the setting needed for the full throttle test.

'Propellor check complete, sir. All satisfactory,' Ben said. 'Ready to run the throttle up to full power?'

The captain scanned the open water ahead. This area of the Solent was designated as a seaplane manoeuvring area, but small boats sometimes strayed into it. The safety boat had gone ahead a mile or so to check the area and now its skipper flashed a green light on his Aldis lamp. 'Looks all clear ahead,' confirmed the captain, placing his right hand on the port inner throttle and his left hand on the flight control wheel. 'Off you go then, Corporal, but open the throttle lever slowly in increments so that I can match your movement with mine, otherwise we'll be all over the place!'

Ben inched the starboard inner engine throttle lever forward, pausing at progressively higher boost settings – three inches Hg, four inches, five and so on – reading off instrument values to Woody as he did so. The engine seemed to be performing perfectly, with no rough running evident. As Ben moved his throttle lever forward, the captain moved his to match it, so that both inboard throttles remained roughly parallel, and the aircraft's direction was held steady as speed increased. The roar of the engines rose to a deafening crescendo and the Sunderland accelerated fast. Ben felt the hull begin to lift, and the aircraft was soon skipping over the wavelets at what seemed like a tremendous rate. At maximum RPM, Ben called out the engine parameters for Woody to record – 'twenty-six hundred RPM, Woody; six-and-a-half inches boost!' He had to shout over the roar of the engines and the slam, slam, slam of the wavelets against the hull. He glanced at the airspeed indicator to see the needle hovering at seventy-five knots. The aircraft could not have been very far from flying speed. He'd never felt such exhilaration in his life! So thrilled indeed, that he must have held the engine at full throttle far longer than he needed to. 'Had enough now?' the pilot called out, laughing over the engines' roar. Ben would have been quite content to have extended the run all the way to Yarmouth. 'Oh, sorry sir! Yes, I think we're done,' he admitted. 'Throttling back now.'

As the throttles were pulled back, the aircraft speed reduced, and the hull settled back down into the water. 'OK Corporal, I'll take her now,' said the captain, taking over the throttles again to turn the aircraft onto a reciprocal heading to head back up Solent. Seeing Calshot Spit move into the windscreen as the turn progressed, Ben realised that they had come a good two miles from where the run had begun. 'Well, if we want to get back in time for tea, gentlemen,' said the captain, thrusting all throttles forward, 'we'd better get a move on! Fun, isn't it!'

Chapter 12

There is something about powerful mechanical machines that put some people, particularly men, into a state of awe at the sight and sound of them, particularly when they are moving under their own propulsion. As a boy, Ben had been fascinated with the little steam engines that had puffed around the shunting yards behind his Backworth home. Now, having experienced the exhilaration of his high-speed Sunderland engine tests, thrashing up and down the Solent, he fell in love with aeroplanes. It was the beginning of a lifelong love affair. Where before, it had been purely their mechanical complexity that had intrigued him, these flying machines now took on personalities of their own, with foibles and fancies, just as might be expected of a beloved steed: some of them, docile and dependable, others, skittish with bouts of disobedience and disorderly behaviour. But Ben loved them all for all their faults and idiosyncrasies. Indeed, so much did Ben come to be obsessed with these magnificent beasts that he took every opportunity to ride the flight decks whenever he was free, and whenever an opportunity arose. His favourite ploy was to lurk around the Ops Room at the end of the afternoon as the following day's flying programme was being chalked up, when he'd catch the flight commander's eye with a keen and hopeful look, which often resulted in Ben's name being added to the roster as supernumerary crew.

He especially liked to fly with Flight Lieutenant Isherwood, who on long flights sometimes allowed Ben to sit in the second pilot's seat and handle the controls (perhaps while the co-pilot took a nap below or was obeying the call of nature?). With some basic instruction, Ben found that he was able to fly straight and level reasonably well and even alter heading, airspeed, and height. On long transit flights, Ben might even be put to work as a sort of human autopilot just to hold the aircraft steady. For Isherwood, it was entertaining to coach his enthusiastic protege and it freed his hands to drink his tea or eat his lunch. One day, he suggested that Ben might have the right aptitude for aircrew, which was both flattering and encouraging. It set Ben thinking, and not long after, he enquired how he might go about transferring from engineering to the aircrew branch. He expected to have his enthusiasm dampened with a cool response but was pleasantly surprised when his enquiry was taken seriously. The relevant application form and procedure could be found in King's Regulations, he was told, and he was encouraged to have a go. Flt Lt Isherwood even offered to act as his referee.

To become aircrew in any sub-specialisation was quite beyond anything that Ben had previously imagined, but it was worth a try, he thought. With a little help from his referee, Ben completed his application and sent the papers up the engineering chain of command for approval. Ben's ultimate boss, the senior engineering officer at Calshot, eventually got to see it and called Ben into his office. He looked distinctly unhappy as his corporal walked in.

'What's all this, Hardy,' he said, sitting at his desk and waving Ben's application form airily as the young corporal stood before him at attention.

Ben told him what he hoped to do.

'You've only been here five minutes, laddie, and now you want a transfer!' the wing commander retorted crossly. 'You know I can't endorse this, don't you?' he said, waving the form in the air again. 'You've spent two years training as an aeroengine technician, for heaven's sake! You can't expect just to pick up your bags and go off on some flight of fancy!'

The SEO didn't seem to appreciate the irony of his words, because it was indeed a 'flight of fancy' that Ben craved! He must have sagged visibly at his superior's outburst, for the wing commander then softened his manner: 'Look Hardy,' he said, 'you're a good engineer, and I don't want to lose you. I'll send your application up the chain to the station commander because I'm obliged to, but I can't give you my support for this, you know. I'm sorry. Now, if I were you, I'd just forget the idea and concentrate on your work here instead. Maybe in a year or two, we can consider it again if you're still keen.'

Ben left the SEO's office feeling deflated, thinking that that would be the disappointing end of the matter. He was therefore surprised two weeks later to be told one morning to report to the station commander's office in station headquarters. The group captain was a greying version of Errol Flynn, with a lantern jaw, a neat moustache, and piercing blue eyes. He was sitting at his desk as Ben was shown in by his PA. The young corporal came to attention in front of the senior officer's desk and saluted smartly but the group captain did not look up, continuing instead to leaf through what Ben recognised at once to be his application form. Ben stood watching the man calmly, his eyes drawn to the pilot's brevet and the rows of medal ribbons on his battledress tunic. In the quiet of this wood-panelled office, surrounded by the trappings of senior rank, Ben felt instantly in awe of this man and began to wonder how he could have had the audacity to aspire to join the old man's aircrew cadre. Eventually the group captain put down the application form and fixed Ben with his powerful glare.

'At ease, Hardy.' Ben relaxed his stance and put his arms behind his back. 'So, you want to be aircrew, eh?' The group captain looked the young aspirant up and down.

'Yes, sir,'

'Hmmm. Well then, tell me why you think you'd make the grade.'

Ben told him of his Sunderland flying experiences and then attempted – probably not very articulately – to explain the sudden lust for flying that seemed to have taken hold. In the august presence of the senior officer, Ben's mind went into such a spin that later he couldn't recall exactly what he'd said. He remembered only that words had tumbled from his lips as they had come into his mind. He also remembered the old man's indulgent smile as he spoke.

'I like to see young men with a bit of pluck!' the group captain said when Ben had run out of steam. 'Take a seat, Corporal.' The old pilot then went on to give Ben quite a grilling to test his motivation, and Ben's responses must have been satisfactory for the group captain's face radiated approval as his interrogation was brought to a close.

'You'll probably appreciate that there's a lot going on in the Service right now, Hardy,' he said finally. 'With all these new aircraft coming along in the pipeline, we're going to need a lot of extra aircrews, especially for

Bomber Command, so you're in with a chance. This war's been a bit slow to get going, but it's going to get very nasty very soon; believe me, we haven't seen anything yet!' Ben sat on the edge of his seat wondering if he should say something in response, but decided against it, instead he simply acknowledged the CO's bleak analysis with a 'yes, sir'. 'It won't be a piece of cake, you know?' the group captain went on. 'It won't all be blue skies and jolly good fun! That time's behind us now, I'm afraid. Anyway, I'm told we're accepting aircrew from right across the Commonwealth, so it would seem a pity not to let one of our own have a go.'

'Yes sir,' replied Ben brightly, realising that that probably meant himself.

The station commander ran his eyes across several pages of Ben's application form again, muttering under his breath as he did so. He put the papers down on his desk and stared at them for a while, apparently in thought. 'You probably know that your CO isn't too keen on letting you become a fly-boy, don't you Hardy?' he said at last.

Ben nodded. 'Er, yes, sir,'

'Well, I disagree with him,' the old man added, making a church spire of his fingers as he leant back in his chair. 'I think your Halton training would be very valuable as aircrew, and therefore I'm going to recommend you for flight engineer training – it's a new aircrew category, and your training would suit you very well for that. Flight Lieutenant Isherwood speaks very highly of you in his reference too – he thinks you're the right sort, and I think I agree with him.' With a theatrical flourish, he picked up the application, scribbled something on it, and placed it firmly into his out tray. 'So, I'll be sending this up to Command HQ with my recommendation! And good luck to you!'

Ben Hardy would have to wait quite a long time for a response to his application. And as the weeks of waiting turned into several months, he began to think that the personnel administrators at RAF Maritime Command HQ had rejected it to safeguard their own manning in the frenzy of the current service build-up. Meanwhile, Ben's work at the base continued much as it did before.

The engineering teams worked a shift system at Calshot – mornings from five a.m. until early afternoon, and afternoons from one o'clock until about nine or ten in the evening, depending on the flying programme and whatever servicing or rectification work was required. This meant that half a day every working day of Ben's time at Calshot could be spent effectively doing as he liked. Located at the southern end of Southampton Water, however, RAF Calshot was miles from anywhere, with not much there to do except spend the evenings in the corporals' mess, watch the weekly film put on in the NAAFI, or take bracing walks along the shingle beach. Some men took up fishing, which Ben did not care for, and others learned to sail the station dinghies. But Ben preferred to look out for opportunities to get airborne, which he managed to do at least once a week when off duty, becoming quite a pest in the flight office when the flying programme was being put up.

Woody was a pest too, but not for flying. The Sunderland engine test that he had done with Ben, thrashing up and down the Solent at high speed, had made him sea-sick and air-sick at the same time and he never volunteered again. Instead, he was always on at Ben to go into town with him for a 'bit of life', which he was known to do himself quite often. By seeking for himself 'a bit of life', Woody really meant drinking beer and/or hunting girls and preferably a bit of both; and that also meant a bus ride into Lymington or a trip on the Hythe ferry across to Southampton.

Chapter 13

After a lot of cajoling, Woody finally persuaded his friend to go along with him on one of his 'adventures' – a trip across the water to Southampton one Saturday afternoon after the morning shift had been completed. Arriving in the town centre, the pair found a dance hall in the High Street where a tea dance was taking place. It seemed that Woody had been there several times before, so knew his way around. Dressed in their smart number-one uniforms, the pair got the serviceman's discount and paid a shilling each to enter. They left their service hats and raincoats with the lady at the cloakroom desk and descended the carpeted stairway to the dance floor below. A six-piece swing band was playing on an elevated stage in the new mellow style of Glen Miller's band, with clarinet and saxophone playing in smooth harmony. Sunlight streamed in from high level windows throwing bright shafts of light across the dancefloor where a handful of couples danced a slow waltz. Tea and cakes were being served from a counter, and the two servicemen bought themselves a cup of tea before making towards a table at the back of the hall where they could sit and survey the scene without coming under too much scrutiny themselves. It was not particularly busy that afternoon. Only half the tables were occupied, a few with couples, a few more with two or three unaccompanied young women in pretty dresses, all made up and looking very alluring to Ben's eyes. Men were definitely in the minority, and of the few who were there only one or two wore uniform. Woody was quick to notice a few appraising glances from the ladies' tables and drew Ben's attention to the interest as they took their seats. So many attractive women, laughing and garrulous, drinking and smoking and apparently enjoying themselves – Ben had to admit that he was excited by the atmosphere. This was his first time in such an establishment ever. He'd been to the occasional dance night in the Halton NAAFI when female students from the local teacher's training college had been bussed in, but those events had been rather restrained affairs. This place looked less inhibited, which was just what Woody liked, of course.

'Come on, Ben,' said he, straightening his tie and running a combe unnecessarily through his crew-cut, 'let's try our luck over there.' He nodded across the room at a table where two young ladies sat by themselves tapping their fingers to the beat of the music. Ben found the sight of the two girls strangely stirring and he thought they looked like nice girls too, girls that he might like to get to know, not 'brassy' or heavily made up. Since splitting up with April, however, he'd become awkward around females and was not at all sure that he was yet ready to re-engage. Once bitten, twice shy might have described his attitude, but he let Woody pull him to his feet, nonetheless. He felt a mixture of dread and excitement as he approached the girls' table in Woody's wake. The two girls had seen the two airmen coming and made a show of looking the other way, but Woody would not be deflected. With the confidence and smooth charm of a Clark Gable, he soon got both men invited to join the young ladies at their table, leading the introductions and raising some laughs with his corny jokes. Ben's conversational skills by comparison needed some honing. He felt clumsy and tongue-tied. Alcohol might have helped to loosen his tongue, but it was not being served at that time of day so he must have seemed dull company.

Woody didn't need any help from alcohol, however, and his audience was soon hanging on his made-up tales of derring-do. Ben sat back meanwhile and let his friend make the running. He knew immediately which girl Woody would make his play for if he thought he had a chance – the tall, black-haired, black-eyed beauty who knew how to flash her long eyelashes and cross her long legs. And it wasn't long before he was on the floor with her doing his version of the 'jive', which involved a lot of high-kicking and arm-waving but wisely stopping short of swinging his girl in the air like some of the others on the floor. The number seemed to go on and on, while Ben meanwhile sat like a lemon, watching his friend's antics in awe. He felt completely out of his depth and was beginning to look for an early escape when his companion leaned towards him. 'Wouldn't you like to dance?' she whispered in his ear. The music had reached fever pitch by now, and she'd had to lean so close that her warm breath on Ben's neck sent shivers down his spine. She seemed a bit put out that Ben hadn't asked her first.

'I'm really not too good at all this, I'm afraid,' Ben stuttered, throwing a frightened glance at the dance floor, which was now a frenzy of waving arms and kicking legs as couples gyrated themselves into oblivion. 'Perhaps something slower?' he offered hopefully.

'Yes, alright,' the girl smiled, sitting back in her chair. 'I'd like that.'

Her eyes sparkled with reflected light as she held Ben's glance for a moment longer. He dragged his eyes away, feeling a buzzing in his ears that had nothing to do with the music. She certainly didn't have the glamour and flamboyance of her friend, but Ben thought she was nice-looking and rather more his type – her pretty face was less made up and she was quieter of demeanour than her friend. With her fair, wavy hair and blue eyes, she reminded him a bit of April. Her clothes were rather plainer than her friend's too: a neat white blouse and a full, flower-patterned skirt pinched at the waist with a broad patent leather belt. He was about to ask her name when the music finished in a crescendo and Woody and his partner returned to the table, both flushed and breathless.

'Hello you two lovebirds! 'About time we saw you on the floor instead of canoodling here!' he said laughing, his face sweaty with his exertions. 'Dot and I are going out to get some fresh air,' he said, as his dancing partner picked up her bag and coat from her chair. 'See you later, alligator!' he said, as he offered the giggling Dorothy his arm in a flamboyant gesture of chivalry. He threw Ben a sly wink as the pair departed.

Ben and his companion were left at the table feeling slightly awkward for a moment. Neither spoke but they caught each other's eyes as the departing couple left the room and then spontaneously burst into laughter. 'I wonder what those two are up to,' Ben speculated unnecessarily, knowing exactly what Woody might have in mind. 'I'm afraid I'm not as deft on the floor as my light-footed friend,' Ben said, 'but perhaps we'd better have that dance now? I think can manage this one.' The band had just struck up a quickstep and he'd summoned up the courage to venture the proposal.

The pair introduced themselves as they walked onto the floor. 'I'm Daisy,' she said, smiling. Ben thought her name suited her slender form and sunny face, caught at that moment in a shaft of sunlight beaming in. 'What's yours?' she asked, examining Ben's eyes as he wrapped his arm around her waist and took her hand in his. 'Benjamin,' he told her as he took his first tentative step. He felt his heart racing. It had been a long time since he'd felt such female closeness, and Daisy's soft curves pressing against him so intimately was electrifying. Ben found himself a bit clumsy on his feet at first, but she was as light as a feather and so nimble on her hers that she followed his unpractised steps without a frown. Suddenly Ben felt like Fred Astaire as his feet fell into gear. His dancing lessons at Halton must have done something for him after all, he thought. He noticed glances from other dancers as he and Daisy traversed the floor with such dizzying alacrity and hoped that the looks were admiring rather than fearful of collision. Too soon, the quickstep reached its finale, and, flushed and breathless, Ben took Daisy's arm to lead her from the floor. 'Not so fast,' she laughed, as she pulled Ben back, 'you're a natural! Time for just one more?'

They must have danced at least three more dances together that afternoon, and, as the band packed up their instruments to go home, Ben realised that he had enjoyed Daisy's company and sensed that she had enjoyed his. 'Next Saturday?' he dared to ask as they left the hall, her arm through his as if they had already become a couple. 'Same time, same place?' he suggested.

'I'd like that,' she replied.

With no news of the progress of his aircrew application, Ben met Daisy most Saturdays at the dance hall during the coming months, often following their dancing with tea in a nearby tearoom and sometimes a visit to the cinema if a good film was being shown. They talked a lot, as young people often do as a friendship develops – learning about each other, probing each other's qualities, likes and dislikes, and testing compatibility – but they laughed a lot too. So far from home, with no family around him, with only the itinerant Woody as a friend, and living on a remote seaplane base at the bottom end of Southampton Water, Ben came to see Daisy as more than an occasional companion and missed her when they were apart.

It turned out that Daisy worked at the Supermarine Aircraft works at Woolston, an art-deco-fronted factory on the eastern bank of the river Itchen adjacent to the 'floating bridge' ferry that linked Woolston with the city on the opposite side. At first, she wouldn't tell Ben what she did there – she'd been sworn to keep 'mum' under the Official Secrets Act, she'd told him. But when she got to know him better, she revealed that she was a fitter on the Spitfire production line. She'd been apprenticed at Supermarine soon after war had been declared when most young men in the area had been called up. She was now a qualified fitter and loved the work. Her parents worked there too, she told him. She lived with them in their family home, a detached house on Peartree Road, a leafy avenue not far from the works. She took him there to meet them one Saturday afternoon. Her mother and father, both well into their fifties, had produced Daisy, their only child, quite late, having not married until the last war had run its course. They too had worked at Supermarine for some years: mother, as a cook in the works canteen, father, as a production line foreman on the factory floor. He'd been an aircraft mechanic in the Royal Flying Corps and proudly showed Ben his campaign medals and photographs of himself in uniform. The two men had a lot in common and got on well.

As the weeks and months of waiting for his fate to be decided dragged on, Daisy's home became a sort of weekend refuge for Ben, which allowed him to escape the bare cold walls of his accommodation block at Calshot. It reminded him of April's home in Backworth and the warm welcome and comfort that he had felt there too. Over time, he came to enjoy the domestic homeliness there so much that he felt rather envious of Daisy's family life and began to think that one day he might want to create such a life for himself. Moreover, he and Daisy seemed so compatible, so comfortable with each other, that he could even imagine settling down with her one day. Although she would never raise his pulse rate in quite the same way that April had, she was shapely and attractive and knew how to please him with her tender looks and touches. It was the first time since his break with April that he had felt that way.

Chapter 14

Bolton Paul Defiant
Gunnery Training at RAF Walney Island

The news of the German advances through the Low Countries and into northern France, and the British Expeditionary Force's rearguard action and subsequent retreat towards the Channel coast was a serious blow to national morale. Until then, Corporal Benjamin Hardy had hardly been touched by the war even as late as the Spring of 1940. As an aeroengine mechanic, working at a non-operational Sunderland maintenance unit at the bottom end of Southampton Water, the war had had little direct impact on his life. He had settled into a regular and not excessively demanding routine, balancing the demands of his work with some recreational pursuits, and splitting his time between RAF Calshot and Peartree Road. When the belated invitation to attend for aircrew selection arrived, therefore, it almost took him by surprise. The letter had been so long in coming that his initial passion to re-train as aircrew had begun to wane. It must be said, however, that this had more to do with his association with Daisy than with any disaffection with flying, of which he anyway seemed to be getting plenty as a frequent supernumerary crew member on Sunderlands. Moreover, having not heard about the progress of his application for so long, he had already reconciled himself to rejection. With the letter's arrival, however, he now realised that the war for him might soon become very real.

With only three days' notice, Ben was requested to report to the aircrew selection centre at RAF Padgate in Cheshire to be assessed for suitability. The selection process consisted of several phases. First, Ben and his fellow aircrew candidates were subjected to thorough medical examinations, including tests of all his faculties: sight, hearing, heart and other bodily functionality. Next, came a series of formal interviews that would probe motivation and character. And finally, and only if those first two phases had been successfully completed, came a full day of practical exercises to test teamwork, initiative, and communication skills. This final phase would see the aspirant aircrew divided into teams of five, of which each member would in turn be asked to lead in tasks that were designed to be difficult if not impossible. When it came to Ben's turn, his assigned task was to get himself, his team, and a forty-gallon oil drum across a simulated 'crocodile infested river', which in reality was the water jump of the steeplechase track on the station sports field. For this task, he was provided with some planks and scaffolding poles, none of which individually were quite long enough to bridge the chasm, and some lengths of rope and parachute cord. The clock was ticking, the assessing officers were watching, and Ben was given ten minutes to come up with a plan. Although it was not a perfect plan, limited as it was by materials and time, it was at least a plan, and he briefed his young team accordingly and then rallied them in their assigned tasks. First, some planks and poles were lashed together to create a sturdy platform. This was then projected from the water's edge as far as it would reach and suspended by ropes, cantilever fashion, from the apex of an 'A' frame braced with guy ropes anchored in the ground behind. Two more planks, just long enough, were then gingerly extended from the platform to span the remaining distance to the opposite bank. With this impressive construction in place, Ben now had to get his team, the oil drum, and finally himself to the other side of the water jump without getting wet. Surprisingly, the first two team members actually did get across unwetted (and uneaten by crocodiles); but the ground was soft, the anchors gave way, the 'A' frame collapsed, and Ben, the oil drum, and the rest of his team were tipped unceremoniously into the water. Such a chaotic pantomime then developed that everyone, including Ben, his team, and the watching assessors fell about in fits of laughter. In the debrief, Ben was awarded good marks for the ingenuity of his approach and top marks for his sense of humour.

Despite, or perhaps because of the competitive element in these tasks, Ben found the whole process immensely enjoyable. Joining with other like-minded young men, while demonstrably holding his own in their company in such testing situations, built his confidence as well as his enthusiasm for the role for which he had applied. It seems that he made the grade too, for, having travelled ten-hours by train to Padgate and ten-hours back to Calshot, he was given just a week before he had to pack his bags again. This time, he would be sent to attend the air gunnery school at RAF Walney, an airfield on a windswept island off Barrow-in-Furness.

The course for which Ben had been selected, he was told, had two objectives. Firstly, it would expose candidates to the rigours and discomforts of flying in a combat aircraft so that those unsuitable for the role could be identified and weeded out; and secondly, it would provide some limited cross-training in air gunnery for rear-crew destined to fly in bombers, for whom such skills might come in handy in an aerial scrap.

Prior to setting off for Walney Island, Ben met Daisy for one last tea dance, and he spent that evening with her at her home. He and she talked long into the early hours about their individual fears and hopes for the future – where the war might take them, what dangers they and their loved ones might face, and what their lives might look like afterwards – a conversation that no doubt echoed those taking place in millions of homes around the country as it prepared itself for war. The future was beginning to look bleak. German expansion across Europe seemed unstoppable, and every day the news got worse.

Over the months of their association, Ben had grown rather fond of Daisy, and he became increasingly fretful as the time for his departure approached, thinking darkly that these moments together could very well be amongst their last. He had no idea yet where he would be sent after his course at Walney, but it was certain that being aircrew would put him in the line of fire. Bombers were sitting ducks in enemy skies, as so many German bomber crews would already testify had they survived encounters with the Spitfires and Hurricanes of Fighter Command only that summer, in what was now called the Battle of

Britain by Winston Churchill. If Ben was apprehensive for himself, however, he was also worried for Daisy. Aircraft factories like Supermarine where Daisy and her parents worked were potential German targets, which would put them in the firing line too. Nothing could be taken for granted.

It was only at the point of their farewell, suddenly taken by a wave of despondency, that Ben thought that he should promise more to Daisy than merely to write. It would be a comfort for them both, he thought, to have something meaningful and optimistic to cling to in the uncertain times that lay ahead. He wondered if she felt the same way. 'D'you think we should commit to being more than just good friends to each other, Daisy?' he asked lightly, as they stood together under her front porch. The question spilled from his lips before he had considered where it might lead. He knew very well that it would be reckless to commit himself to anyone at times like this, yet the desire for some certainty was overwhelming. And having got the ball rolling with his question, so to speak, he was now propelled purely by its momentum.

Daisy examined Ben's expression seriously, her bright blue eyes searching his for meaning. 'But we are more than good friends, Ben, aren't we?'

'Yes, but…' Ben hesitated, searching for the right words without really knowing what he wanted to say. 'Could we give a name to what we are to each other, sweetheart?' It was the first time that he had used that term of endearment, but it was what his heart seemed to be telling him in these last heady moments before their parting. 'I mean, could we make a promise to each other, Daisy? Perhaps that we'll keep ourselves for each other?'

She didn't answer, but simply smiled and stared up into Ben's eyes enquiringly.

'What is it that you are asking me, Ben?' Daisy asked, still smiling, her expression, contrivedly innocent. She knew exactly where this was leading and was revelling in the moment.

Ben took a breath, took her hands in his and lowered himself onto one knee, laughing at the theatricality of his gesture as he did so. 'Will you be mine, Daisy? Not now, of course,' he interjected quickly as a sudden pang of doubt overtook him, 'but as soon as this wretched war is over and as soon as we can see a safe future for ourselves ahead?'

Daisy wrapped her arms around Ben's head and brought it to her soft belly where he could hear her heart beating as loudly as his own.

'You are a *lovely* man, Ben! I've felt the same way myself for weeks and wondered if you'd ever ask. Yes, of course I'll be yours!' she said, laughing, with pure joy in her voice.

Ben raised himself to his feet, wrapped his arms around Daisy's shoulders, kissed her lightly on her lips, and said: 'Then wait here just a moment; there's something I have to ask your father!' And with that, he left her standing on the doorstep, strode back down the hall, and entered the living room. Daisy's father would, of course, give the pair his blessing.

As soon as Corporal Ben Hardy arrived at RAF Walney Island, he was told that he would not be there for long. Most courses at the airbase were combined wireless operator and air gunnery courses lasting up to eighteen months, but Ben and half-a-dozen other chaps like him destined to become bomber flight engineers, had been assigned to the short air gunnery course lasting only a month. Their course would cover just the essentials of aerial gunnery, enough to be able to load, point, and squeeze the trigger if they had to take the place of a dedicated air gunner who'd been wounded from an attack in enemy skies. Bombers generally had two, and sometimes three, gun turrets depending upon the aircraft type, so it made sense to have some cross-training between the rear crew. For new boys like Ben, the gunnery course would also serve as an aerial baptism by fire – and it would almost literally be just that. Flying was not a task that everyone would take to, especially flying as a rear crew member. Frozen to the core on a filthy night and thrown around the sky strapped inside a narrow metal tube wasn't always going to be a load of fun! Even this relatively benign initial training course would have its casualties – two of Ben's fellow trainees were so air-sick that they couldn't continue, and another broke a leg slipping off a wet wing while climbing out of the aircraft.

After a week's ground school and some practice firing from a static gun turret on a rifle range, Ben and his compatriots were given six flights each in a Bolton Paul Defiant, during which they would each shoot off over twelve hundred 20mm rounds. The Defiant aircraft was a bit of a hybrid. It had the rotating gun turret of a bomber on its upper fuselage just behind the pilot's cockpit, but it looked a little like a Hurricane. In fact, it was powered by the same Merlin engine as the Hurricane, but it was heavier, less manoeuvrable, and had no wing-mounted guns, which made it vulnerable to head on attacks. In theory, the gun turret (in which the student gunners would do their training) gave all-round cover, but the guns weren't allowed to fire directly ahead or directly astern to protect the propellor, the tail plane, and the pilot! The concept sounded quite good in theory and was moderately successful against unescorted German bombers, but when German fighters started to accompany the bomber waves, Defiants became easy prey.

On the six training flights that Ben flew from Walney, his practice rounds were mostly shot at the sea (which was difficult to miss!) and at banner targets towed by another aircraft on a very long cable (wisely)! He also practised tracking Spitfires that carried out simulated attacks on his Defiant – using camera film rather than bullets. But his guns had to be aimed so far ahead of the speeding Spitfire's fight path that it became a bit of a guessing game and Ben's gunsight camera hardly recorded any 'hits' at all. In a real attack, the use of tracer rounds would have helped because their trajectory could be seen and brought to bear on the target. Even so, there still wouldn't have been much time to think, especially if the attack came out of the sun. In those sorts of situations, all Ben could do was swing his turret roughly in the right direction, squeeze the trigger, and hope for the best! For the Spitfire pilots, it was a turkey shoot and a lot of fun!

Nevertheless, at the completion of his course, Ben was given an 'average' assessment, which was fine by him. Being seen to be too good as a gunner might have given the RAF the idea that that was what he should become. He needn't have worried though – his posting notice had already been written – to RAF Waddington in Lincolnshire for flight engineer training on the brand-new Avro Manchester.

Chapter 15

Corporal 'Woody' Green had just completed his morning ablutions and was buttoning up his shirt in front of his mirror when Ben entered Woody's bedroom in the RAF Calshot Corporals' accommodation block. Woody seemed surprised to see him.

'Didn't think I'd see you again so soon,' Woody said, straightening his tie. 'What the hell are you doing all the way down here, anyway? Seen sense at last, I bet! Being a flyboy's not all it's made out to be?'

Ben laughed. 'Not pleased to see me then!'

Woody's uniform jacket hung on his wardrobe door and Ben noticed the shiny new corporal's chevrons on its sleeves.

'Hmmm!' Ben pointed at the new insignia. 'Made it after all! I'm impressed!'

'I got your old job, Ben, thanks very much,' said Woody. 'And you're not getting it back! So don't even think of it.'

Ben grinned broadly. 'Don't worry, Woody, I'm not here to stay. I've been posted to Waddington. I need to clear from here, and then,' he added, rubbing his hands vigorously, 'I've got a week's leave before I start. So, how about I take you out for a beer once we're finished today? I think I owe you one.'

'What? For my introduction to that girl of yours? Hah! Yes, you do, don't you!'

'We've got ourselves sort of hitched, Woody, so you and I are going to drink to that. How about it?'

Calshot had remained Ben's parent unit while he completed his short course at Walney, and there was now a 'clearing' procedure to be completed. 'Clearing' was a tedious administrative procedure, which had Ben traipsing around the base from office to office, handing back equipment and manuals, settling outstanding bills, and signing off. When he eventually reached the station mail room, there was a letter waiting for him. It was his mother's reply to his own letter, written before he went to Walney, in which he had told her of his selection for aircrew training. *'Your news makes us both very proud of you, son, but do take care,'* she'd written briefly in response, and then gone on to give Ben her regular update of affairs of state in Backworth: news that the new Baptist minister had arrived; that Frank had started working at the pit; and finally: *'your Da is back in uniform again! He's joined the Backworth Home Guard, God bless him'.* Interesting as it was to be kept in touch, not much of real note seemed to have changed in the parish – except for one matter about which Ben's mother seemed intent on keeping him regularly informed.

'Oh, and your April's got herself engaged,' she wrote as a postscript, 'to that chap I told you about – the one that her father doesn't much like. It's in the papers. They'll be married in the summer, the paper said.'

Ben wanted to shout out loud that April wasn't his anymore, that he was now engaged to Daisy, and that his life was moving on in a different direction entirely. All this was true, of course, but later in his life when he recalled these frequent updates on his former girlfriend's movements, he would come to realise that mothers sometimes know their sons better than they do themselves.

Woody was on duty for the morning shift that day and did not finish until early afternoon, by which time Ben had completed his clearance procedure and been signed off. The two men met up again in time to catch the mid-afternoon bus to Lymington. Arriving in the town, the pair made their way down to the Ship Inn on the quayside, a popular half-timbered hostelry of attractive character and excellent beer. It was a warm day, and so, with pint glasses in hand, the pair seated themselves outside to enjoy the sunshine and the view of the river. Flushed with a modest sense of achievement in passing his gunnery course, Ben told his friend all about it – until Woody's gaze began to wander. 'Can't say that it would appeal to me,' said he, interrupting Ben's enthusiastic monologue and stifling a yawn. 'Anyway, let's talk about something more important!' said Woody, brightening up. 'Tell me about you and Daisy. I knew you'd tied the knot, by the way – Dorothy told me. She and Daisy work the same shift at Supermarine and there're no secrets between them. Trouble is, Dot's getting ideas now too, so I'll have to watch my step!' He rolled his eyes. 'I've always known that you're a braver man than I am, Ben, but getting yourself hitched is a bit quick, isn't it? What on earth's got into you, man!' Woody looked incredulous.

'I don't know, Woody. Must have had a rush of blood to the head, I think.' Ben laughed then suddenly turned serious. 'It was on the evening I left for Walney – when we were saying goodbye at her parent's place. A vulnerable moment, I guess you might say. The idea just popped into my head as the right thing to do.' He shrugged his shoulders. 'You know, Woody, with me becoming aircrew and about to be sent off to the far-flung edges of the known universe and all that!' He smiled haplessly, then gazed for several moments at a sailing boat moving down river on the ebb tide. 'And she loves me, Woody – amazingly! Which is a good start, isn't it; and we do get on well, you know.' A furrow on his brow came and went. 'I just wanted to have some certainty in my life, that's all. Things are going to get a bit rough if the balloon really does go up – especially with me flying bombers. And I guess I wanted someone to be there for me when I come back – some normality to look forward to. That make sense?'

Woody looked dubious. 'That last bit does, mate. I guess I feel the same sometimes – even if I shan't be as likely as you to be shot out of the sky! But what about that other girl of yours?' he said. 'The one up north? You used to talk about her a lot, you know. Is she completely out of the picture now? You sure this isn't one of those frying pan and fire situations or a rebound thing?'

Ben recalled his mother's letter with the news of April's engagement. 'No. April's definitely out of the picture for good now, Woody,' he said firmly. 'She's doing the sensible thing and marrying a banker, and I can't say I blame her. Not many women would like the life of a service wife – trailing around after their men like a nomad – especially when children come along! I still think about her though – first love and all that – but time moves on you know; and I can't spend my life wishing things were otherwise.' Ben took a mouthful of beer then let his gaze wander again in a moment of thoughtful reflection. 'Daisy's different though,' he said eventually. 'She's easy-going and seems to like the RAF too, which is a bonus. And it helps that she's in the aircraft business, I think. We can speak the same language…' Ben chuckled as he grasped the irony in what he'd said. 'Hah…well, maybe my accent's still a bit of a challenge for her! But don't worry, Woody, we're not rushing into it,' he insisted, 'and we'll think it all through again when this war is over – to be sure that we know what we're doing before we walk down the aisle.'

Ben himself may not have been aware of what he was revealing in the earnestness of his explanation, but it was clear to Woody that Ben's feelings for Daisy fell a little short of love. It may have been fondness or a good friendship, perhaps a refuge in choppy seas, or even the comforting embrace of being loved in a time of loneliness, he thought; but was that enough? He wondered what his friend really felt for Daisy. But then, 'What is love, anyway,' he asked himself, 'if not the sum of all those things?' He gave Ben one of his long hard looks. 'Ok my friend,' he said, at last. 'Let's drink to that!' And he raised his glass and downed what was left in it in a single gulp. 'My round, I think!'

With plans to spend his week's leave with Daisy and her parents in their home in Woolston, Ben had intended to catch the early bus to Fawley station for a train to Hythe from where he would take the ferry to Southampton. His outing to Lymington with Woody the previous afternoon, however, had turned into a late night that had had its consequences. It was therefore late morning when he finally left Calshot and already well past noon when he took his seat in the cabin of the little ferry to cross Southampton

Water to the city's quay. It was 24th September 1940, a date that the population of Woolston and Northam will mourn forever. German bombers had been targeting Southampton on and off since the June of that year, but most of the bombs had been targeted on the city's docks and the railway infrastructure at nearby Eastleigh. The dull thump of bombs exploding and the pom-pom-pom of anti-aircraft fire had sometimes been heard even as far away as Calshot, but the scale of those raids had been relatively small.

Things were about to change.

Fighter Command's 'Battle of Britain' victory during the summer of that year may have stymied Hitler's planned invasion, but now that his Luftwaffe was operating from the airfields of northern France, his bombers could nip across the Channel under the radar and attack coastal ports practically at will. That day, at the very time that Ben was crossing to Southampton on the ferry from Hythe, their attack would take the city completely by surprise.

The ferry was about half-way across the mile-wide stretch of water when Ben first heard the drone of aircraft engines. He would have recognised the sound of the Sunderland's four Pegasus engines or the Spitfire's Merlin and knew at once that the drone he heard was from neither of those. Grabbing his holdall, he left his fellow passengers in the cabin and climbed up onto the open deck. From there, he had a clear view down Southampton Water and across the Solent to the distant Isle of Wight, and he swept his gaze around the southern horizon. The drone of engines increased steadily in volume and soon Ben's ears were able to distinguish the throbbing of multiple propellors. The unusual sound was as sinister as it was foreboding. Then, low on the horizon, coming up fast from the south only just above the treeline, Ben spotted a number of twin-engine bombers in sections of two or three, stretched out in long line astern. Although he could not identify the aircraft by type, they were like nothing he had seen before. He was certain that they must be German bombers. Those in the cabin must have seen the aircraft too for the little boat lurched to starboard as many rushed to the seaward side to get a better view.

Grabbing the handrail to steady himself, Ben swept his eyes forward along the bombers' projected flightpath trying to predict their route. The aircraft seemed at first to be following the eastern shoreline of Southampton Water towards the city centre, but as they passed the prominent clock tower of Netley Hospital, they banked to starboard and increased height. It was then that he saw the black crosses and loaded bomb pylons on the underside of their wings. His worst fears were now confirmed. Worse still, he could see now that their targets must be the Supermarine works on the river Itchen, only a mile or so ahead of the leading formation. Ben prayed to God that neither Daisy nor her parents would be on shift at the factory as scores of torpedo-shaped projectiles dropped from the attackers' wings in graceful yet deadly arcs. Their multiple impacts created waves of rippling percussions that pummelled his eardrums and threw huge volumes of smoke and debris high into the air. The ferry scurried for cover, and Ben's view of Woolston was obscured by the warehouses on the quayside. He could not see if the bombs were hitting their mark, but multiple detonations continued to split the air.

With his pulse racing and desperate to reach Woolston and find Daisy, Ben leapt off the ferry even as the vessel was still closing on the quay. He practically threw his holdall into the ticket office as he passed it, shouting to the clerk that he'd be back. The bag was packed with all his worldly possessions and there was no way he'd have been able to run while carrying its weight. Ben ran as fast as his legs would carry him. He knew the route well. He'd walked it many times before on his way to Daisy's home, but he was sprinting along that same route now as if his life depended on it. Explosions were still hammering his ears as the acrid smell of cordite reached his nose. Drifting smoke and fragments of falling debris gave the place a desolate air. Trams and vehicles sat abandoned. The streets were otherwise empty. The people had run for cover. Only now did the air raid sirens wind up to an echoing wail as the anti-aircraft batteries opened fire.

Too late, Ben thought!

Chapter 16

By the time he reached the Itchen riverbank, the bombing had ceased and the skies over Woolston were no longer full of menace. He saw the last of the bombers disappearing southwards at high speed, but they had left behind an almost unbelievable scene of devastation. Not more than two-hundred yards from where he stood at the river's edge, fires raged along the length of the opposite bank. Black smoke, embedded with crimson and orange flames, billowed upwards in great volumes that darkened the sky. One end of the Supermarine works had been destroyed completely, its structure now a smoking heap of bricks and bared and burning roof timbers sticking up like the charred fingers of a dead hand. Swinging his gaze upriver, he saw that many of the residential streets had suffered even worse, the skyline was now jagged with remnants of chimney stacks and collapsed roofs. Fires burned amongst the ruins; palls of dust and thick white smoke wafted on the wind; the reek of burning rubber and spent explosive assaulted Ben's nose and choked his lungs. The scene was otherwise strangely silent as if it itself had been stunned by the sheer onslaught. There was no movement, no sign of life.

Ben was desperate to get across the river. Not at all sure what he would or could do once he reached the other side, his mind was set on one thing and one thing only: he must find Daisy and her parents. The floating bridge that ferried pedestrians and vehicles across the river lay nudging the far foreshore with its ramp down and several cars still aboard, their doors left open as their occupants had run for cover. Evidently, the vessel's skipper had run for cover too. The vessel would be going nowhere for a while. Ben scanned the near shore. Several small rowing boats sat on the mud, their painters running to mooring rings on the sea wall. He clambered down onto the shingled beach and ran towards a small tender that still had oars in its rowlocks. He quickly released it and slid it into the water, pushing off and hopping into it as it became waterborne. Within moments, he had both oars thrashing the water as he set off across the river.

The ebb of a neap tide was in its last sixth, so there was not much current to lay off. It took Ben only a few minutes to reach the opposite foreshore. He beached the boat below an upturned jetty at the southern end of the town, adjacent to the smoking ruin of a warehouse. As quickly as he could, he made his way along the rubble-strewn streets towards Daisy's home on Peartree Road. The bombing seemed to have been indiscriminate. If the aircraft factory or the nearby Thorneycroft shipbuilding yard had been the German targets, the raid had only been partially successful. More damage seemed to have been caused to surrounding residential housing than the works themselves. Rescue parties and ARP men were soon appearing amongst the ruins, pulling out casualties and helping survivors to safety. An ambulance came slowly towards him, ringing its bell as it picked its way around the debris that littered the road. Choking smoke and dust hung heavy in the air.

As Ben turned into Peartree Road, a fire engine came screeching up behind him, its crew leaping into action to couple up its hoses. 'Stay clear!' shouted one of the firemen as the hoses were run out. Ben's first sight of the bomb damage stopped him dead in his tracks as he took it in. Through the drifting smoke and falling ash, his gaze swept along the road as he counted off the frontages to find the one he sought – Daisy's bay-windowed home in a row of others similar in what was once a quiet and leafy avenue. But Daisy's home and those that had stood on either side of it were simply no longer there, their former bricks, mortar and timbers reduced to piles of rubble. Beyond the smoking debris, amazingly, other houses in the road still looked structurally intact, though some windows had been blown-out and several roofs had lost half their tiles. It seemed that only one bomb had struck Peartree Road, and Daisy's home had been its point of impact.

Ben's legs refused to move as he stood, dumbstruck, surveying the wreckage of what was once the home he'd come to love almost as his own – picturing it still standing there as he had last seen it. If Daisy and her parents had been in it at the time, they would have perished instantly. When he'd first spotted the German bombers flying up Southampton Water towards the Supermarine factory, he'd prayed that Daisy and her parents had not been there. Now he prayed to God that they had not been at home. Supermarine had got off relatively lightly, whereas their home had been totally destroyed. The firemen had by now worked along the road ahead of him and were already hosing down the fires. Rescue parties and ARP men soon arrived, and Ben followed them down the road, picking his way through the scattered debris beneath trees that had been stripped bare by the blast.

'You alright, mate?' one of the men asked, taking Ben's arm. Ben's uniform was covered in dust. It must have looked like he was a survivor too.

'That house there,' he said, almost incoherently in his daze, pointing at the ruins. He could not finish his sentence.

'You wait here, mate, we'll take a look. Not much hope I'm afraid.'

Ben stood back and watched as several of the rescuers picked carefully amongst the rubble, lifting timbers, peering into cavities, listening for signs of life. But Ben already knew that if anyone had been inside the house, they could not possibly have survived. He waited for a while longer as the men continued their search, but he could see that there was no hope. Eventually, becoming impatient for action, he called out: 'I'm going back to the factory! They could have been at work today. It's possible that they got to the air raid shelters in time, so I'm going back to check.'

Thrusting his worst fears to the back of his mind, Ben headed back in the direction from which he had come, but he had only gone a short distance when he saw Daisy, a lonely figure coming towards him. She was still dressed in her overalls and headscarf and running in such wide-eyed panic that she didn't seem to recognise Ben standing in her way. Ben had to grab her as she made to dodge past him. She struggled to free herself, craning to look over his shoulder into the road where her home had once stood. She had seen the smoke and the fire engine, and her frightened eyes went wild. Ben could feel her heart thumping against his chest.

'The house has gone, Daisy,' Ben said gravely, tightening his hold to stop her breaking from his grip. 'No, no, no..!'

she cried, wriggling in his arms. 'Let me go, let me go!' she screamed.

Ben took her firmly by the shoulders and shook her. 'Think Daisy! Think!' he shouted, looking her full in the face. 'Were your parents with you at the works today?' The fierceness of his look captured her attention and seemed to calm her. She shook her head. 'No, they were on the early shift today. They would have left at about one o'clock, I think, but they may not have come straight home.' There was some hope in her tone now as her eyes came into focus. Her face had drained of colour.

'Is there anywhere else your parents could have gone before the raid, Daisy? Might they have gone to the shops? Family? Friends?' Ben shot these suggestions at her, wanting to turn her thoughts to more hopeful possibilities and away from the bleakness of her worst fears.

Daisy returned Ben's stare blankly. He had to repeat his questions before she responded. 'My grandparents' place,' she said, at last. 'Yes,' she said, her voice now lifting in tone, 'yes, they might well have gone there. They often do.' Her face lit up.

Daisy's grandparents lived in a detached Edwardian-style house in Bitterne, another east-of-the-river suburb of Southampton, located about a mile up the hill from Woolston. Daisy had taken Ben to call on them before, so he knew the way. In his race to get there, he left Daisy trailing behind and was first to enter the old couple's front garden. He found them closing the front panels of their Anderson shelter. They must have heard his footsteps on the gravel path for they turned expectantly. Ben saw their expressions change from hope to disappointment the instant they recognised him – he was not who they most wanted to see.

'Are Daisy's parents with you!' Ben shouted hopefully as he neared; but the anxious looks that passed between the old couple told him all he needed to know. He was in the middle of telling them what he'd seen in Woolston as Daisy caught up. She was still catching her breath. Immediately recognising the situation for what she most feared, her eyes began to well up. By this time, the couple too were beside themselves, having just received Ben's report. They said that they had tried to telephone Supermarine once the 'All Clear' siren had sounded but that they'd not been able to get through. Nothing had been heard from anyone since the bombing. They'd decided to remain where they were in case their son or daughter-in-law called, but as time had passed, the lack of contact was becoming more and more frightening. Surely, they would have been in touch by now if they were alright?

Ben urged them all not to lose hope. 'Look, there's a good chance that they'll have taken cover somewhere,' he said. 'There'll be air-raid shelters at the works – they'll have taken cover there for sure.' He was trying to reassure them, though he felt less than confident himself. 'They might even now be making their way here,' he added, throwing a glance back towards the front gate as if Daisy's parents might suddenly appear. It was a vain hope, and after a moment's further thought, he decided that he would have to do more to ease their anguish. 'I'll go back down to Woolston to see what I can find out.' Ben's desire for action was once again coming to the fore. 'I suggest that you three go inside, make yourself a cup of tea, and wait here in case they turn up. If they're still down in Woolston, I'll find them.' He produced a notebook and pencil from his pocket and handed them to the old man 'Here,' he said, 'write down your telephone number for me, sir, I'll call you when there's something to report.'

With only the slimmest of hopes that his search would be successful, he left the worried threesome and raced back down the hill, deciding to start his search at the site of Daisy's home. If her parents had survived the bombing, he was pretty sure that they would have gone there first.

Peartree Road had already been closed off when Ben arrived, and an elderly warden stood at a barrier on guard. The white letter 'W' on his helmet, and a row of campaign medals on his battledress tunic identified him as a veteran member of the ARP volunteers. Behind him, the rescue and firefighting teams that Ben had seen earlier were still working amongst the rubble. 'Any luck?' Ben asked the warden as he approached the barrier. The veteran shook his head. 'Not yet,' he replied. 'But I suppose it's good news that they've not found any bodies,' he added dryly. 'But then, they've not found any survivors either. And I don't think they will now. If anyone had been inside those houses when the bomb hit, they'd have been blown to bits. Anyway, what's your business here, corporal? Do you live in the road?' he asked, consulting his clipboard which had several sheets of paper attached to it.

'Well, no, not a resident exactly, but I'm connected to the people who lived there,' Ben replied, pointing at the wreckage of Daisy's home. 'Their daughter's my fiancée. She's safe with her grandparents up in Bitterne now. It's her parents I'm worried about. I'm hoping they might have taken shelter somewhere. Can I leave a message with you in case they turn up?' The warden turned his clipboard round for Ben to view. 'What's their name and address?' he asked.

Ben ran his finger down the list of names and addresses in the road and tapped Daisy's. 'This one,' he said. 'Can you make a note that their daughter, Daisy, is with her grandparents in Bitterne.' He dictated their contact details, which the warden noted.

'I'd better have your name too, corporal.' Ben gave it as his eyes wandered to the pile of rubble that was Daisy's home and shook his head despondently. 'I hope to God they're safe,' he said. 'I'm going to go back to the Supermarine works now in the hope that I'll find them there; it's where they worked. With luck, they'll have taken cover in a shelter there.'

'Well, best of luck, young man,' said the warden, as Ben turned to leave: 'And being a man in uniform,' he added, 'you don't need to be reminded of the dangers of all this debris lying around, do you? So don't go poking about!' Ben acknowledged the warning with a grim shake of his head and strode off with the intention of backtracking the route that Daisy's parents might take if they were making their way to Peartree Road. He had not gone more than half a mile, however, when the distant drone of aircraft engines once again caught his attention. Stopping to listen more closely, he immediately recognised the same throbbing beat of multiple aircraft propellors that he'd heard from the ferry earlier that afternoon. Even as he'd watched the German bombers scuttling southwards after they'd dropped their deadly loads, it had crossed his mind that they might be back. Now, sure enough, here they were again! The distant drone became louder by the second and Ben sensed from its direction that he must be in the bombers' path. He glanced about frantically for somewhere to take cover. Unluckily, he was crossing open ground at that moment and there was no obvious hiding place nearby. But fifty yards off to his right, across a strip of meadow, a line of mature trees and bushes marked the riverbank. With no time to think and seeing nothing better, he made a dash for it. But the engine noise came upon him so quickly that it drowned out the pounding in his chest as he sprinted through the long grass at full pelt. Glancing over his shoulder as he ran, he was terrified to catch sight of three, twin-engine bombers coming fast across the rooftops, not a hundred yards behind. He knew then that he could not possibly make the cover that he sought, yet he kept up his desperate sprint, his lungs screaming for air. The engine noise mounted quickly to a thundering crescendo as the lead aircraft came upon him, its shadow darkening his path like that of a raptor's wings – with Ben, the fleeing prey. He heard the shrill whistle of falling bombs then felt the aircraft's pressure wave as it passed directly overhead. Then came a monumental blast that seemed to lift him bodily into the sky. He felt himself tumbling in space then saw the ground rushing up to meet him. Then everything went black…

Chapter 17

In the moments before Ben regained full consciousness, images of his headlong dash across the meadow kept replaying in his mind like a repeating film loop. In his semi-conscious state, however, it was not enemy bombers that threatened but some unseen aerial terror that was swooping down upon him with claws outstretched. Sheer panic urged his legs to sprint, but they felt as heavy as lead and his muscles had given up the fight. He was stuck in a quagmire, the shelter of the riverbank never came closer, and the shadow of the terror turned day to night as its claws plucked him up and tossed him into the air like carrion. It was as the green grass rushed up to meet him like an express train that he came back into the conscious world with a cry that brought a nurse to his bedside.

Ben would not remember exactly what he uttered when a woman's kindly face first swam into focus before his eyes, but it was probably something predictable like 'where am I!', because she told him that he was in the medical centre at the Thorneycroft shipyard. In his state of confusion, Ben stared up into her face uncomprehendingly at first, his mind still full of nightmarish images, but as she explained and as his mental fog began to clear, he began to understand why he was where he was. It seemed that he'd been very lucky. The exploding bomb had not been close enough to do him any real damage and he'd got away with mild concussion and some superficial flesh wounds.

He'd been found near the riverbank only yards from the Thorneycroft works (which, she thought, the bombs had probably been aimed at) and brought to the medical centre on the back of a lorry on its way to the yard. The centre normally only dealt with minor injuries, the nurse told him – the sort of minor workplace injuries that were frequent where such heavy work took place – and since it seemed that first-aid and rest was all Ben needed, they had decided to keep him. The hospitals in the city were anyway too busy with more serious casualties to take him in, she said, and so Ben had become their special guest.

It was only then that Ben noticed the time. The hands on the clock pointed to ten o'clock, and from the bright sunshine that streamed in through the windows, he was shocked to realise that he must have been unconscious for some time. 'Since yesterday afternoon,' she told him. 'But the RAF has been notified,' she said. Ben asked how she had his details. 'Your dog tags', she answered. 'Your uniform was a bit of a giveaway too,' she smiled. 'It's being cleaned, by the way; you'll get it back in the morning. We're going to keep an eye on you for another night in case anything develops from that bang on your head, but you should be alright to leave us tomorrow.'

Ben spotted his holdall lying in the far corner of the room and asked how it had got there. The last time he'd seen it was when he'd left it at the ferry terminal in his rush to find Daisy. The nurse told him that the ticket clerk had given it to the police who'd tracked Ben down through the ARP. Ben's name, rank, and service number were on the bag's label. Ben marvelled at the efficiency of all this despite the obvious chaos that must have reigned in the city following the raid. It was the nurse's mention of the ARP that reminded him of his conversation with the warden on Peartree Road, and suddenly he remembered the mission that he'd been on. He sat up rather too quickly, and it made his head spin. 'I've got to make a telephone call,' he said, clutching his head, 'some people will be wondering where I am.' He made to get up, but the nurse restrained him. She was stronger than she looked.

'Calm down,' she said firmly, 'we found a telephone number in a notebook in a pocket of your uniform when we stripped you – Bitterne 317. I talked to your fiancée's grandparents last night. I told them where you were and that you were alright and that I'll call them again when you're ready to leave. So don't worry!'

'Did they say anything else?' Ben asked. 'Anything about Daisy's parents? We were worried about them.'

The nurse shook her head. 'No,' she said simply.

Ben feared the worst. Nevertheless, he did what he was told and stayed in bed for the rest of the day, feeling a bit of a fraud but accepting the nurse's advice. Later, someone brought him the evening newspaper which contained an account of the previous day's raids. It read:

Southampton Daily 25th June 1940

'Yesterday's raid came in two waves...the bombs straddled the railway embankment, and, tragically, hit the air raid shelters just as the Supermarine workers were arriving there, killing 24 and injuring 75. The factory was only slightly damaged and the effect on production is therefore

likely to be small. Some damage to railway lines and private property and numerous small fires were also caused. Total casualties in the two raids – 33 dead, 69 seriously injured and 120 slightly. Workers had to dig out people who had been buried because of the bombing and administer first aid as best they could. Female ambulance drivers then ferried the injured to the Royal South Hants Hospital showing great courage as they also had to drive through the second raid later in the afternoon.'

Ben was still reading it when Daisy arrived.

'They've been found,' she said from the doorway as she entered the room.

'Oh, thank God!' Ben replied too quickly, thinking that her parents must have survived after all, but then realised from her face that that was not at all what she meant.

'They were in the air raid shelter that got hit, Ben. They're gone.'

Daisy's words came from a face devoid of expression and from which all colour had drained. The dark shadows under her eyes suggested that she had probably not slept since Ben last saw her. She walked across the room and collapsed into the chair beside his bed, her eyes hardly leaving his. Ben could see her tears welling up as she lowered her head onto his bed where he could comfort her. He put an arm across her shoulders and stroked her hair gently as she wept into his blankets, her muffled sobs drawing simultaneously from him the most tender feelings of protection and the most intense anger at her loss. No words seemed necessary or appropriate. These two wounded souls must have fallen asleep in that consoling embrace because the next thing that Ben became aware of was the arrival of Daisy's grandparents at the side of his bed. They had come to take her home.

The following morning, a grey-haired lady wearing a wrap-around pinafore and a tied-up headscarf came into Ben's room carrying his uniform over her arm. She'd taken it upon herself to have it cleaned and pressed, she explained, as she hung the garment on a hook on the back of the door. She'd cleaned Ben's shoes too and washed the rest of his clothes, which she placed neatly on top of his holdall. She introduced herself as the medical centre's 'cleaner, tea lady, and general dogsbody'. Her dear husband had been in the RAF too, she said quickly, interrupting Ben just as he began to express his surprise and pleasure at her thoughtfulness. 'I can't have you leaving the Centre looking like something that the cat dragged in!' she said. 'Why, it'd let the side down, wouldn't it?' she protested in her Southampton drawl. Ben thought she must have taken a bit of a shine to him and offered to pay her for her trouble. 'Oh no, no; I couldn't let you do that,' she objected, a cross frown wrinkling her brow. 'It was something I wanted to do for you, darlin', so don't be daft.' And she went on to explain that Ben reminded her of her grandson who was also in the RAF. Intrigued, and believing that she wanted to tell him more, Ben asked her about the boy. 'He was a mechanic at the fighter base at Tangmere,' she told him proudly, and spoke for some minutes about her 'lovely boy in blue'. But it was not long before some recollection or memory brought a catch into her throat, and she faltered. Instinctively, Ben reached out and squeezed her arm. His touch brought a coy smile to the old lady's lips as she brushed a tear from her eye with her finger and then took hold of herself again with a resolute puffing up of her slender chest. 'Anyway, young man,' (her voice now back to its earlier robust vigour) 'you take good care o' yourself, you hear!' she said, patting Ben's arm affectionately before she turned and left the room. When the nurse came in to see Ben later, she told him that the cleaner's RAF grandson had been killed in a German strafing attack earlier that summer when Tangmere had been attacked. He'd only been eighteen.

Ben was pronounced fit and discharged from Thorneycroft's medical centre the following morning. Reunited with his holdall and dressed in his newly cleaned and pressed uniform for which he'd left the lady a little gift of money in gratitude for her kindness, he made his way back up the hill to Daisy's grandparents' home. Bitterne Village was only a mile or so's walk up the rising ground from Woolston, and yet it seemed entirely untouched by either of the German bombing raids. From its higher elevation, however, his view back down towards the river and the city beyond was a shocking scene – a dystopian panorama of drifting smoke, bomb craters, and the skeletons of wrecked buildings. Where before there had been tidy rows of red-tiled roofs, tree-lined streets, and tended gardens, there was now dusty devastation. As his eyes took in the scale of the damage, Ben found himself outraged at the enemy's wanton and indiscriminate brutality. The newspaper account had recorded the number of dead and injured resulting from the two raids, but seeing the physical impact of the bombing for himself now made it horrifyingly real. He found himself incensed at such cruel obliteration of life and property. No one would have considered Ben belligerent or vindictive before, quite the contrary in fact, but all that had happened in just these last two days had overturned his natural disposition to civility, replacing it with an angry lust for revenge.

From that moment on, Ben vowed that he would throw himself wholeheartedly into any duty that would contribute to German defeat. The Nazis had swept across Europe and now it seemed that they were trying to destroy Britain and everything it stood for. He found himself consumed by an intense urge to hit back in whatever way he could. If he had needed a flame to ignite the dormant patriotism within him, the smouldering scene upon which he now gazed could not have been more incendiary. It was in that frame of mind that he came to decide that he must forego his remaining days of leave and travel up to Waddington immediately to join the fight. He knew that trains left Southampton for London every hour, with connections via Kings Cross to Lincoln. If the floating bridge was back in operation, he could be at Southampton railway station by two o'clock, London by four, and Lincoln by early evening – still not too late for transport to the airbase. His blood was up, the bit was between his teeth, and having made his decision, he must take his leave from Daisy as sensitively as he could.

Chapter 18

When Ben arrived at Daisy's grandparent's house he was met by two drawn faces as the front door was opened to his knock. He went inside, embraced the old couple in turn and sat with them for some minutes in the sitting room. But no words that Ben could offer could ease their grieving, and after a decent interval of quiet reflection with the pair, he told them of his intention to leave for Waddington immediately. They concurred without a moment's hesitation that he should go – indeed, they encouraged him to do so: 'Don't worry about Daisy, Ben, we'll look after her,' the old man said. 'Your lot's got to teach those bloody Germans a lesson!' he added angrily, throwing a wistful look at some silver-framed photographs on the piano, which Ben recognised straight away were photos of their son at different stages of his life and of Daisy as a young girl. 'She's in the little bedroom on the left at the top of the stairs,' he said, catching Ben looking at the photographs too, and added: 'That room's always been Daisy's – since she was a toddler – whenever she came to stay.' He flicked his head in the direction the stairs. 'Go on up to her, Ben. She'll understand why you have to go.'

Daisy opened the door to his quiet knock and threw herself into his arms, burying her face in his shoulder. Her cheeks and eyes were red from the tears that she had shed. There would be many more to come, Ben thought, as he held her and comforted her in his embrace. They stood like that in a sort of silent communion for several minutes before moving across the room to the bay-window seat. The curtains were still drawn, which made the room as gloomy and as sombre as their mood. More minutes passed as they sat together without many words passing their lips, but when the time seemed right, Ben told her of his decision to travel to Waddington that afternoon. Though his heart was telling him that his staying longer would bring Daisy comfort, it could not shake his resolve. He told her what he had read of the bombings and what he himself had seen of the damage done – and of the anger that had boiled up inside him that had brought him to decide that he must go. She listened silently, her head bowed, her hands held with his in her lap, their fingers entwined. By the little movements of her eyes, Ben could see that she was taking in what he was saying. After some moments of consideration, she brought her eyes up to meet his squarely, and nodded resolutely.

'You're right, Ben,' she said. 'You have to go. This is something that I've got to get through by myself and be here for nana and grandad because they're grieving too. Your staying here for a few more days won't help any of us; and perhaps it's better that you're not here anyway. You can't do my grieving for me, can you? And you'll do more for all of us by doing your bit to help put an end to this stupid war.' She squeezed Ben's hands then let them go almost as if she were sending him on his way. 'Go on, Ben, go and catch that train!' she said, smiling bravely. 'Do what you have to do; I'll be thinking of you wherever you are.'

A lump came to Ben's throat. To hear such resolution in her voice filled him with admiration of her stoicism, but it also released him from any lingering sense of duty to stay. He hated to leave her in the state she was, but with a comfortable home to live in and her grandparents to look after her, she could not be in a better place. Not wanting to prolong the unhappiness of parting, he kissed Daisy's cheek, stood up and left her to her thoughts, promising to write and to get back as often as he could.

Getting back to see her, though, would come less often than he thought.

Ben Hardy ran down the hill to Woolston as fast as the weight and awkward bulk of his holdall allowed and stepped onto the ramp of the floating bridge just its engines revved up to pull away. Several motor cars, goods vehicles, and foot passengers were already aboard for a crossing that would only take a few minutes. Surprisingly, the vessel was back in normal operation despite the damage to many of the buildings along the waterfront. Arriving on the west bank, Ben took a tram to the city centre then made his way down to the railway station. Though the roads had been cleared of debris, mountains of fallen masonry and brickwork lined his route, with several fire-gutted, half-standing buildings looking like relics from the dark ages. Firemen were still hosing down; blown-out shop windows were being boarded up; and ambulance crews and ARP personnel were still picking gingerly amongst the rubble. It was the usual aftermath of a bombing blitz. The centre of the city had been badly hit but people were out salvaging belongings, and municipal clearing-up operations were already underway. The city was bravely pulling itself up by its bootstraps.

The arrival of London-bound train was being announced on the loudspeaker as Ben reached the Southampton railway station to exchange his travel warrant for a ticket.

His train surprisingly was only a few minutes late departing, and although the bombing had damaged the Portsmouth railway line around Woolston and Northam, the main line to Waterloo was unaffected. It was a two-hour journey to the capital and Ben hit the London underground at the start of the rush hour. Crossing London by underground therefore felt a little like being in the centre of a rugby scrum with so many people rushing home from work. He arrived on the Kings Cross concourse with just enough time nevertheless to make his connection.

It was early evening and beginning to rain when he arrived at Lincoln railway station, and his first thought was to organise transport to take him to the base. Spotting an empty telephone kiosk on the pavement opposite the station entrance, he made a dash for it, joining the race with other arriving passengers who clearly had the same idea. On his way, he passed a newspaper-seller shouting out the latest headlines but wasn't listening at first – until he heard the word 'Southampton'. He skidded to a halt to listen again as the newspaperman repeated his broadcast: 'Evening Echo,' the man shouted, 'more bombs on Southampton, more killed, read all about it!' Ben went back, put a threepenny bit in the newspaper-seller's hand, and took a copy. Finding a bench inside the station entrance, he sat down and turned hurriedly to the page-two report heralded by the headline. His eyes raced along the lines, picking out the salient points:

Lincoln Evening Echo 26 September 1940

...another raid on Southampton two days after the last ... enemy formations of about 100 aircraft ... targeting the

Supermarine Aircraft Works. Factory sirens heard around 4pm... 60 Me 110 fighters protecting the 60 Heinkel 111 bombers attacked in two waves along a North-South attack line. Approximately 200 bombs were dropped but only 7 hit the Woolston factory. A large number of bombs, however, hit residential areas and the factory air-raid shelters again causing a significant number of casualties. Production is suspended... 3 nearly completed Spitfires destroyed and 20 damaged ... Casualties: 36 killed; 60 seriously injured.

Ben's heart sank. 'Oh God, oh God!' he muttered to himself, and threw the paper down onto the bench as he leapt up, his first reaction to the frightening report being to telephone Daisy or her grandparents. The rush for empty telephone boxes was over by then and he entered the nearest, picked up the handset, and dialled 'O' for 'operator'. A woman's quick and efficient voice answered:

'Number please, caller?'

'Long distance please, operator. Southampton area – Bitterne 317, it's urgent!'

'Trying to connect you, caller. One moment please.'

Ben could hear background chatter in his earpiece coming from hubbub in the telephone exchange as he waited impatiently for a connection. It seemed to be taking longer than normal. He could hear the operator muttering to herself in a manner that suggested some frustration.

'Hello caller?' she said eventually, 'there seems to be some problem on the lines in the Southampton area. I'm just going to call central control to see if there's a fault. Hold the line please.'

Ben hung on hopefully. Taking some coins from his pocket, he separated copper from silver and arranged them neatly on the shelf above the telephone directories, ready to insert as soon as the connection was made. As he waited, a motor vehicle's clumsy gear-change accompanied by the throaty roar of its exhaust announced the arrival of a grey-blue Bedford single-decker omnibus on the station forecourt. To see the miniature RAF roundel above the vehicle's radiator grill and the words 'ROYAL AIR FORCE STATION WADDINGTON' in the destination windows above the driver's split windscreen was a relief. He wouldn't need to make another call now. The vehicle swung around the station forecourt and juddered to a halt just a few yards away from Ben's kiosk. Several airmen and NCOs in RAF blue raincoats then appeared, seemingly out of nowhere, and began to board it. Ben leant out of his kiosk door as far as the handset cord would stretch and called out to the last few climbing aboard: 'Hold that bus for me, please, chaps! I've got an urgent call to make! I'll be right with you,' he said, hoping for a quick connection.

Just then, accompanied by an electric crackle, a metallic voice in his right ear spoke up: 'Hello caller?'

'Go ahead, operator,' Ben replied hopefully.

'I'm sorry caller,' the operator said, 'it seems the lines are down in some parts of Southampton due to the air raids, and I'm not able to connect you; would you like me to try another number?'

Thwarted, Ben thought quickly. Daisy and her grandparents lived in Bitterne, a good mile or so away from the Supermarine works, so there was a good chance that they had escaped the bombing. He was anxious nevertheless to have his hope confirmed.

'No, thank you operator, but I'd like to send a couple of telegrams instead, please,' he said. 'One to an address in

Bitterne, Southampton, the other to RAF Calshot. Can you take this down as I dictate?'

With the bus driver glaring at him with impatience through his windscreen, Ben dictated his two messages hurriedly: the first to Daisy's grandparents, the second to Corporal Bill Green at RAF Calshot, both asking for confirmation that all was well in Bitterne (the one to Woody as a back-up in case 'all' was not well in Bitterne). Both recipients were to reply by telegram to RAF Waddington post office for his collection. With payment hurriedly inserted into the apparatus from his waiting pile of coins, Ben boarded the bus.

Chapter 19

When Corporal Ben Hardy arrived at the guardroom at RAF Waddington's main gate to sign in, it was already dark. He presented his ID card and announced himself to the duty Corporal who duly consulted his list of expected arrivals.

'Ah yes, Sergeant Hardy,' the corporal said, ticking Ben's name off on his clipboard. 'You're not expected until next Saturday, Sarge, but I expect the Mess can find you something to eat and somewhere to bed down for the night. Just let me give them a call.' Ben was puzzled as well as flattered by his apparent promotion but knowing that the twin chevrons on his uniform would give the game away, he protested: 'I think there must be a mistake,' he said, pointing at his sleeve. The duty corporal checked his list again. 'That's what it says here, sarge; it's got a capital 'A' in front of it,' he added, 'so that means you've been given acting rank. I wouldn't question it if I were you; you may as well get the extra pay! I'll make that call to the mess.'

Ben was given directions to the sergeants' mess and entered the lobby rather apprehensively, acutely aware of his corporals' stripes and fearing embarrassment as an imposter. A mess steward wearing a white monkey-jacket stood behind the reception desk. Alerted to Ben's imminent arrival by the guardroom, he had an envelope with Ben's name on it already to hand. Ben opened the letter straight away to find a buff-coloured Air Ministry letter inside, which not only confirmed his acting rank and new pay grade but also his entitlement to flying pay and the flight engineer's brevet. As he re-read the letter a second time, still thinking that there must have been some administrative error, Ben sensed the steward still hovering expectantly behind his desk. Ben met the man's gaze questioningly.

'You're not the first,' the steward responded. 'There've been a few of you chaps coming here from gunnery courses over the last few months, and you've all been given acting rank. Didn't they tell you at Walney?' He looked surprised as Ben shook his head. The steward handed Ben another envelope that was bulkier than the first. It was unsealed. 'And this is for you too,' he said, peering inside the envelope. 'Clothing stores must have been told even if you weren't. They've sent your stripes and brevet – and a hussif! Very thoughtful of them! Looks like you've got some sewing to do before breakfast! It's in the dining room at 0630 by the way and Met Briefing's in the Ops Room at 0730. There'll be other aircrew heading in the same direction in the morning, so just follow the flow.'

The mess kitchen had closed, but the steward rustled up Ben a light cold supper in the dining room before he retired to his room. He was late to bed that night, nevertheless, and late asleep too, not only delayed by the chore of his necessary needlework, but also kept awake worrying about Daisy and her grandparents. He eventually fell asleep, but it was a fitful slumber interrupted by periods of wide-eyed wakefulness in his impatience for the night to pass.

RAF Waddington was originally built as a Royal Flying Corps airfield some twenty-five years earlier, but it had doubled in size in the time since. The layout was typical of many RAF airfields of the time. The flight line was formed by a crescent of four large aircraft hangars which bordered a broad, concreted aircraft movement area – the 'apron' in RAF parlance. Aircraft would be towed out of the hangars and parked there after servicing, and then tugged or taxied around a concrete perimeter track to a dozen or more dispersal pans where they'd be fuelled and bombed-up ready for flight. The flying field itself was a relatively level area of about six-hundred and fifty acres of mown grass lying within the peritrack. It was criss-crossed by three take-off and landing strips marked by boards for day flying and paraffin-fuelled goosenecks for night. Each of these runways measured between four and six thousand feet long and were arranged in an 'A' pattern, their orientation reflecting the dominant wind directions. The whole base – all the buildings, the hangars, and even some of the concrete hardstandings – were camouflaged with black and green paint schemes to break up their outlines and confuse any German bomb-aimers who got this far.

The airbase had begun the war equipped with the twin-engine Handley Page Hampdens of No. 44 and No. 50 Squadrons. Both squadrons had been in action on the day of Britain's war declaration, attacking German naval targets at Kiel. They were also involved during the late summer and early autumn of 1940 attacking the French and Belgian channel ports where barges were being assembled as part of the German invasion fleet. No 50 Squadron with its fleet of Hampdens had since moved from Waddington to RAF Lindholm to make room for the arrival of No 207 Squadron, the first squadron scheduled to receive the new twin-engine Avro Manchester bomber. When Ben arrived at RAF Waddington, 207 Squadron was in the process of being reformed at the base in preparation to receive the new aircraft. It was to this squadron that he was to report.

As Ben left the sergeants' mess the following morning after breakfast, he was immediately aware of a general air of earnestness about the base. It was, after all, wartime, and although its targets were very distant, Waddington was effectively on the front line of it. Vehicles and people moved about the base with haste and purpose, and the pervasive rumble of aircraft engines on the distant flightline created a sense of urgency. Ben followed other men in uniform walking in the direction of the aircraft hangars, whose tall zig-zag roofs formed a jagged backdrop to the sprawl of single-story buildings of the camp. He was the last to enter the Operations Room, a prefabricated 'Seco' building whose windows had been boarded-up for security. He hoped he had come to the right place, for the doors were closed immediately behind him by a military policeman, and there was suddenly no easy escape. The room was already packed with a hundred or so seated aircrew sporting a variety of brevets on their tunics. Ben took the last empty seat at the end of the back row. There was a lot of noisy chatter which was amplified by the A-frame ceiling above their heads.

'New boy?' His neighbour had to raise his voice above the din as he leant towards Ben and held out his hand by way of a greeting. 'Dick Crozier! Welcome to the madhouse!'

Ben shook the man's hand. 'Ben Hardy, sir,' Ben replied. 'Arrived yesterday evening late.' Ben's neighbour was a dark-haired, brown-eyed flight lieutenant in his late-twenties with a pilot's brevet on his tunic and a white silk scarf around his neck. His keen eyes had a penetrating look as he examined Ben's face. 'No need for any of that 'sir' stuff, Hardy. We're all in this together. In the air, it's 'Skipper', on the ground its Dick.' He eyed Ben's battle dress tunic, which now sported a brand-new half-wing brevet with the capital 'E' at its centre. 'Oh, you're one of the new flight engineers, eh?' he remarked, raising his eyebrows. Ben nodded, but before he could reply, the room suddenly fell quiet, and everyone stood up as a group captain, a wing commander, and a flight lieutenant entered the room and processed in silence to the front row. 'We'll talk later,' Ben's neighbour whispered, bringing a finger to his lips, as everyone resumed their seats. 'That's the station commander.' He flicked his eyes to the front. 'Digby Allen. He's a good sort. Good pilot too.'

The briefing followed the usual format. First up onto the dais was the met officer who gave his best guess at what the day's weather would bring, with his predictions of cloud coverage, freezing level, and winds from surface to altitude. Second to stand up, was the air traffic controller who rose to announce the runway in use and the state and serviceability of the radio and navigation aids. This was followed by a briefing on the day's flying programme by Wingco Operations, with details of aircraft and their missions with estimated times of take-off and sortie length. All this was now routine stuff for Ben having been introduced to the format at Calshot and Walney, but it was unusual in his experience for the station commander to have anything to say. Today, however, as the wing commander resumed his seat, the group captain stood up, stepped up onto the dais and turned to face his audience. Group captain Allen was a short, heavy-set man with an archetypal handlebar moustache, bushy eyebrows tinged with grey, and bull-dog jowls. He cleared his throat. 'Morning Gentlemen,' he said, speaking in a gravelly voice. 'You'll be pleased to hear that the new Avro Manchesters for 207 Squadron have at last started to arrive from Woodford. Those of you not too bleary-eyed this morning may have seen two of the new machines sitting out there on the dispersal pans. They arrived yesterday and are being given the once-over now by Eng Wing. Those Hampden crews transferring to 207 for conversion to the Manchester will be joined by air and ground crews posted in from Cottesmore in due course, and the plan is to build the squadron up to full strength over the next month or so as more aircraft arrive. We all know that the Manchester has had a few teething problems, especially with its engines – which is why it's late – so, 207s first job will be to sort those problems out and get the aircraft ready for ops as quickly as it can. The Manchester's a big bus compared to the Hampden, as will be obvious when you get up close to it. She may not be as fast and manoeuvrable, but she can carry a lot more and go a lot further. And importantly, she has some room in her for crews to move around, so you Hampden Navs and WOps especially will enjoy a new freedom to get up and stretch your legs.'

A little murmur of approval ran through the room as the group captain continued.

'And pilots converting to the Manchester will appreciate the extra crew member you're going to get up front to look after the engines and the systems for you. As we know too well, the Hampden's systems are quite a handful for a single pilot, and the Manchester's are an order more complex yet. So, in their wisdom, the Air Ministry is introducing a new aircrew category of flight engineer for these new big bombers to look after that side of things for us. They'll sit alongside the pilot to help with all the knobs and tits, and they'll also be getting some basic pilot training so that they can bring the machines back home if the pilot gets hit. You'll also be glad to know that the new bird has an Elsan down the back – for which some of us longer-in-the-tooth aircrew will be especially grateful!' At this remark, a ripple of laughter erupted, at which the group captain smiled knowingly. He raised his hand to regain order. 'Some of these new flight engineers are already with us and more will be arriving soon. They'll bring with them a lot of engineering expertise to help 207 with bringing the Manchester into service, so please make them welcome.' He looked around the room enquiringly. 'Well, that's all for now, gentlemen. Wingco Ops will take any questions,' he concluded, leaving the dais to resume his seat.

A few questions were raised from the floor and answered by the wing commander, mainly regarding the timetable for conversion and the composition of the crews. When this came to an end, someone called out loudly: 'Stand please!' at which the assembly rose to its feet and stood respectfully in silence while the senior officers exited. A general buzz of conversation broke out immediately they had left the room as the aircrews surged towards the exit too. Being closest to the door, Ben and his neighbour found themselves first out, the pair falling into step as they came out into the morning sunlight.

'I expect you knew all that?' said Crozier.

'First I'd heard,' said Ben. 'But now I know why I've got these,' he said, pointing at his sergeant chevrons and his flight engineer's brevet, all pristine and vivid in their unsullied colours.

Crozier laughed. 'Looks like I'll be joining you on 207,' he said. 'I'm one of those lucky few moving over from 44. Like the groupie said, the Hampden's a great aircraft to fly but a horrible one to fly *in*, especially for the rear crew. It's really like a sardine can flying on its side. Once you're in the thing, you're stuck! And managing the engines, the fuel, the hydraulics and so on with one hand while you're flying with the other makes for quite a high workload, especially when things go wrong. It's quite a handful at times! And the Manchester's going to be even more complicated and yet it's still only got a single pilot! So, to have someone like you in the crew to manage the aircraft's systems will be very comforting – especially if those Vulture engines start misbehaving, which apparently, they're quite prone to!'

Picking up the general drift of the flight lieutenant's thoughts, Ben sensed a potential opening. He quite liked the idea of crewing up with this amiable man and, not wanting to lose an opportunity to make his number, he chipped in: 'Yes, I can believe it, sir,' he said thoughtfully, (not ready yet to switch to first-name terms). 'I flew a lot as supernumerary crew in Sunderlands whilst I was at Calshot, and they have two pilots *and* an engineer aboard! I don't suppose the Manchester's much less complicated than the Sunderland, either. I'm guessing that a pilot would be hard pressed to manage everything by himself *and* keep his mind on flying.'

Crozier nodded sagely then fell into a thoughtful silence as they walked on. 'The CO's asked me to form an operational evaluation crew for the Manchester, Ben,' he said eventually. 'I'm the squadron QFI – that stands for qualified flying instructor, in case you didn't know – and I've flown a few other operational types too, like Whitleys and Wellingtons, mainly at the Central Flying School as an instructor – so the wingco thinks I'm the best man for the job.' He gave out a sort of non-committal snort. 'I'm not so sure that he's right about that, but anyway, I've been asked to put together a crew and I'll want a good flight engineer to join it. How'd you fancy joining me? Are you any good, Ben?' he added with a smirk.

'The best!' replied Ben, his face splitting with a beaming grin. 'Sounds just like my cup of tea.'

In the 207 Squadron crew room later, Ben made himself known to the Squadron adjutant, a middle-aged RAFVR flight lieutenant with a drooping moustache and thinning hair that made him look a little like a walrus. He had single campaign ribbon on his chest but no flying brevet, which suggested that the man was a veteran of the interwar years, most likely having held some administrative function or perhaps air traffic control.

'Hardy? Oh yes. Hmmm! You're not expected until the weekend!' the officer said, sounding slightly irritated. He did not seem to be in the best of moods.

'I had no reason to hang about, sir,' Ben replied, not wanting to go into detail. 'So thought I may as well come up and get started.'

'Well, alright sergeant, you may as well!' was the adjutant's stiff reply. 'And you can start by getting your arrival procedure done today and drawing your flying kit. Find yourself a locker in the changing room through there to stash it,' he said, pointing at a side door. 'You'll be joining 'B' Flight, so introduce yourself to Flight Lieutenant Crozier, the 'B' flight commander, when you get back to let him know you're here.'

'Very well, sir,' Ben replied as he took his leave, not bothering to tell the adjutant that he and the 'B' Flight flight-commander had already become acquainted.

The arrival procedure was the reverse of the clearing procedure that Ben had completed at Calshot just a day or so before, and, like then, it had him traipsing around the base from section to section collecting signatures and filling in forms. He reached the clothing store by midday where he was issued with his flying clothing. The storeman ticked off the items on his list, muttering to himself as he did so, taking them from the shelves and placing them one by one on a long bench:

Holdall, blue, aircrew – one;

Helmet, leather, flying, with electric headset and leads – one set,

Oxygen mask, tubes and connectors – one set;

Overalls, flying, cold-weather – two,

Thermal undergarments, flying, combination – two,

Boots, flying, leather, fleece-lined – one pair;

Jacket, flying, leather, sheepskin – one;

Gloves, flying – one pair;'

And so on. All of which Ben crammed into his new 'Holdall, blue, aircrew,' which he then carried back to his newly allocated locker in the squadron aircrew changing room.

It was not until late afternoon, after Ben had handed in his completed arrival form at the admin office in station headquarters, that he had time to call by the post room. Two telegrams awaited him. The first was from Daisy; it read:

'ALL SAFE HERE COMMA BUT WOOLSTON HIT BADLY AGAIN STOP TELEPHONE LINES STILL DOWN STOP WILL WRITE SOON STOP LOVE DAISY END.'

The second telegram came from Woody in Calshot:

'SUPERMARINE WORKS AND CITY HIT AGAIN STOP DOROTHY AND DAISY OK STOP BOTH MET IN BITTERNE TODAY AND REPORT ALL WELL STOP GIVE 'EM ONE FOR ME BEN EXCLAMATION WOODY END'

Ben slept better that night.

Chapter 20

Ben as Flight Engineer
RAF Waddington

The 'Met Man' would tell the aircrew assembled for the 0730 met briefing the following morning that a clear and sunny day lay ahead, but at 0710 hours, as Ben set off from the Sergeant's Mess, the whole camp was shrouded in early-morning mist. The September air was still and dew lay heavily on the grass. By the time Ben reached the broad expanse of concrete of the flight line, however, the sun had begun to work its magic. A light breeze had sprung up, and the windsock had begun to stir as if waking from the dead. Patches of pale blue sky were beginning to appear through the thinning haze above his head, and far across the airfield, shadowy forms of aircraft were appearing like spectres emerging from the mist. Ben recognised their outlines straight away as the Hampdens of No 44 Squadron, but sitting amongst them, like cuckoos in the nest, were a couple of the new, much larger Manchesters, their triple tail fins identifying them as Mk 1 versions of the type.

Ben had been assigned to No 207 Squadron, and his first task was to get himself up to speed on the Manchester's operating systems and the Rolls Royce Vulture engines that powered the new aircraft. As the only Halton-trained aero-engine engineer joining the embryo squadron at that early stage in its operational build-up, Ben had been earmarked by the squadron commander to join the operational evaluation unit even before Flt Lt Crozier had spotted the young flight engineer as a likely candidate.

The Vulture was a new 24-cylinder engine designed to deliver the very high power levels required for future heavy, twin-engine aircraft like the Manchester. Its design combined four, 6-cylinder blocks in an 'X' configuration joined by a common crankshaft to deliver nearly eighteen hundred horsepower. Unfortunately for the Vulture, however, Rolls-Royce had been instructed by the Air Ministry to prioritise its engineering effort on Merlin engine development and manufacture instead. The Merlin was the trusted 12-cylinder, 'V' configuration engine that powered the Hurricanes and Spitfires that had distinguished themselves in the 'Battle of Britain' that summer. Vulture development had, therefore, been sidelined and starved of the engineering focus required to sort out it's teething problems – which were many. Apart from delivering a lot less power than specified, mainly because of de-rating the engine to put it under less strain, it also suffered from overheating. The engine had also experienced several serious mechanical failures during its initial development and testing phase. These warning signs should have delayed the engine's introduction into service until the problems had been resolved, but normal engineering prudence seems to have been over-ridden in the rush to bring the Manchester into service. This would not bode well either for the engine or for the Avro Manchester.

———

As directed by No 207 Squadron's CO, Sergeant Benjamin Hardy was assigned to the Manchester operational evaluation team, which was given the task of putting the aircraft through its paces, identifying its problems, and making recommendations on how best to deal with them. The tasking instruction had been easy to formulate but its implementation would be rather more difficult to execute. Flt Lt Dick Crozier was to be the unit's trials leader and also the pilot of the test aircraft. As an experienced flying instructor with flying time on several other heavy bomber types in his logbook, he was well qualified. His crew would be Flying Officer Peter Wilde as navigator, Flying Officer Ted Guy as wireless operator, and Sergeant Ben Hardy as flight engineer. The gun turrets and the bomb-aiming stations of the aircraft would not be manned in the early stages of the evaluation, which would concentrate on engine and aircraft handling rather than on weaponeering. Several weeks of intensive technical instruction on the Manchester followed, which for Peter Wilde and Ted Guy focussed on the aircraft's navigation and radio equipment, while Ben concentrated on the engine and ancillary aircraft systems. Dick Crozier received a technical briefing on all aircraft systems as an overview, but concentrated his attention on cockpit procedures, aircraft handling and performance, and emergencies. The courses were delivered by specialist engine and systems technicians of Waddington's engineering wing who themselves had been trained by Avro and Rolls Royce. Crozier's team also visited the Rolls Royce and Avro works to talk to the test aircrew, the design engineers, and the men and women who worked on the assembly lines. The latter meetings were more to do with motivating the work force than for further learning, but it was instructional nevertheless to see how the individual parts were manufactured and put together. By the time the team was programmed to conduct its own flight trials, its members knew the aircraft, its systems, and its engines literally inside out.

The team's first flight of the first of the production Manchester Mk 1s to arrive at Waddington was scheduled as a simple acceptance and shake-down flight as well as familiarisation for the crew. By 1100 that morning, the autumnal mist had cleared, the reported visibility was better than ten nautical miles, and the cloud was five-tenths broken cumulus with a base at around 3,000 feet.

The pre-flight technical briefing was given by the senior engineering officer, a young squadron leader, who ran through the detail of the acceptance flight-test schedule, which he unfolded page by page on the chart table for the crew to scrutinise. The flight profile was to include tests in different configurations and conditions across the aircraft's flight envelope from take-off, climb, and level flight, to stalling and maximum speed dives. A lot of data would need to be recorded to check the performance of the aircraft and its systems. Ben was to concentrate on engine and ancillary systems while Dick Crozier would assess general and asymmetric aircraft handling. As flight engineer and data recorder, Ben would also manage the progress of the tests, calling out the required flight conditions point by point, and then recording the resulting data from aircraft instrumentation. Any subjective comments or observations made by any of the crew were also to be noted. Ben raised his eyebrows as the officer finished his extensive briefing. 'Shouldn't take us long then,' he quipped with an ironic smirk.

The crew were then transported to the aircraft, which sat waiting on one of the perimeter dispersals already fuelled and plugged in to the ground-power electrical trolly. The pilot, navigator, and wireless operator climbed aboard leaving Ben to do his walk-around pre-flight external inspection with the flight sergeant servicing engineer. 'Anything particular to tell me, Flight?' Ben asked, as the pair set off to check the aircraft over. The aircrew pre-flight was a relatively superficial last-minute visual check for anything obviously out of place like control locks, pitot covers, and unfastened access panels. The technical boys of engineering wing would have completed a thorough servicing schedule before clearing the aircraft to fly, and the aircrew depended upon their diligence.

'Nothing serious,' said the flight sergeant as they made their way slowly around the aircraft while Ben checked every item on his list. 'We did another run-up on the port engine this morning. It was running a bit hot yesterday, but it seems to have settled down now. They're both new engines, of course, so they probably needed a bit of bedding in. I'd advise you to keep an eye on the port engine especially, though. If it starts to run hot again, reduce power and bring her home. No point in taking any chances.' By this time the pair had completed their walk-around and, both being satisfied that all seemed in order, the flight sergeant handed Ben the aircraft's technical logbook for a final acceptance signature. 'She's all yours,' he said.

Ben scanned the relevant pages of the logbook carefully, checked that all the necessary trade signatures had been appended, signed it himself then handed it back. 'Thanks Flight,' he said. 'We'll try not to bend it!' He then climbed aboard, pulled up the ladder, secured the rear hatch, and made his way up to the cockpit where he strapped himself into the fold-down 'dickie' seat, alongside the pilot. 'All clear to go, skipper,' he said.

Engine starts, taxy, take-off, and climb to ten thousand feet were accomplished without incident, and the subsequent scheduled tests of services went entirely according to plan. Next came the high-power tests, which included accelerations under maximum rated power, high speed dives and simulated evasive manoeuvres, followed by low-speed handling in the clean and landing configurations, with checks of stalling speeds. Nothing particularly untoward was noticed.

'Hmmm. So far so good,' said the skipper over the intercom, as he levelled again at 10,000 feet and trimmed the aircraft. 'She's got quite nice handling, Ben,' he added for the record. 'But a little bit squirrely directionally, and a bit heavy on the controls. Have you got all your data down, Ben?' Sitting alongside the skipper, Ben was bent over the clipboard on his lap, scribbling notes and numbers on his test sheets. 'Just about, skipper,' Ben replied cheerfully, looking up. 'It's the fuel consumption tests next – ten thousand feet; four inches boost; RPM 1800.'

They were not long into the cruise-speed fuel-consumption test runs and two hours into the flight in total when Ben noticed that the port engine cylinder head temperature was running slightly hot. He wondered if there might have been a malfunction in the automatic operation of the cooling gills and radiator shutters, and so, easing himself from his fold-down seat and securing it out of the way, he moved behind the pilot with his binoculars to take a closer look. As best he could see from this cockpit viewpoint, nothing seemed out of order.

'Port cylinder head temperature's running a bit high, Skipper,' he reported, as he returned to his seat. 'Gills and shutters seem to be operating normally on auto, but I'll try manual opening to see if that makes any difference.' He operated some levers.

Ben monitored the engine instruments closely over the next few minutes, but whatever he did to adjust the cooling airflow, the port CHT remained high – about twenty degrees hotter than the starboard CHT for the same power, engine speed, and mixture settings. The difference between the two engines' operating temperatures was small but, in view of the engine's troublesome history, any difference was a cause for concern and should be investigated. Remembering the crew-chief's advice to bring the aircraft back if overheating was encountered, Ben's cautious mind suggested that they turn at once for home. He switched on his microphone. 'CHT's still running a little high, skipper,' he said, tapping the gauge. 'I've tried manual control, but it makes no difference I'm afraid. Suggest we head for home to be on the safe side. We can still get some useful data on the way back.' The pilot replied: 'Roger, Engineer, understood. Navigator, did you get that? Let's head back. Give me a course to steer, would you?'

Chapter 21

The aircraft was put on its new course as tests and engine monitoring continued, but after a few more minutes Ben began to feel a slight vibration through his seat. He thought at first that he might be imagining it, or perhaps that it might be air-turbulence, but then the wireless operator's voice crackled over the intercom. 'Sparks here, skipper: you getting this vibration? I can feel it in the wing spar!' Ted Guy was an unflappable sort who only spoke when he had to. His wireless station was at the rear of the flight deck just forward of the main wing spar, one of the two structural beams holding up the wing. Using the beam as his back rest, he would feel any vibration transmitted from the engines more keenly than anyone else in the crew.

'Engineer here, skipper,' Ben chipped in quickly, 'Yes, I'm getting the vibration too. Something's up. Recommend we reduce power. I've got a nasty feeling in my water about this.'

Crozier throttled back both engines and started a cruise descent. But even at the lower engine power, the vibration seemed to get worse not better. 'I don't like it skipper,' Ben said glumly, catching the pilot's eye and shaking his head warily. 'I think we should close it down. It's not going to last long like this.' To emphasise the point, he tapped the port CHT gauge again, which now showed the port engine temperature rising steadily. From his 'dicky' seat, Ben could reach all the main engine controls; indeed, his job was to manage the engines whenever the pilot needed both hands on the control wheel.

Then, without further warning, the whole aircraft shook as the engine coughed, spluttered, and backfired loudly. 'Jesus skipper!' Ben yelled out. 'We have to close her down NOW,' he shouted; 'She'll seize up otherwise!' And getting a confirmatory nod from the pilot, he reached for the port engine master cock and pulled the lever down to OFF. Time, however, had already run out. A few seconds later, even as the engine RPM ran down, Ben's premonition of catastrophic failure became fact. In rapid succession, several loud retorts like shotgun fire were followed by a metallic clattering sounding like nuts and bolts being shaken in a tin biscuit box (which was not far from the truth of the matter!). In that same instant, the aircraft slewed violently to port as the propellor came almost to a complete stop. Crozier reacted almost instantly to counteract the yaw, slamming his right foot forward on the rudder pedal and wresting the control wheel to starboard sharply to counteract the induced roll. The Manchester's flight controls had no hydraulic power assistance, and Ben could see that the pilot was struggling to hold the forces. Less secure on his fold-down dickie seat, Ben had been thrown sideways, hitting his head hard on the canopy frame. Thankfully the blow was cushioned by his leather helmet. He pulled himself back into position and swung his gaze to the port wing to assess the damage. Thick black smoke mixed with yellow and orange flames was now pouring from every orifice in the engine cowling, its alloy panelling punctured and torn in several places, the skin of the nacelle peeling back like the lid of a sardine can.

'Bloody hell, skipper,' Ben exclaimed, 'it's blown itself to bits!'

Having already closed the port engine master cock, the drill now was immediately to close down everything else possible on the port engine to starve the fire of fuel, air, and ignition: port throttle – closed, port fuel lever – OFF, port engine magnetos – OFF; then press the fire extinguisher button. Ben accomplished the drill in seconds almost without thinking, having rehearsed it time after time during his training. Next, he had to feather the propellor which had run to coarse pitch as the engine had died. He pressed the port feathering button. The selection should have turned the four propellor blades of the seized engine into line with the airflow and thus reduce the asymmetric drag that was causing the pilot so much trouble. But the blades remained obstinately like a flat plate to the airflow, the prop simply continuing to windmill lazily, and causing yet more drag. Meanwhile, the pilot's leg, fully extended on the starboard rudder pedal, was shaking under the strain and his fists were clamped on the control wheel like vices.

'Can't get enough rudder on!' the pilot yelled, his voice grunting with the effort. 'I can't stop her yawing!' He eased the starboard throttle back a little to reduce the asymmetric force, but the drag from the port prop was still too great to hold the aircraft straight even with a boot full of corrective rudder and two armfuls of rotation on the wheel. With reduced engine power and such extreme control deflections, the airspeed washed off rapidly and the aircraft began to shudder and shake as the stall approached. They were in imminent danger of literally dropping out of the sky. Both the pilot and the aircraft were very close to their limits.

Ben shouted: 'The feathering mechanism must have jammed, skipper!' The roar of the sideslipping airflow and the banging and rattling of torn metal in the wind nearly drowned out his voice. 'If we can spin-up the prop, it might free it,' he shouted. 'Push the nose down to get some airspeed.' It was not his place to prompt the pilot, but he could not stop himself blurting it out.

'I'm bloody well trying to!' the skipper shouted back in a strangled voice, clearly doing his utmost to control the shuddering beast he now had in his hands. 'Help me, Ben, quick!'

The lack of slipstream combined with the extreme sideslip was reducing the effectiveness of elevators and rudders to a dramatic extent. More elevator deflection was required to get the nose to go down, but with his right leg stretched to its limit and his arms across his chest still struggling for control, Crozier seemed unable to exert enough forward force on the control wheel. Seeing this, Ben braced himself on the cockpit frame with his right hand, reached over to place his left on the centre of the pilot's control wheel, and pushed forward with all the strength he could muster. The two men's combined forward force was enough to push the control column just an inch or so further forward, sufficient to deflect the elevators just a degree or two further downwards. It was as much as the pair could do between them, but slowly, very slowly, the nose began to drop and the airspeed correspondingly to edge upwards. Having come almost to a complete stop, the port prop began at once to spin up like a windmill, which must have released the stuck feathering mechanism and allowed it to do its job. The blades at last turned into line with the airflow and came to a stop. It took only seconds for the pilot to regain full control as the asymmetric drag reduced. Crozier's crew had been lucky. Catastrophic engine failures such as this on other twin-engine types had resulted in the loss of the aircraft and its crew.

'Port propellor's fully feathered, Skipper,' Ben called out in relief.

The skipper's sigh was audible over the intercom as he wound the trim wheels rapidly to reduce the remaining out-of-balance control forces effectively to zero. Ben, meanwhile, noted that the black smoke that had engulfed the port engine had turned to a diminishing stream of white vapour. The flames too had disappeared. Ben's quick action to cut off the fuel supply and operate the fire extinguisher seemed to have had the desired effect; but the shrapnel damage from the explosion was now revealed to be extensive, suggesting a real risk of collateral damage to adjacent systems and controls. Ben opened the cross-feed cock and transferred fuel from the port fuel tanks to the starboard just in case; a leak of high-octane gasoline onto a red-hot engine was the last thing the crew needed right now.

For some minutes, the crew fell silent while they took stock, realizing how close they had come to disaster. The Manchester's problems, however, were not over yet. Even if the fire had been extinguished, the crew still had to get the aircraft back on the ground in one piece. Prudence suggested that they should do so in haste, and since the Manchester with a dead engine could barely maintain level flight, they wouldn't have much choice.

'Navigator, give me a heading to the nearest suitable airfield,' requested the captain. 'We need to get this heap down on the ground tout suite!'

'Steer two-zero-zero degrees for Binbrook, Skipper – twelve miles.' called the navigator without a moment's hesitation. 'That's the closest suitable.' He had clearly anticipated the request.

Crozier's crippled Manchester was only some thirty nautical miles northeast of home base, but even that was too far to risk. With confidence in the Vulture engine shattered by their narrow scrape, it would be reckless to bank on the remaining engine holding out, especially since higher power settings would now be required to compensate for the loss of the port engine.

RAF Binbrook was home to two other bomber squadrons, Nos 12 and 142, the former squadron flying the twin-engine Vickers Wellingtons, the latter, the single engine Fairey Battles. If the Manchester had to land away from home, landing at another bomber base with its crash rescue and fire-fighting facilities geared-up for large aircraft was a prudent choice.

After a rapid descent and with Binbrook in sight ahead, the skipper levelled out at fifteen hundred feet. Ted Guy's voice suddenly piped up on the intercom with a crackle: 'I've alerted air traffic of our problem, skipper,' he said. 'They've cleared us for a straight in approach and told other aircraft to hold off. The sky's ours, skipper.'

'Thanks, Ted,' replied Crozier, then, addressing the navigator: 'Ok Peter, let's have the landing checks now please.'

With no further mapwork to do, the navigator was the least employed on the flight deck and thus best placed to read out the check list.

'Autopilot?' called the navigator.

'OFF,' responded Ben, having checked the switch was in the off position.

'Supercharger?'

'LOW GEAR,' replied Ben.

'Fuel?'

'Port -200lbs; Starboard – 3000lbs. Cross-feed cock now closed.'

'Air Intake?' '- COLD.'

These first three checks had been for Ben to carry out. The following checks were for the pilot.

'Brake Pressure?' called the navigator. '250 to 300 psi,' replied the pilot.

'Airspeed?' 'Below 200 Knots,'

'Flaps?' '20 degrees selected,'

'Undercarriage?' 'Selecting down...waiting for the lights...,' said the pilot.

Then, after a rather longer pause: 'Hmmm. We've got a red light on the port undercarriage, Enge. I guess that shouldn't be a surprise, should it?' His tone of voice was matter of fact, but everyone knew that a red light meant trouble.

The Manchester's two main wheels were housed in the lower part of the port and starboard engine nacelles. Indicator lamps on the pilot's console – one for the port undercarriage, one for the starboard – indicated undercarriage position. The lamps would be unlit when the respective undercarriage legs were locked in the up position; red lights indicated that the undercarriage was unlocked or travelling; and green lights would show that the undercarriage was down and locked. For a safe landing therefore, two green lights were required. On this occasion, however, only the starboard green lamp was lit, while the port indicator lamp remained an unsettling red.

'Take a look, Enge, looks only half down to me,' suggested the pilot, glancing over his left shoulder while he inched the starboard throttle forward to compensate for the extra drag of gear and flaps.

Ben slid out of his seat again and positioned himself behind the pilot's seat where he could get a better view of the port engine and wing.

'It *is* only half down, skipper,' he reported. 'The tyre's blown and the struts look damaged too,' he added, after a closer inspection with his binoculars.

'Just our luck!' Crozier exclaimed drily. 'What's the hydraulic pressure doing?'

Ben checked the gauges on his panel. 'Port system pressure's way down,' he said. 'Pipes must have been ruptured when the engine blew itself to bits!'

'What about using the pneumatic system to blow it down?' asked Crozier.

'If the pipes are ruptured port-side, skipper, the air probably won't work either. It'll just vent to atmosphere through the rupture,' Ben said. Then, following a moment's further reflection, he added: 'And since there's mechanical damage, the leg won't lock down anyway. On top of that, skipper, the pneumatic system's a one-shot system for both legs; if we use it, the starboard leg will lock down too – and we won't be able to get it back up.'

'Hmmm, yeah,' said Crozier, immediately understanding the consequences of Ben's analysis. 'I see what you mean. Better a belly landing on the grass than landing on one wheel then?'

Ben nodded his agreement. Landing with only one main wheel down carried a very high risk that the unsupported wingtip, port in this case, would dig itself into the turf and either rip the wing off or turn the aircraft on its back. Both possibilities carried an attendant risk of rupturing fuel tanks and fire. Neither scenario seemed especially appealing.

'Right then!' muttered the skipper, after taking stock. 'Get back into your seat Ben, and strap in tight. We'll go round and set up for a wheels-up approach.' He moved the starboard throttle lever forward to increase speed, then raised the undercarriage lever, observing that only the starboard leg retracted fully. The damaged port leg with its blown tyre and distorted structure still dangled half-down in the airstream. There was no doubt that it would collapse the moment the aircraft made contact with the ground.

Nearly full power was required on the live engine to fly the aircraft around the landing pattern again for a second approach. It was just as well the aircraft was lightly loaded.

'Ted! Tell air traffic that we're setting up for a wheels-up landing!' said Crozier. 'We'll do an extended downwind leg while we're dumping fuel. If they've got other aircraft holding off nearby, suggest that they might be able to get them back on the ground before us if they're quick about it – I'm afraid we're going to make a bit of a mess of their field!'

It was on occasions like this that the usual banter and chit-chat between the flight crew died away to bare essentials. Each knew the risks of putting an aircraft down without its wheels – anyone else would call it a crash landing – and each of the men fell into a state of semi-introspection while they went about their separate preparations for a potentially uncomfortable return to earth. Ben dumped all unnecessary fuel, leaving a small margin for a further approach if the first had to be aborted. Reducing fuel weight would reduce the landing speed as well as the fire risk. Landing checks were then completed and the drill for the wheels up landing rehearsed: 'As I flare at the threshold, Ben,' said Crozier, 'you close down and feather the starboard engine and shut off its fuel supply. I'll bring the aircraft down to a few feet above the grass and hold off as the airspeed decreases, and then... ' here he paused, twisted his lips and raised an eyebrow before going on, '...and then I'll ease her down onto her belly so gently that you won't even know we're on the ground!' He grinned, but he knew that he faced a difficult task. 'Pete and Ted: no point in you two coming along for the ride if you'd prefer to bail out! I'll do my best to get her down in one piece, but I can't guarantee it. It's up to you.'

Both elected to stay with the aircraft and take their chances. It seemed a more comfortable proposition in the moment than leaping out into space and dangling under a handkerchief of flimsy silk. Besides, negotiating the length the fuselage to reach the rear hatch encumbered with harness and parachute was a bit of an obstacle course.

If this was Crozier's carefully considered plan for the coming wheels-up reunion with terra-firma, the reality turned out to be rather different. Just to make things more difficult for him, the wind was gusting twenty knots at the time, and although he lined up directly into it for the landing, he found it a struggle so close to the ground as airspeed decreased to maintain the steady level attitude that he intended. Instead, some slight over-controlling on his part while feeling for the ground, combined with an untimely gust of wind led to the tail wheel hitting the ground heavily before the belly was ready to go down. The tail impact was so fierce that it bounced the rear fuselage back up into the air, rotating the Manchester bodily about its centre of gravity and pitching it down to such an angle that it could not be corrected before impact with the ground. The shock of the collision felt like a punch in the nose to the four occupants who were thrown violently forward in their seats. Fortunately, they were all strapped in tightly and rode out the ensuing roller-coaster ride, but the nosedive shattered the bomb-aimer's plexiglass and scooped up a large roll of airfield turf. It was just as well that the forward gunner and bomb aimer positions were not manned. As it was, leaving a broken-backed aircraft behind them as the fire crew doused it down as a precaution, all four of the crew walked away with only minor bruises. The aircraft, however, would never fly again.

Chapter 22

Despite the evaluation team's near catastrophe, and several other engine failures similar though never quite as dramatic or as consequential as the first, the squadron continued to build up its fleet of Manchesters to full strength. Of the thirty or so flights that Ben made as flight engineer in several different Manchester airframes, six concluded with single engine landings – half of those at alternate airfields because there wasn't enough power on the remaining engine to reach home. Of the rest, the aircraft rarely returned without reportable snags. Though poor serviceability was a constant issue that limited the size of the operational fleet, the squadron managed nevertheless to raise enough aircraft for some meaningful bombing raids in northern France the following year. But few of Ben's fellow squadron members came to trust the Manchester, and in the Spring of 1941 and again in the Summer of 1942, the entire Manchester fleet was grounded due mainly to further engine problems. The Vulture engines never would become reliable in the Avro Manchester. Moreover, even had both engines functioned perfectly, there was still barely sufficient power between them for a heavily loaded aircraft; and if one engine failed or was shot out over enemy territory, the aircraft would never make it home. On that first test flight, Flt Lt Crozier's evaluation crew had only managed to get back to Binbrook because they were flying at light weight and didn't have far to go. If they'd been over France or Germany at the time with a full crew and an operational load, they'd have finished up in the drink!

The Manchester had come to No 207 Squadron with a shaky reputation, but the squadron aircrew had given it a fair chance to redeem itself. After such a dismal record of mishaps, however, all confidence had been lost. When news came that the aircraft would be withdrawn from operations the following Summer, everyone breathed a sigh of relief. Its successor would be the Avro Lancaster, which was in effect a four-engine version of the Manchester with a bigger wing and re-designed tailplane and fins. Importantly, instead of the two unsatisfactory Vulture engines, four tried and tested Rolls Royce Merlins would take their place – and no one would lament the Vulture's passing! It was this bit of re-design wizardry by Roy Chadwick, Avro's design engineer, that would completely transform a lame duck into a superb flying machine. The Avro Lancaster, offspring of the Manchester, would live on to earn a distinguished place in aviation history.

As for Ben, by surviving so many mishaps and near misses, it seemed that he had built up a reputation as a proficient and, perhaps more importantly, as a lucky flight engineer, which soon earned him his commission. It was as Flying Officer Hardy that he and the same three members of the Manchester evaluation crew were given the task of carrying out evaluation tests of the first Lancasters to come off the production line. From the beginning of their familiarisation, initially flying the aircraft out of the A.V Roe works in September 1941, everyone knew they had a winner. Crozier, Wilde, Guy, and Hardy would arrive back at Waddington in the Spring of the following year, bringing the first of the Lancasters with them.

With all this going on, Ben's contact with Daisy, either by telephone or by letter, had taken a bit of a back seat. His first and all-consuming priority had been to hit back at Nazi Germany; indeed, it had become a bit of a personal crusade. Every day, in newspaper reports and on the wireless, the news of bombings across the country was increasingly grim. For Ben, the German bombing campaign felt almost like a direct and personal affront. The mounting death toll of his fellow aircrew and of innocent civilians was horrific enough to contemplate, but the flattening of cities and the loss of so many irreplaceable British landmarks left Ben feeling both desolate and bitter. Southampton, the city that he had come to think of as his second home, had had its heart torn out; Newcastle, his place of birth, a strategic target for its docks, shipyards, and steelworks, had been pounded much the same. Cinema newsreels of the London blitz had made it all horrifyingly vivid. It felt as though the country's very identity and culture were being systematically targeted. Ben would never have thought himself vindictive – nor would his closest friends – but underneath his calm exterior, he was vehemently determined that Germany would pay for what it had done. It was this determination that drove him day in day out – almost to the exclusion of everything else. Even Daisy.

Throughout all this, Daisy and Ben had continued to exchange letters, but his to her had become slower and slower in the sending and less and less fulsome in their tone as time went on. Telephone conversations were also hit and miss, for she was often still at work when Ben was able to call her. And when she tried to call him, he was often in a pre-flight briefing, or airborne, or being debriefed – and sometimes celebrating his safe return in downtown Lincoln. When they did manage to reach each other, their conversations seemed increasingly stilted – awkward even – and sometimes frustratingly interrupted by problems on the line. Security also forbade talk about their work, and so the words that passed between them often seemed to have no substance – so much so that calls became more a duty and less a pleasure. A slight distance thus grew between them.

Absence was certainly not making Ben's heart grow fonder. Quite the contrary in the stressful circumstances that prevailed, and his aspirations for and view of his own future was changing dramatically too. He soon began to question the wisdom of his hurried proposal – a proposal made in the heat of the moment on the eve of his going off to join the war. Perhaps, in asking for Daisy's promise that day, he was seeking a foothold on firmer ground, something real to cling to in the madness of a world order that seemed to be unravelling before his eyes. He had always been prone to rush headlong into things without thinking, obeying instinct or heart rather than logic. But even if he'd sought counsel on the matter from wiser heads, assuming anyone would presume to offer it, it is unlikely that he would have taken any notice anyway. It is also true that things had changed so much for Ben since he and Daisy had exchanged promises that he had become a different man. He had established himself in his new role, he had won his commission and the respect of his peers, and, it seemed, he had gained the prospect of a future professional career.

Youthful ego was no doubt also playing a part in Ben's thinking, but it may be that he no longer needed that 'something real to cling to' that he had once sought by proposing to Daisy? Perhaps some archetypal male reserve prevented Ben from expressing his feelings, or maybe he hadn't entirely made up his mind about where his future lay? Daisy may have been just as unsure about her future too. She'd been orphaned, her home had been destroyed, her workplace and city were German targets, and her days and nights must therefore be lived in fear. All this would be turning her world upside down as well. Whatever the case, month by month, their bond loosened and things between them started to drift, with neither of them writing to nor calling each other sometimes for weeks at a time, both claiming the demands of their work as an excuse.

Meanwhile, Ben's present existence was a living roller-coaster, which seemed to have little room in it for Daisy or even for his own family. Night after night he was sent into battle in hostile skies, squatting in the cold, cramped aluminium fuselage of a bomb-laden Lancaster set upon a deadly mission. Dawn after dawn, he returned, fatigued and beset by doubts, yet exhilarated to be in a life still lived – and celebrated too – until the dreadful reckoning came when he counted the empty chairs at his breakfast table. The constant proximity of death is certain to have warped Ben's thinking in those dark times when he lay awake in the early hours trying to make sense of it all and yearning for peace and the freedom to do as he liked again. A simple, untroubled life would be a just reward, he thought, for the horrors that he was having to endure; but when he tried to picture this version of his future self, Daisy was not at his side. The truth is that Ben was unable to see any future for himself at all while he was so occupied with the war. He could only live in the present, day by day, and sometimes minute by minute. He would eventually come to understand himself better and to know what he wanted in life, but at the time he was at least wise enough not to burn any bridges or break the promise he had made.

Chapter 23

With all this churning in his mind, Ben might, therefore, have felt relieved to receive Daisy's letter, which put into her own succinct words the very notions and uncertainties that Ben felt himself. But he was hurt by it, nevertheless.

'Ben, my love,' she began, 'I think we both know that our engagement will not survive this war, don't we?'

Ben felt a sudden sharp pang of loss on reading Daisy's opening line. Preoccupied with his own feelings and his own precarious life for so long, he had neglected to think of hers. Now came the reckoning, and for a moment he was on the verge of replying immediately in protest. Only when something taken for granted is lost is its value truly appreciated, and this was never truer than at that moment for Ben. That Daisy should have felt this way was an arrow to his heart, and at first, he railed at the very idea of ending a relationship that he now realised had been so dear. As he read on, however, he came to feel that she may be right.

'The truth is, Ben,' she went on, 'my life here is so very different now. The factory, my production line, and me with it, are all to be moved away from Southampton to protect us from the bombings. I cannot tell you any more in this letter, but these changes will mean a new start in a new place for *me after a very unhappy time. Our prolonged separation has not helped to settle me, of course. Even now, I still mourn the loss of Mummy and Daddy, and I think that this move will help me at last to draw a line under a period in my life that I would rather forget.*

Your life too seems so different from your time at Calshot. Both of us were very different then, weren't we? You talk about your flying now in such a single-minded manner that I think you need a clear run at it without worrying about me. We had a visit the other day at the factory from some Spitfire pilots. I think it was to thank us for our work and make us feel that we were important to the war effort too. They talked to us about what they do and how they fight the Germans. I think you boys are so brave! Winning this war must be your mission, my dearest Ben, and I so admire you for it and wish you God's help in fulfilling it.

Perhaps one day we shall have peace again, and things between us might return to what they were? But for now, I think that it is best for both of us to go our different ways and let fate plot our course ahead.

Please forgive me if this catches you by surprise. I will always remember our good times together and I am still your friend, so please don't forget me.

With love,
Daisy x

Ben left it some days before replying, while he let his feelings settle. Although he and Daisy had never got round to exchanging rings, they had regarded themselves as promised to each other. She had not only been Ben's undeclared fiancée, but her parents had also occupied a familial role in his life. Their home had practically become his during his time at Calshot, at least at weekends, and this had given him so much comfort, especially since he had been so far away from his own. The Southampton bombings and their deaths had tragically brought all that to an end. Now, in her letter, Daisy was suggesting a yet looser relationship with no promises and no expectations on either side. While he had slowly been coming to the very same conclusion, it seemed that he was not as ready for the break as he thought, and for some days Ben felt as if he had been cast adrift on an empty sea. As the time passed, however, he came to feel relieved that he no longer had to make the difficult decision himself, from which he had unconsciously shied away.

He eventually replied.

My dearest Daisy,

I must admit that your letter did take me a little by surprise, and please forgive me if I have not been as attentive as I should. I was remiss in not writing to you or telephoning you more often and I am sorry for it. You are very dear to me too, but the truth is that this horrible war seems to have taken me over rather. I am glad to hear that you will be moving away from Southampton, which seems to have come in for a bit of a pasting, doesn't it? You will be safer out of it, I think, and I hope that the change of scene will offer you the fresh start that you are looking for after suffering so much sadness in your life. I remember your parents with so much fondness and share some of your grief at their loss.

With all that is going on in both our lives, I do agree with some reluctance and more than a little sadness that it might be better to let fate have its way with us as you suggest – and, at least for the time being, that we should go our separate ways. Let us see what that fate will bring.

No, I will never forget you either. I too will always remember our good times together. One day, if better times eventually come, we may be able to think again.

With love,
Ben x

PS: Please give my kindest regards to your grandparents.

'You're looking a bit glum, Ben,' said Peter Wilde, finding Ben brooding over a beer alone at the bar in the officers' mess one evening a day or two later. Peter had become a friend as well as a fellow crew member of the Manchester and the Lancaster evaluation teams, and they had flown together operationally since on several bombing raids over northern Germany. Peter was a bright-eyed, sharp-witted Londoner with tight, curly hair that looked as if it had been permanently set. Older than Ben by five years or so, his antennae were well tuned for picking up Ben's mood. 'Let me guess,' he said, wrapping an arm around his young friend's shoulders, 'I'm betting it's that girlfriend of yours in Southampton?'

'She was supposed to be more than that, Pete,' Ben muttered, gulping back the last dregs of his beer. 'But she isn't anything anymore. We've just decided to go our different ways.' Ben gave his friend a wry smile. 'I'm just drowning my sorrows. Want to join me?' He ordered two pints of Theakston's Best from the corporal steward standing behind the bar in his smart white monkey-jacket. The young NCO pulled two pints into fresh glasses, noted the purchase in Ben's bar book, and then returned to his housekeeping chores – drying beer glasses with a tea towel and hanging them on hooks above the bar. It was still early in the evening and the spacious, wood-panelled saloon was otherwise empty. Later, it would fill up as squadron aircrews wandered in for an evening of beer, bawdy jokes, and mess games – a not untypical officers' mess evening for aircrews when off-duty or when flying had been cancelled for the night. Life, and what young men expected of it in those strange times, was far from that of peacetime present day. Most of the aircrew were young and single, and with no female influence to steady them, booze and raucous behaviour were the relief valves for the fears and tensions that built up on operations.

'Truth is, Pete,' Ben said, as the pair carried their pints across to a table in a quiet corner of the room, 'I think I'm better off not having any romantic entanglements just at present. Got too much other stuff on my mind.'

'Don't tell me about it, mate, my love life's a bit of a disaster area too. Though I can't say I'm surprised *you've* split up, Ben. Women need a bit more attention than you've been giving that girl of yours. I mean, when was the last time you went down to see her? It's months, isn't it?'

Ben stuck out his lower lip and nodded, acknowledging the criticism thoughtfully. He knew he had been remiss, of course, but since becoming aircrew, everything else on his list of priorities had been relegated. He hadn't even written home in months.

His friend smiled indulgently. 'Not having much luck where the fairer sex is concerned, are you, old chap?' Wilde said, sounding sympathetic. 'That other girl of yours up north you told me about – she gave you the old heave-ho too, didn't she?'

'Thanks for the reminder, Pete!' Ben retorted with a forced grin. 'You're a real friend! You're supposed to be cheering me up!' Ben took another swig of his beer. 'Anyway, c'est la vie, as they say.'

Peter Wilde gave his friend a playful nudge in the ribs with his elbow. 'Life moves on, old boy,' he said, laughing. 'You'll get over it. Come on, drink up! I think a few more beers are what you need.'

Ben raised his glass. 'Aye let's drink to that!' He smiled lamely, then emptied his glass ready for another.

Eventually retiring to his bed that evening after spending much longer in the bar than he had intended, and feeling rather the worse for it, Ben lay awake pondering the evening's conversation. His friend had been right: he was certainly not having a lot of success with the fairer sex. He'd now clocked up two broken relationships: his first with April, his second with Daisy – severed in different ways for different reasons. Both break-ups, nevertheless, had had the same effect – a sudden lonely emptiness at the very centre of his being, like the feeling of being homeless on a cold night. Whose banner would he be flying now when he flew into the battle zone, he asked himself; who now would be praying for his safe return? 'His parents would do that, of course,' said his rational mind; but parental love would never be enough for a grown and independent man. It was the love and companionship of a woman that he really craved, the kind of love that he had felt before, the kind of love that had electrified his spirits and warmed his heart. Morose and with too much beer inside him from his late night with Peter Wilde and the other squadron aircrew who had later joined them in the bar, he now mourned the loss of his two lovers. How could he have been so careless, he wondered? He knew very well, of course! The plain fact of the matter was that both his loves had needed more from him than he was able or willing to give.

As he lay in his bed musing gloomily, he came to the conclusion that the pursuit of love in wartime was a waste of time. And in concluding this, Ben found himself mildly piqued that women should expect so much. He was after all a decent chap on a worthy crusade (at least in his own estimation), and in fighting the Germans he was fighting for April and Daisy too. 'Such is the price I have to pay,' he thought, resignedly, as he stared at the ceiling in the early hours, unable to vanquish such dismal thoughts. 'I may have lost their love, but maybe they'll respect me for serving my country?' It was a pious thought, but respect was as much as our young Ben could now hope for as far as his two old flames were concerned. Drifting off eventually into slumber, he would dream of the love and companionship that he might one day again enjoy, conjuring a dreamy scene in his mind's eye of some domestic rural idyl with a loving woman as his companion in life. Waking to the dawn the following morning with the content of his dreams still vivid in his mind's eye, Ben realised that the women at his side in those imagined scenes were sometimes Daisy and sometimes April. Though neither no longer seemed to be within his reach, their presence in his dreams had become interchangeable.

Chapter 24

Avro Lancaster
No 44 (Rhodesia) Squadron, RAF Waddington

Ben's wartime service as a Lancaster flight engineer was exemplary and distinguished, but he would never speak of it outside the circle of his close and diminishing number of veteran colleagues. He was eventually persuaded in his later years, however, to write something down of his experiences for a historical compilation of reflections produced for a veterans' magazine. Ben wrote it reluctantly, keeping it brief and avoiding too much detail, but the account nevertheless revealed something of his feelings about his flying and about the war. It reflected what many of his colleagues felt too. This was what he wrote:

I am not going to describe the horrors and discomforts of my first thirty-seven bombing missions over Germany, or the twenty-five that followed in my second operational tour. It is not something that I remember happily or with pride. To me, it was a necessary if abhorrent task. In those first few years, it seemed that bombing Germany was the only way that we could take the war to Hitler and give him a bloody nose for the damage that he was inflicting upon us all. But it also slowed down his production of war machinery and armament and gave us more time for ours to catch up. I believed in what we were being sent to do then. Later, I lost faith in a bombing campaign that continued to wreak death and destruction on German cities even when Germany was in full retreat. If our bombing could have been more accurate and aimed more strategically, I could have believed that it was bringing the war to a faster end. At the time, we did what we were told to do coolly and professionally to the best of our ability – with our blood up, in fear of our lives, and with pure adrenaline flowing in our veins. But since that time, reflecting and remembering, I have found myself unable to speak of it without feeling uneasy. I saw first-hand what we did, and the horrible memories of those burning cities will never leave me.

That you are reading this will tell you that I lived through it, unlike thousands upon thousands of my fellow Bomber Command aircrew who lost their lives, and despite my own Lancasters being strafed by enemy fighters and holed, burnt, and bloodied by triple-A.

As a Lancaster flight engineer, I sat alongside the pilot and assisted him in managing the aircraft's engines and systems. The Lancaster was quite a handful during take-off due to the swing forces that occurred – all to do with the torque, slipstream, and gyroscopic forces of the whirling Merlins – which you can look up if the phenomenon interests you. Each of the four Merlin XX engines developed one thousand two hundred and eighty horsepower. Imagine holding the reins of over five thousand unruly horses stampeding down the runway! That's sometimes how it felt on take-off! To hold the aircraft straight and to prevent it from careering off-piste into the long grass, the pilot needed deft right-handed fingering on the throttles and super-quick reactions with his feet. My job was to take over engine control once he was satisfied that we were going in roughly the right direction, and then raise the undercarriage and flaps for him once we were clear of the ground.

At the other end of the flight – on approach and landing – the pilot needed both hands on the control wheel to keep the aircraft on an even keel, especially when asymmetric or in turbulence, so he'd call out what he wanted from the engines (in manifold pressure units of boost), and I'd give him what he wanted by adjusting the throttles. Not quite captain Kirk and Scottie of the 'Enterprise' but something a little like it. Flying the Lancaster was definitely a two-man job. Throughout the flight, I also had to manage the fuel, the electrics, the hydraulics, the superchargers, keep an eye on the engines, and sort out anything that went wrong. I was given ten hours pilot training on the Airspeed Oxford and about the same on the Link Trainer, so if the pilot was wounded, I could take over the controls and fly the aircraft back – as long as the Navigator gave me the headings to steer! I could also take over a set of guns if we lost a gunner for which I had also been trained on the Defiant.

My two tours of operations on No 44 (Rhodesia) Squadron were for seven and ten months respectively, flying two-hundred and eighty hours on the first and a hundred and sixty-five on the second – including fifty-four bombing operations in all. That meant fifty-four flights into enemy territory against heavily defended targets at night, more often than not in large bomber formations where mid-air collision was yet another hazard to keep us on our toes. Cramped, icy cold, ear-achingly noisy from the constant drone of our four mighty Merlin engines and thrown around like loose biscuits in a box by turbulence and enemy flak. We had to suffer this living purgatory for up to ten hours at a time. Fifty-four take-offs, followed by nearly as many returns with all four engines still working and with all seven of us more or less in the same state as when we took-off – if frozen to the core and a little weary and bleary-eyed.

However, it wasn't all plain sailing. We had to limp home on more than one occasion with our metalwork ripped to pieces by flak or strafing. One night, a Junkers 88 night-fighter crept up low behind us and hit us from below setting the bomb bay hydraulics aflame. It was a dark night with no moon and the tail gunner hadn't seen him coming until it was too late. Fortunately, our bombs had gone by then. With a bomb bay fire, the procedure was to open the bomb doors and dive steeply in the hope that the blast of airflow would blow out the flames. For good measure Dick Crozier, the skipper, also threw in a high-G corkscrew manoeuvre, which shook off the Junkers at the same time. On another, I had to take over the mid-upper gun turret after the gunner was blinded by shattering plexi-glass from a Me109 strafing attack. In the moonlight, I could see two of the nasty things circling us like sharks waiting to come in for the kill. The tail gunner and I gave them everything we had. While I don't think we managed to hit either of them, the streams of tracer from our guns must have frightened them off, for they left us alone after that.

On yet another occasion, I had to take over the controls for the skipper when his left thigh took some shrapnel during a Messerschmidt Me 210 encounter, which also took out the hydraulics and the two inboard engines. The Nav, Peter Wilde, and I pulled the skipper from his seat, and I took over *the controls while Ted Guy, the W/Op, administered first aid on the cockpit floor. Peter gave me the headings to steer to get us back across the North Sea. We were losing height all the way, and with all the shaking and groaning from the damaged fuselage and flying surfaces, the aircraft was a real pig to fly. Fortunately, the skipper was able to struggle back into the driving seat eventually, which was a great relief to me because I wasn't sure that I could handle a landing with two engines out. We were still losing height as we made landfall at dawn, and we could see that there was no way we were going to make it to an airfield. Fortunately, we found a stretch of flat, firm beach at low tide, and Dick Crozier managed to put our battered Lancaster down smoothly on its three wheels in a remarkable bit of flying, despite his leg wound. We all walked away from it with only minor cuts and bruises, but we had to abandon the old girl (Y-yorker) to the incoming tide.*

Overall, however, our crew got off comparatively lightly, which was just the luck of the draw. Many other bomber crewmen did not fare so well. In fact, fifty-five thousand of my Bomber Command colleagues were killed during the war – over half of those who flew. And only half of those who survived got off entirely unscathed, though it would have taken a psychologist rather than a surgeon to have spotted some of their wounds.

Between my two operational tours and again following the completion of my second, I was given 'rest' tours as an instructor, when I could take enough leave sometimes to make it worthwhile to get home to Backworth, where my father still hacked out the vital black stuff underground and my mother still made his tea.

My first 'rest tour' was as an instructor on the Lancaster Finishing School at RAF Wigsley, teaching new recruits to become flight engineers; my second, at the Bomber Command Instructors School at RAF Syerston, teaching battle-hardened flight engineers to become instructors like me – God help them! So, by the end of all that, I think I knew what I was doing as far as the dear old Lanc' was concerned and I had had the opportunity to try out my skills on the Halifax and Wellington aircraft too.

Forgive me if I don't make too much of all this or make my story into a Boys' Own adventure yarn. While I often look back and think of good times and good friends, the camaraderie of service life and the exhilaration and celebrations of a successful homecoming, my nights are often troubled by the darker episodes, and I would prefer not to dwell upon on them. Those were frightening times. I lost too many friends and the country lost too many good men.

When the war in Europe ended in 1945, I was a twenty-six-year-old squadron leader with the purple and white medal ribbon of a Distinguished Flying Cross and half a dozen campaign medals on my battledress tunic.

A year later, I was a twenty-seven-year-old civilian and unemployed.

Chapter 25

Squadron Leader Benjamin Hardy DFC, RAF(Retired) returned to Backworth in the early Spring of 1946. He looked somewhat out of place as he stepped off the train at Backworth railway station wearing his customary officers' off-duty rig of sports jacket, squadron tie, and flannel trousers (a 'uniform' that would soon be shed in favour of something less conspicuously 'not from around here'). With an RAF-blue raincoat over his shoulder and all his possessions in a bulging RAF holdall, he carried with him all he had in the world. Not much of a legacy for ten years' service, is it? he thought, as he walked lop-sided from the station weighed down by his asymmetric load. With some accumulated savings from his pay and his demobilisation gratuity in the bank, however, things did not look too bleak. Finding suitable employment would become a priority in due course, but for the moment, he had other things on his mind.

There were no taxis and no busses and no one to meet him at the station. Not having made up his mind until the last minute about whether to head north to Backworth or south-west to Southampton, he had told no one that he was on his way. He walked home slowly, swapping his heavy bag every few minutes from arm to arm to ease the strain on his shoulders, noting that nothing seemed to have changed much in Backworth since his last visit more than a year before. Except that everything seemed somehow smaller, dirtier, and more run-down than he remembered.

His mother was in her little garden when Ben lifted the latch of the back gate and went in. He entered just as a shunting engine rumbled and hissed along the track that ran just beyond the rear fence. It was hauling a long train of loaded coal wagons behind it. His mother was on her knees, trowel in hand, picking out some weeds that were springing up amongst a small cluster of primroses that were coming into bloom. She raised herself awkwardly to her feet as the engine passed and threw a wave at the driver who returned her gesture with a peep on his whistle. Susannah hadn't yet noticed her son standing at the back gate waiting for the noise of the passing wagons to abate. Unseen, Ben watched his mother fondly for a moment. She seemed shrunken somehow, her form frailer; her hair had now turned almost pure white, yet it was still swept up into her customary knot at the back of her head.

'Hello Ma!' Ben called from the gate as the noise of the passing wagons died away. Coal smoke and warm steam from the engine wafted into his face and assailed his nostrils – the smell of home, he thought. His mother hadn't heard him calling out, so he took a step closer and called again. 'Hello Ma, I'm back!' He didn't want to come too close for fear of startling her. She heard him this time and turned, a frown appearing on her forehead as she looked behind her. Then in an instant, her expression changed to one of sheer delight as she recognised her son standing before her. She threw down her trowel, wiped her hands on her apron, and raised her arms to embrace him as Ben came towards her.

'Oh Ben!' She reached up and took his head in her hands, pulled it down to her level, and kissed him on the cheek. 'You are a neglectful, thoughtless boy!' She put on her cross face but then smiled indulgently. 'I was beginning to think you'd forgotten your Ma and Da! Becoming a bit too posh for us, eh?' she huffed. 'Anyway, come in, come in, son.' She took him by the hand and led him into the parlour. 'Put your things in the corner there and sit yourself down, boy,' she said, practically pushing him into father's empty brown-leather armchair. Ben sank into it obediently while his mother fussed about, laying the table with her best tea set, which usually only came out at Christmas. 'I've got you all to myself until your Da and brother come home, so you can tell me in private what you're going to do with yourself' now that the war's over. I know what your Da'll be hoping for.'

Ben thought his mother must be hoping that he was back for good and that he would be looking for work somewhere not too far away. He didn't want to disabuse her of that notion, for he wasn't yet sure himself of what the post-war future might have in store for him and what opportunities might arise. One thing he was quite certain of, however, was that he wouldn't be staying there for more than a few days. His mother already had enough on her hands with two miners to feed and look after, and their two-bedroom cottage was too small to accommodate him as well (at least, not in the comfort to which he had become accustomed). He'd stay a few days at most, he thought, and Frank would have to put up with having his brother sharing his precious bedroom.

Ben was recounting some of his tales over a second cup of tea when the colliery whistle sounded, signalling the end of the day shift and the start of the next. 'That'll be your Da and Frank on their way back now,' said Susannah, levering herself out of her chair with some evident pain in her joints. 'I'll get their tea on the table.' Ben noticed her face contorting with every step as she made her way slowly to the stove. 'My old bones!' she puffed crossly, as if some explanation was required. Ben offered to help but was firmly refused, so he left her to it and went into the front room where he stood at the window to watch for the two returning men to appear in the street. He spotted them as they turned the corner, walking amongst a loose straggle of other home-coming miners. They all looked much the same – grubby jackets, flat-caps, hands in pockets and roll-your-owns hanging from their lips. Frank had not followed Ben into the RAF as he had once declared to be his ambition. Like most of his school-leaving contemporaries, he had become a coal miner after all. It was a bit depressing to see him so black-faced and grubby, just as Ben himself had looked all those years before. But it was pleasing, nevertheless, to see Frank apparently happy with his lot, joining in the banter and the laughter with his fellows as they tumbled along the street. Ben could see him soon married with children, living in a colliery cottage of his own with free rent and free coal. In some ways, Ben envied the predictability of his brother's life, though certainly not his work. He watched the shambling cohort as it drew closer and he smiled at the obvious camaraderie that existed between the men. It was a Friday afternoon after all, and a free weekend lay ahead, no doubt with Backworth FC playing at home and some housey-housey at the Welfare club? Their high spirits reminded Ben of the band of brothers to which he had once belonged, and of the sense of inclusion and identity that he'd enjoyed in the RAF. For just one brief moment, he wondered if he had been reckless to cast himself adrift from all that. But there was now no going back; in resigning from the Service, his instinct had been to forge a more stable civilian life for himself where he would have control of what he did and where he went and not forever be subject to postings and deployments. His moment of doubt passed quickly. He knew that he must hold firm and trust that instinct now.

The two men burst through the front door still laughing, as if finishing off some bit of banter started in the street, and Ben's presence in the sitting room surprised them. 'Hello Da, Frank,' said Ben, greeting the new arrivals with a beaming grin. 'Good God, man, it's the prodigal son returned!' Exclaimed his father, taking his number-one son by the shoulders and holding him at arm's length as he swept his eyes up and down the height of him. 'Very smart! And you've lost weight, me bonny lad!' he said, chuckling. 'You'll need to get some of mother's good cooking in you while you're here! Mother!' he shouted into the kitchen, 'the boy'll have some o' that cake o' yours for a start!'

'And so will we!' added Frank, with a hint of pique in his voice as he took his brother's hand and returned the firm grip. 'That is if our war hero 'ere don't mind us ordinary folk sharing it with him,' he said with a look that was half joking and half cynical. Ben did not feel his brother's welcome was entirely fulsome.

Over tea, the conversation remained respectful and light to start with, but after mother left the table, talk between the men became strangely restrained. Awkward silences soon developed, which made Ben think that there was no longer much common ground between them. He'd been hailed as a 'war hero' in the local newspaper when he'd received his DFC from King George, and while he felt himself to be nothing of the sort, he still thought it strange that neither his brother nor his father had congratulated him or asked anything at all about the little part he'd played in the country's victory. He understood their reticence. As photographs of flattened German cities had appeared in the press, the destruction wreaked on some of the German population centres, even when the war was all but won, had come in for some public censure. Talk of it even seemed to have become taboo, a tainted subject tinged with embarrassment and shame. Ben sympathised with the sentiment; he'd been on the Dresden raid himself and had seen the horrors of those devastating firestorms first hand. He could not help but feel uncomfortable to have been a part of it. It was a subject best avoided, he soon realised, even within family circles.

But that would not be the only issue to make Ben feel uncomfortable during his short stay. Coal mining had ben vital to the war effort too. Many young men had been conscripted into mining rather than into military service as 'Bevin Boys', so-called after Earnest Bevin, the then Minister of Labour and National Service who'd sent around ten percent of all male conscripts into coal mining – many unwillingly. Most miners felt that coal had been as important to victory as Spitfires, tanks, and battleships, and so it hurt their pride that they had been unsung compared to the lauding that the fighting men received – especially when so many of them would have volunteered for military service if they'd been allowed to sign up. There was, therefore, a lingering sense of injustice if not resentment amongst some miners that their contribution had not been recognised. Being from mining stock himself, Ben had noted the lack of recognition too and it made him feel uncomfortable about his own award. To win it, he, like they, had just been doing his job. So, when he accompanied his father and brother to the Backworth Miners' social club that first evening, he was not surprised that his reception was muted, almost chary. His former workmates, by then veteran miners happy in their own company, hardly acknowledged him as he, Levi, and Frank found empty chairs amongst the throng. Ben's father and brother were soon joining in the banter as the ale and laughter flowed, but though trying to engage, Ben got very little response. It felt almost as if he were not entirely present, more like a visitor than a returning Backworth son. Even Frank seemed unable to hold Ben's gaze for long when the brothers' eyes met across the beer-glass cluttered table. Ben was hoping for a bit of brotherly encouragement or at least some indication of approval. Instead, he felt himself almost to be resented by his brother. He wondered where Frank's ambition to do better for himself had gone.

Ben paid a visit to Jack Palmer's motor workshop along Springfield Road one afternoon a few days later in his short stay. It had been Ben's work in Mr P's workshop, though part time and unpaid, that had allowed Ben to claim he was a motor mechanic when he applied to join the RAF back in 1936. To call himself such had stretched the truth, but it had probably won him a place at Halton to train as an aeroengine engineer. He therefore owed Mr P quite a lot for the leg up (and for the glowing reference) and regarded the man as a friend. But there was an ulterior motive for his visit, which was to catch up with news about April and her new life. He knew by then, of course, that she had married her senior bank clerk and that any feelings that she might have had for Ben must necessarily have now been consigned to history. Yet, despite the passing of time, there was a corner in his own heart in which she still resided and where the flame that he carried for her still burned. His breath even shortened as he entered the workshop thinking of the affection that he and April once had for each other, feeling her presence in the places she used to sit watching him and her father working together in their oily overalls.

As usual, he found Jack P under a vehicle, his legs protruding this time from under the front bumper of a Rover saloon. The smell of old engine oil and gasoline evoked fond memories of younger days and simpler times. Jack's workshop was so familiar and filled with such pleasant recollections. Some part of him longed for those days again – those carefree days when he used to tinker with engines and serve at the pumps, those halcyon days of his rose-tinted memories.

'Hello Jack!' Ben called, squatting down on his haunches and shaking one of his former mentor's protruding boots. Recognising Ben's voice instantly, Jack P emerged with a wide grin upon his face, wiping his hands with a grubby rag that can't possibly have served any purpose other than ingraining oil further into the grooves of his skin. The two men chatted amiably for a while, catching up with each other's news, until Ben gently steered the conversation to the underlying subject of his visit.

'Well, you know she's moved up to Alnwick now, don't you?' Jack replied. Ben shook his head. 'About two years ago, it was,' Mr P went on. 'Bought themselves a little terraced house on a back road near the castle. It's quite a way, so we don't see so much of her now. The bank promoted Bob to deputy manager of the Alnwick branch, and she was transferred with him – on promotion too – as senior counter clerk, which she loves. She likes meeting the clients, you know, face to face over the counter. She's got that sort of a personality, hasn't she? Much better for her than being stuck in the back office operating the calculating machine and keeping the books like she used to do down here. You know what she's like, don't you, Ben?' He chuckled fondly. 'But she had to give it all up when the bairns arrived. They've got two now, one of each.'

Ben smiled too. 'I expect she's happy being a mum now,' he replied, lightly. 'Probably busier with two babes than when she was working!' he said, laughing.

'Snowed under!' Jack chuckled. 'But, yes, she does seem to be happy, Ben.'

Jack Palmer had developed an eerie ability to read the mind of his former assistant and must have detected the more than superficial interest behind Ben's questioning. 'She never lost her interest in you though, Ben,' he confided, taking Ben's arm and squeezing it gently. 'She always asks for news of you, you know, whenever she meets your mother in the street.' He smiled. 'Sometimes it's a bit too obvious of her, I think!' he added, the wrinkles around his eyes creasing. 'I'd have loved to have had you as a son-in-law, Ben, but there it is,' he said flatly. 'She could have done worse. Her man's a decent bloke, and that's a blessing.'

Ben nodded sagely. 'Well, pass her my best wishes when you see her next,' he said.

The two men chatted for a while longer over this and that, but, throughout their conversation, Ben's mind kept flitting back to memories of the times when he and April had been together in that very place. If there had been any lingering hopes in his mind that he might find her free again and of somehow rekindling their relationship, the report of her new family in Alnwick had extinguished them completely. That he had harboured such flimsy and ill-considered thoughts of reconciliation now seemed stupid and naïve, and he berated himself for such idle romanticism. Moreover, if April still had any feelings for him at all, he thought, his reappearance on the scene could be unsettling – and that would be unfair.

'On second thoughts, Jack,' he said, as he took his leave at last, 'perhaps it would be better, after all, not to tell April of my visit. I'd hate to rock the boat.'

'I wasn't going to, Ben,' Mr P replied flatly. 'Yes, I think it's best for all of us to move on now.'

A knowing look passed between the pair as they shook hands in farewell. 'But don't be a stranger,' the older man called as Ben turned and walked away.

Chapter 26

Two days later, Ben left Backworth and headed back to Southampton. With nothing now to keep him in Northumberland, he was drawn back to the only other place where he had felt at home. In that frame of mind, his thoughts turned back to Daisy. There was nothing fickle in the suddenness of his decision to go south and try his luck again with her, and Ben would not want anyone to think that Daisy was his second-best girl. In his way, Ben had loved her too – and he knew he could come to love Daisy just as much as he had loved April. With his wartime crusade over, he craved the comforts and warmth of womanly companionship after being too long deprived. In his mind, there was no duplicity in his abandonment of one doubtful pursuit and his quick adoption of another. He was driven purely by a desire to settle down as if some primeval chemistry in his blood compelled him to do so. Put simply, he sought a compatible and loving companion in his life, and that is surely what any good man desires?

Ben hoped that he and Daisy might pick up where they had left off before their mutual decision to part ways. In their last letters to each other, they had entrusted themselves to fate while both separately had coped with the demands of the difficult wartime years. Perhaps the time had come at last, he now thought, to give fate a hand. April had been his first love, and she would always occupy a special place in his heart as first loves often do. But in discovering that she was settled now, that door had been firmly closed. It had been whimsical for Ben to have harboured such fragile notions of April's love recaptured, but far sillier thoughts have been nurtured in the name of love.

In Daisy's last letter to Ben, she had told him that the Spitfire works was to be relocated and dispersed to protect it from the bombings in Southampton, and that she was to be relocated with it. Wartime secrecy, however, had prevented her from telling Ben to where she would be moved. His first task, therefore, was to track her down.

He'd taken the overnight sleeper southwards and arrived in Southampton shortly after ten. It was a Saturday morning, and hoping that Daisy might have returned to her grandparent's home for the weekend, he tried to telephone from the station. Getting no reply, however, he decided to make his way there instead. Impatience might have been his middle name if not his first.

His heart was in his mouth as he knocked on Daisy's grandparents' door, hoping that Daisy herself might open it. But it was not Daisy but her grandmother.

'Oh, it's you, Ben.' She said after a few seconds' hesitation, soon recognising the young man standing before her so expectantly. 'Come in, come in!' She said, stepping back to make way for him to enter. 'Grandfather's gone down to the Dell to meet his football friends,' she explained. 'They meet for a beer before the game. He's got a season ticket, and 'The Saints' are playing at home this afternoon. Basingstoke, I think?'

Ben followed the old lady into the kitchen, and the two sat themselves at the breakfast table. After some pleasantries, Ben learned that their granddaughter only visited infrequently since moving to Salisbury when

Supermarine had dispersed its operations. 'We've visited her up there once or twice,' she said. 'It's a pretty place,' she added, 'it's got a lovely cathedral with a very tall spire and lots of half-timbered buildings.' She went on to tell Ben that Supermarine, had continued Spitfire construction throughout the war in secret factories dotted about that old city, and that Daisy had taken digs nearby. She gave Ben her granddaughter's address.

'She'll be glad to see you, Ben, but I'd better warn you that she's been a bit poorly lately. She won't tell us what it is, but she looked a bit pale and fragile last time we saw her.'

Ben frowned. He hadn't expected this. 'Hasn't she told you what's wrong with her?'

'Her grandad and I have tried to get it out of her, but she won't say. She's been in hospital several times for tests apparently,' she added, as if that was explanation enough. 'I'm sure she'll be alright though; she's a strong girl.' The old lady's tone was positive, but her expression was less certain.

'Hmmm. Well, hopefully she'll tell me when I get to see her,' said Ben.

In his impatience to keep up momentum, Ben bid the old lady a polite farewell and made his way back to the station and caught the next train to Salisbury. Arriving there late afternoon, he deposited his holdall at the station's left-luggage office and made his way directly to Daisy's address. It was a top-floor flat in a three-story Edwardian terraced house on Wilton Road, just a short walk from the station. The front door to the house was opened by a middle-aged and rather well-built lady, wearing a headscarf and pinafore, who folded her arms as if to block his way. She eyed her visitor up and down.

'We're a ladies-only lodgings,' she said, somewhat abruptly. Ben told her why he had come. 'Well, she's not in,' the landlady continued, only half descending from her high horse. 'She went out for a stroll with her young man,' she added; 'He called for her at about two.' With this last detail, the woman looked down her nose as if to say: So, you're too late mate! 'She often goes out for a stroll with him on a Saturday afternoon,' the landlady went on, softening her tone a little. '…sometimes to the pictures if there's a good film on, or to do a bit of shopping. She's usually back by six though, if you want to come back. Who shall I say called?'

Ben felt deflated. After a two-day trek from one end of the country to the other, his hopes to reconnect with Daisy looked likely to be thwarted. *She's found another man*, he thought dismally, and would not have blamed her for one minute if she had, for he had been away and out of contact for far too long. He doubted himself for a moment, wondering if he should bow out gracefully and simply move on. But after only a slight pause for thought, he resolved not to give up so easily – faint heart … etc, he thought, vaguely remembering a maxim often quoted by a distant aunt. 'Then could you please tell her that I called by. I'm Ben Hardy, an old friend of hers. She'll remember who I am,' he said. 'Tell her that I'm planning to stay in Salisbury overnight and would love to see her this evening – if she's free, that is.' Ben had passed a decent-looking pub on Wilton Road as he'd made his way to Daisy's lodgings and had noted it as somewhere that he and Daisy might meet. 'Tell her, I'll be in the Horse & Groom just down the road at half past seven this evening. If she'd like to come and meet me there, we could have a drink and a chat.'

Ben thought that he'd said enough, but then, attempting to touch the lady's heart and secure her cooperation, he decided to bare his soul. 'I'd be really grateful if you'd tell her that, Ma'am,' he said, summoning up his politest tone. 'Daisy and I were practically engaged some years ago, but sadly our relationship didn't survive the war. My fault, I think. I was up in Lincolnshire in the RAF – on Lancasters – and I got rather wrapped up in it all. I also didn't get back to see her as often as I should when she was having a bit of a hard time of it herself. So, we eventually agreed to go our different ways. Then when she moved up here to Salisbury with the Spitfire works, we lost touch completely. I should have tried harder, I suppose, but I'm afraid the war took me over, rather.' From the lady's expression, Ben sensed that his honest words were having the desired impact. 'Anyway, now that that's all behind us,' Ben continued, 'I'm hoping there might be a chance for Daisy and me to have another go at it.' He shrugged his shoulders and gave the lady a hapless look. 'I'd be really grateful if you could pass on my message.'

The landlady softened visibly. 'Seven thirty at the Horse & Groom, you say?' she said. 'What was your name again?'

Ben collected his holdall from the station and found inexpensive lodgings nearby. Installing himself, he unpacked, rested awhile, then spruced himself up, spending much of this time mentally rehearsing and re-rehearsing what he might say to Daisy when and if he saw her. It had been nearly two years since their last contact, and he realised that appearing out of the blue like this, hoping to get their relationship restarted, was a very long shot. Ready to depart too early for his rendezvous, he sat on the edge of his bed in the gloomy light of his dingy garret imagining the meeting. He could not be confident that she would even turn up, and was worried, that even if she did, the meeting would be strained and uncomfortable. He wondered if impetuosity had got the better of him again. He knew himself too well, and perhaps she knew him too well too and wisdom would counsel her not to come. If her outing that afternoon with 'her young man' was more than casual, a meeting with a former lover could throw her feelings into turmoil. Ben began to doubt himself, realising that Daisy might see it as crass of him simply to have turned up and knocked at her door. It would have been much kinder and more sensitive to have written to her instead. It would have given her time to assess her feelings before deciding whether to meet, rather than be put on the spot. It was typical that he had rushed in like the proverbial bull in a China shop, without thinking. Now it was too late for doubt. The deed was done; he had suggested the time and place for their meeting and not to be there for her would be unforgiveable. 'If anyone should have to experience the rejection of a no show', he said to himself, 'it should be me rather than her.'

Continuing this circular and fruitless debate with himself, he made his way to the Horse & Groom in the cold air of that early-Spring evening. The sun was still quite high in the sky as he arrived at the pub's front door a few minutes early. With no sign of Daisy approaching, he entered, bought himself half a pint of bitter, and seated himself at a table in a quiet corner of the saloon bar. It was a cosy room with low oak beams, dark Victorian furniture, and tobacco-tarred ceilings. A log fire blazed in the inglenook, in front of which three men sat around a low table playing dominoes, their pieces lined up before them like little walls, their faces intent on their play. Now and then, there came the clack-clack of pieces being slammed down on the tabletop, accompanied by good-natured cries of dismay and muted laughter. A few couples stood at the bar, drinking, smoking, and chatting amiably. It was a warm and subdued atmosphere – just right, Ben thought, for his nervously anticipated meeting.

He settled down to await Daisy's arrival, apprehensively throwing glances at the nearby grandfather clock as the appointed time approached. As the clock chimed the half-hour, the door to the saloon opened with a clunk of its wooden latch, and his heart skipped a beat as he began to rise, anticipating that Daisy's face would appear. But it was a middle-aged couple entering, and so he resumed his seat, disappointed, and returned to the contemplation of his beer. His reaction was the same each time the latch was lifted as several other patrons entered and the minutes passed. When the clock struck eight, Ben's glass had been drained and refilled, yet he was still sitting alone at his table. The minutes went on passing as the clock's hands inched around its face well beyond the hour, and more people came in. Yet there was still no sign of Daisy. Ben must have struck a lonely figure, brooding over his glass as he sat alone in his corner, attracting curious glances from the regulars in the saloon.

Eventually, the clock struck the quarter hour, at which time Ben gave up trying to persuade himself that she might still come. *Perhaps it's for the best,* he thought gloomily, as he reconciled himself to a lonely walk back to his dingy digs. *At least I've given it my best shot and can't blame myself for not trying,* he thought. April and now Daisy both lost! In that moment of reflection, he believed he would have been happy to spend the rest of his life with either. It made him wonder about himself. Perhaps both women had spotted the same flaw in him, and it had put them off? Perhaps he was destined to spend his life a bachelor? Thinking those depressing thoughts, he drained his glass and bid the barman a good night.

Arriving on the pavement outside, Ben decided that he would strike further along Wilton Road in the direction of Daisy's lodgings rather than return to his garret bedroom straight away. He had no particular plan in mind but thought he might risk knocking on Daisy's door to seek a confirmation from her landlady that his message had been passed on. He realised that in doing so he might look like a lovesick fool appearing at her door with such a plaintive enquiry, *but hell,* he thought, *what more could I lose...* As it happened, however, he never did reach the house, for as he walked along the pavement, facing a dusk sun that was by then settling on the distant rooftops, he spotted a figure walking in his direction on the opposite pavement. Dazzled by the sunset, it was at first difficult to be sure, but the figure seemed so familiar that he thought it must be Daisy making her way to see him after all. And, of course, it was Daisy; and she had recognised Ben too.

They came closer, then stopped as they came abreast of each other on opposite sides of the road waiting for the traffic to pass. She looked thinner than he remembered, which reminded him of her grandmother's concern about Daisy's illness. Her expression was mildly quizzical. She wore a dark blue coat with her collar up and had her hands thrust deeply into her pockets. She'd left her warm coat unbuttoned, so it had fallen open at the front, providing a glimpse of a blouse above a flower-patterned skirt, a combination which Ben thought attractive. With a silk scarf arranged loosely around her neck and wearing stockings and high-heeled shoes, she had clearly made an effort to look her best.

'Stay there, Daisy! Too much traffic,' Ben shouted. 'I'll come across.

As Ben waited for an opportunity to cross the road between the vehicles passing, a delivery van pulled up on the kerb immediately in front of where he stood and blocked his view. It was as he took the few steps required to manoeuvre around the vehicle, that he heard the harsh screech of braking tyres followed by a dull and sickening thump. His heart came into his throat as he quickened his pace, moving behind the rear of the vehicle quickly to obtain a clear sight of the road. Some dreadful instinct told him what he would find even before he saw it. Daisy now lay in the road like a discarded rag doll, her limbs twisted, the front bumper of a black Morris inches from her bare feet, her shoes and handbag scattered as if they had been carelessly thrown aside. Ben froze. His legs would not move as his eyes took in the terrible sight. The driver of the vehicle, an elderly woman in a tweed jacket and skirt, threw open the car door and stood beside her vehicle, her hands to her mouth, working herself up into a hysterical state.

'She just stepped out into the road as if she hadn't seen me coming,' she cried, as she gazed down in horror at Daisy's crumpled form. 'I tried to stop and steer out of her way but didn't have time. My God, my God,' she screamed, 'what have I done.'

Ben came to his senses, spurred his legs into action, and ran over to kneel at Daisy's side. Her eyes were shut. Blood pooled under her head. She had clearly taken a hard knock. Ben felt her neck for a pulse. Nothing.

'Someone! Quickly! Call for an ambulance!' he shouted, raising his eyes and calling to the small cluster of residents who had emerged from their front doors. 'Quickly! Please!' he shouted again when no one seemed to move.

'I'll go,' shouted a young woman as she broke away from the group and dashed inside a nearby front door. Other vehicles were now stopping in the road from both directions, and within minutes a small crowd had gathered.

Kneeling at Daisy's side, one hand holding hers, the other cradling her head, Ben felt helpless. He knew that a back injury was the most likely consequence of a motor car impact, and that moving her might make things worse. Afraid to move her body, there was nothing he could do. 'Does anyone know if there's a doctor or a nurse anywhere near?' he shouted in desperation, his voice breaking as he took off his jacket to cover Daisy's still form. But something inside told him that it was already too late. No one from the surrounding crowd of onlookers came forward to offer help, and Ben was still kneeling by Daisy's side, still holding her hand, when the ambulance arrived.

Chapter 27

Daisy was buried two weeks later in the Anglican Church of the Holy Saviour in Bitterne, where Daisy's grandfather was a church warden and her grandmother, the sacristan. The coroner's court had concluded that she had died an accidental death. The report suggested that in stepping out into the road, she may have been blinded by the low sun and thus may not have seen the vehicle approaching or perhaps she had misjudged its speed. Whatever the reason, Ben held himself responsible. If he had not come to Salisbury to find her, had not invited her to meet him that evening, or if he had been quicker to cross the road himself, she would still be alive. If only, if only…These guilty thoughts would haunt him for the rest of his life.

The wake was held in Daisy's grandparent's front room. It was a modest affair, restrained and sombre by its very nature. This was no celebration of a long life well lived, the kind of wake that might mark the passing of an aged and eccentric aunt with fond smiles and anecdotes of funny times. Daisy's death had been sudden and violent. A young woman taken in her prime. There was no humour in the room on this day, nor levity, nor any animated conversation. Sombre faces and the sober hubbub of quiet talk made the atmosphere feel heavy. The old couple, visibly still in shock at the loss of their only grandchild, had invited a few of Daisy's closest friends and some of her cousins, uncles, and aunts to attend. The vicar and, of course, Ben attended too, and Dorothy had brought Woody Green along. Food rationing had limited what had been put on the table, but some of the guests had contributed coupons from their own ration books, so the spread didn't look too sparse when it was laid out in the dining room. Ben sat sullenly in a corner much of the time, neither eating nor drinking and rarely engaging with the other guests. Daisy's grandparents sat quietly too, smiling weakly at offerings of condolence but averting their eyes when Ben caught their glances from across the room. Ben was sure that they blamed him for Daisy's death, and the burden of guilt sat heavily on his shoulders. Even Woody's consoling words failed to pull him out of the pit of his gloomy introspection.

'Sorry Woody,' Ben said, quietly, 'thanks for trying old chum, but I think I need some time to mull things over now.'

Indeed, it would take some weeks before Ben reclaimed anything resembling his earlier persona. Following the wake, he returned to his lodgings in Salisbury where his landlady took pity on him and mothered him, bringing to his room the little food and drink he would consume and other essentials necessary for his comfort. Ben allowed himself to descend into a morose and uncommunicative state, hardly ever leaving his little room and abandoning himself to recriminations and self-pity. He lost weight, skimped upon his personal hygiene, and looked an unkempt wreck on the few occasions he braved himself to sally forth into the light of day.

During those weeks of self-imposed mourning, Woody called upon Ben several times. Ben's old friend from his Calshot days had recently received a posting to the

Aeroplane and Armament Experimental Establishment at nearby Boscombe Down to take up a new post created there as part of its post-war reorganisation programme. A Halton graduate and a former flight-line technician, Woody was an obvious choice as a flight-line supervisor in the Technical Services Division there. The airfield lay just outside Amesbury, a small town only ten miles north of where Ben had his lodgings, and so Woody was able to visit his friend every few evenings and at weekends. He would have to be patient with him. The meetings between the pair turned out to be as lifeless and depressing as Ben's garret, with Woody departing feeling almost as low as Ben.

'It was fate, my friend,' he'd told Ben on more than one occasion, trying to lift his mood. 'There's nothing that you could have done to stop it happening. Don't beat yourself up about it, mate. Life must go on.'

'Fate!' Ben replied scornfully, remembering his words to Daisy and hers to him in their last letters to each other. 'Fate was supposed to bring us back together!' His face was as pale as parchment.

It was not until mid-summer's day that Woody managed to precipitate a change in his friend's mood. The change would not be sudden or revelatory, but it would be a start to Ben's recovery. Woody had taken it upon himself to view the coroner's report, which had eventually been made available to the public in the city's council offices. In it he read that Daisy had been suffering from a rare kidney disease for which she had been receiving treatment at the Salisbury Infirmary for more than a year. From the consultant's notes attached, it appeared that the treatment had not been successful in arresting the progressive failure of that vital organ and that the prognosis, therefore, was pessimistic.

Woody passed all this on to Ben in as sensitive a manner as he could.

At first, the coroner's report provided no solace for Ben whatsoever. Indeed, he felt even more guilty to have been absent during what must have been a really difficult time for his former sweetheart. He kept seeing Daisy's face as he had last seen it, as she came towards him on the opposite side of the road – the road that moments later would claim her life. She was smiling then with a hand raised in greeting, apparently pleased to see him after so long apart. He had re-lived that moment over and over again, wanting to wind back time. *'If only I had not invited her to meet me? If only I had known she was ill,'* he thought. *'I might have…I might have…'* But he didn't know what he might have done to prevent the train of events that followed. Young warriors like Ben are often filled with egoistic arrogance, and his had been further reinforced by his survival of fifty wartime missions. It had endowed him with an almost unshakable conviction that all problems were within his power to solve, all bodily weaknesses within his power to heal by mental strength and resolve alone. With such belief in his power to control events, he was convinced that he could, by sheer force of his own will and influence, have changed the way that events had played out for Daisy. But he had failed her. Had he not been so consumed by the war, had he been with Daisy through her illness instead, he might somehow have brought about some transformation – or at least some alleviation – of Daisy's symptoms, or made what remained of her life happier and more comfortable. He had failed her, sure enough. Worse, by inviting her to meet him that evening, he had been instrumental in her death, and he condemned himself bitterly for it, heaping blame upon blame on himself and allowing himself no mitigation or excuse. He found himself guilty in the trial of his own court.

All this time, Woody had acted as a sort of silent sounding board as Ben had unloaded his innermost thoughts, but eventually he tired of his friend's unrelenting self-indictment. 'Come on, Ben,' he said at last, with some impatience. 'It's very sad what's happened, and I feel for you, my friend; but you of all people should know that accidents happen. A roll of the dice and your number's up! Something's going to dispatch all of us sooner or later. Just think what you've been through. Just think of Daisy's parents in those Southampton bombings. What's done is done, old friend! You can't put back time, there's nothing you can do about it now. Daisy's quick death may even have been a blessing. She'll not have to suffer now.' Ben leant forward in his chair, put his elbows on his knees and cradled his chin in his hands. 'Oh Woody, I don't think I'll ever get over this,' he said with a sigh.

But he would get over it, at least to all outward appearances. Although it would take some weeks and months yet for all Ben's feelings to find some rational order in his troubled mind. The chemistry of grief does odd things to one's thinking, but by degree he began, if not to absolve himself of his guilt, then to put his part in Daisy's death in a more reasonable context and to think more positively about his life ahead. Decisions regarding his own future needed to be taken. Rent and subsistence were eating into his small reserves, and he could not go on living on tears and sighs forever.

Waking up to a bright and breezy Autumn morning some days later, Ben threw open his dormer window, wondered at the beauty of the sky and the sun-bathed wheatfields on the distant horizon, and took a deep breath of fresh Wiltshire air. In that moment, he decided that it was indeed time to move on. It was not his intention to forget Daisy or to shed his grief and guilt about her death, but more to park these troublesome thoughts in a quiet corner of his mind where they would not interfere too much with the rest of his life. It was a cathartic moment.

Only the previous week, Woody had brought him details and an application form for a new post he had seen advertised at Boscombe Down for which, he thought, Ben would be ideally suited. Ben's interest in the post had been mildly aroused at the time, but in his self-destructive mood he had simply put the papers aside. Now, at last, with that fresh Wiltshire wind blowing in through his attic window, ruffling his hair and stirring his spirits, Ben pulled himself together and picked them up.

Ben's application and subsequent appointment to the post was the turning point he needed. And such was the pace of his induction and training over the following months that he would have little time to think of anything else. In this respect, it was liberating, a new beginning. To be given the chance to work directly for the nation that he had helped to defend filled him with an enlivened surge of pride – a sort of patriotic fervour – though his Englishness would have prevented him from articulating it as such. Contributing to the country's testing programme for new defence equipment and helping to build a fighting ability that would deter another belligerent country from picking a fight with Britain was a cause he could believe in. It would be something he could commit too, something positive and substantial that would displace the personal miseries of his past. It pushed the past horrors of his wartime service aside too (perhaps into another of corner of his mind?) and filled him with hope for a new and brighter future.

Ben would often reflect on his life's journey – the journey that had brought him to where he had now arrived – from pit boy in the Backworth coal mines to senior RAF officer with a distinguished flying cross. From a background almost fated to lead into a life of manual labour, to a career as a professional technical officer at a national aeronautical experimental establishment. He knew too that he had been miraculously lucky to have survived the war when so many of his contemporaries had perished. Despite the regrets and sadnesses of his private life, the upward course of his professional life navigated through the first quarter-century of his existence seemed almost too incredible to be true.

Chapter 28

Ben's Cottage in the Wiltshire Countryside

A nd so began another chapter in Benjamin Hardy's life. At the time of his arrival at Boscombe Down, the Aeroplane and Armament Experimental Establishment was in the middle of a reorganisation. The Establishment had only been in residence at the airfield since 1939, having moved there from its original Suffolk home on Martlesham Heath to put a bit more distance between itself and German bombers. The airbase was one of the original grass aerodromes built on and around Salisbury Plain during the First World War for the Royal Flying Corps, and when A&AEE took up residence there it was still relatively undeveloped. As it moved in, the Establishment had to make do with what it had found, but facilities had been improved throughout WW2 as its testing role had expanded. It was not until 1945, however, the year before Ben arrived, that a concrete runway had been laid. Two more would be built later.

The Establishment's primary role was to carry out acceptance trials for all new service aircraft and their armaments, equipment, and systems. Prototype and pre-production aircraft and equipment of all shapes and sizes designed to meet new military requirements needed government acceptance before being approved for general service use. A & AEE would establish whether military requirements for the equipment were likely to be met, and if not, to quantify the shortfall so that the respective service – RAF or RN – could decide whether to accept the new product and make do with it – or send it back to the drawing board.

At that time, A&AEE came under the Ministry of Supply and was staffed mostly by civilian scientists, engineers, and technicians, but there was also a sizeable cohort of service personnel, mainly the aircrew who would fly the trials aircraft and the specialists who would test its armament. The scientists and engineers were grouped into divisions according to areas of aeronautical specialism, and there were four flight-test squadrons testing different categories of aircraft.

The usual tiresome arrival form-filling and induction procedures of Ben's first few days were followed by briefings on current and anticipated projects. Ben realised immediately that he was in for an exciting time. Engineering Division, the division to which Ben had been assigned, was responsible for evaluating engine performance and primary and secondary aircraft systems. In this sort of work, Ben was immediately back on home ground having operated and evaluated such systems in his wartime days. It would not be long, therefore, before he would be given trials of his own to devise and direct, working with and alongside the technicians and test aircrews who would perform the tests.

Russia, a wartime ally had turned belligerent soon after the war. The new Union of Soviet Socialist Republics seemed to most western eyes to pose a threat that demanded a strong retaliatory capability for credible deterrence. A cold war of posturing and sabre-rattling thus began – the beginning of an arms race that would last for decades. Consequently, new types or marques of aircraft and new equipment were arriving at Boscombe by the dozen every year, each requiring to be evaluated and cleared for operational use.

It was during his early years at A&AEE that Ben was also given the opportunity to train and qualify for his private pilot's licence. This was a scheme designed to give trials officers some piloting experience so as better to understand the demands they might be making of the test aircrew. Ben's earlier RAF training had included some flying instruction on the Airspeed Oxford and the Link Instrument Trainer so that he could pilot his wartime Lancaster back to safe territory should the captain be injured or killed. But such limited training would not have given Ben the competence to navigate the craft himself or to perform advanced flying tasks. He was a quick learner, however, and with his licence soon under his belt, he became an enthusiastic weekend flyer, continuing his private flying as a member of the Establishment's flying club.

All this would make Ben's professional life interesting and rewarding, and over the coming three decades he would progress from his entry grade in the civil service to principal technical officer, the equivalent of a Royal Air Force group captain. The aircraft on which he would conduct trials would range from multi-piston engine transports and maritime patrol aircraft to turbojet-powered bombers and fighters. He would test new engines and systems, check that they met the performances required, and ensure that they were safe to fly. He would devise the flight test schedules and analyse and report on the data collected in flight. If something was going to go wrong (which it almost invariably would), it would be Ben's job to ferret it out, and then come up with workarounds or fixes, or suggest operating limitations that would minimise risk in flight. And when not actually directing or participating in flying trials himself, Ben would have to write reports and make recommendations for the decision-makers higher up the chain of command. Professionally, he could not have made a better choice of future career, and he threw himself into it from the start.

———

But we are getting ahead of ourselves in the telling of Ben's story. What has just been described is merely a glimpse into Benjamin Hardy's professional future – a short summary of his working life to come. Interesting as that might be, the professional side of Ben's story is but one strand in an existence that had already suffered several emotional twists and turns. Having now dealt with the relative success that Ben would enjoy in his future working life, let us flip back the pages of the calendar and look at his continuing emotional development – that strand of his life that had been nipped in the bud, so to speak, with Daisy's sad demise in the traffic accident in Salisbury – a tragedy that had abruptly stunted Ben's emotional development before it had really matured. How Ben's relationship with Daisy might have turned out is now anyone's guess.

Had it not been for her illness, it certainly had the makings of a potentially fulfilling matrimonial future, one that might have matched and complemented his professional development. Sadly, that was not to be. Daisy's loss was a wound that had left a permanent scar, but Ben was already beginning to find a degree of contentment in being single and unattached.

Although Boscombe Down employed several thousand staff, few in Ben's professional circle were female, and so the opportunity for romantic interaction with women hardly ever arose. Even when it did, Ben's reaction was to shy away from anything more than the briefest of encounters – like a two-year-old refusing at Becher's Brook in its first race at Aintree. He found himself unwilling to pursue relationships for fear of exposing himself again to the agonies of loss that he had already twice suffered – partings for different reasons admittedly, yet each as painful and as laced with regret. Fond memories of his two lost loves never seemed to dim. Their ghosts drifted into and out of his mind constantly – intruding upon his thoughts whenever nothing more pressing took his attention – a preoccupation which, in his darker moods, sometimes made him seem introspective and self-absorbed – and not especially good company.

Outside work, Ben chose to live a solitary life in a small two-up, two-down former woodman's cottage at the end of a long track. The cottage was located on the fringe of a Wiltshire village, with a swiftly flowing chalk stream running along the length of its long plot. It was an ancient seventeenth-century hovel built of chalk, flint and clay under a straw roof. Sheltered from the prevailing wind by drooping sycamores and rising ground yet having an open aspect and a sunny garden, it had a picturesque south-facing front elevation with hollyhocks and roses framing its front door. The estate agent's brochure had made it sound idyllic but, having been abandoned to the elements for years before Ben's acquisition, neglect had taken its toll. The low price for its freehold of only two-hundred pounds reflected its poor condition but had brought it within Ben's means – as a 'project' for him to 'do up' over time and as income and his limited DIY skills would permit. Gravity had bent the cottage out of true, damp had risen in its cob walls (as it would), and small creatures from the surrounding fields and woodlands had taken up residence (as they do). It had no mains water or drainage, no heating other than one small open hearth, and its electrical lighting dimmed to a flicker whenever the cooker was turned on.

In the early years of his occupation, there had been much work for Ben to attend to – even to make the place habitable let alone comfortable. While Ben might sometimes have wondered at the wisdom of taking on such a monumental project alone and largely unaided except for a few craftsmen who brought in the skills that Ben himself could not master, he never regretted it. This ancient hovel would become his home and his castle – his own estate, not occupied at the whim of some landlord. Moreover, its location was secluded and tranquil, and the rustic isolation provided the peace he sought. A long-haired, coal-black moggy was his only residential companion (apart from those other creatures who had been reluctant to move out when he had moved in), and she was as choosy about her company as Ben himself. They were made for each other.

Living and working so far away from the county of his birth and early upbringing and being so totally absorbed with his work and his bucolic domestic life, it was rather too easy for Ben to forget his past and fix his attention instead on his present and his future. As has already been said, he seems to have developed an ability to bury uneasy memories in the backwaters of his mind, just as he had buried memories of April's rejection and Daisy's untimely death. Only by doing so, had he been able to move his life on. The human brain seems to be quite good at stashing unpleasant or awkward memories away in places where they do not become too troublesome. It is, no doubt, a helpful protective mechanism, but Ben was accumulating a lot of these dark places in his mind, which may explain why he devoted so much time to his work and why he buried himself in a remote cottage deep in the Wiltshire countryside.

He was also a lamentably neglectful son, especially neglectful of a mother who still wrote to him from time to time, and to whom, to his later shame, he rarely replied with more than a few desultory lines. In his new 'professional' role, his way of life had changed so completely that his mind was occupied with so many other things that he hardly gave a thought to home and family. News from Backworth, he thought, was anyway largely everyday scuttlebutt about his old domain and the former acquaintances who populated it – information merely of passing interest and soon forgotten.

The news of a pit collapse at the Backworth Colliery thus came with an uncomfortable jolt, which proved that family ties were stronger than he thought. It was received by telegram, the arrival of which was announced by an insistent rap-rap-rap on the windowpane of Ben's half-glazed kitchen door. Still in his jacket and tie having only just returned from work that early evening, he was seated at the kitchen table with a cup of tea and a slice of toast and Marmite on a plate before him. Startled by the sudden noise, he turned to see a shadowy face peering in. It made him jump. In his rural isolation, it was rare for Ben to have visitors, except his daily cleaning lady and the occasional villager who might pass by using the footbridge that connected him with the nearby village, and very rare for anyone to call so late. The dusk light was already fading outside on this mid-October day, and it was therefore only by the kitchen's light shining outwards through the glazing that the face was visible at all. It was an eerie image that alarmed Ben at first, until he recognised his visitor as the postman who by this time was mouthing something unheard and incomprehensible while waving an envelope in his hand. Ben grinned a greeting at the figure, pushed back his chair and went to the door.

'Paul!' exclaimed Ben, throwing the door open (he knew his regular postman well by now). 'What's this? Special delivery?' Any post delivered to Ben's cottage was usually received in the early morning or early afternoon, and so to see the postman standing at his door at this late hour had taken him by surprise.

'It's a telegram, Mr Hardy,' said the visitor somewhat needlessly, for the small, buff-coloured envelope flapping in his raised hand was clearly just that. In the absence of a telephone (which Ben had not yet got round to installing), telegrams were the only way that urgent messages from afar could be conveyed. He knew that this message would therefore either be good news or bad news, and there was something in the man's manner that suggested that it was the latter. Ben felt his stomach turn. His brow creased as he took the envelope from the postman's hand and ripped it open. It read:

PIT COLLAPSE AT BACKWORTH COLLIERY STOP YOUR
FATHER AND BROTHER AMONGST THOSE TRAPPED BELOW
STOP CONTACT MADE STOP RESCUE UNDERWAY STOP YOUR
MOTHER ASKS YOU TO COME HOME STOP REGARDS FROM
YOUR OLD FRIEND TIM AT BACKWORTH COLLIERY END

Ben had feared that the message would contain bad news, but this news was a shock. He studied the text again as he backed slowly into the kitchen re-reading it and seated himself at the kitchen table. The postman coughed gently. 'I read the message as it came off the teleprinter, sir,' he admitted. He was still standing in the open doorway, the crimson sky of a setting sun behind him now making a silhouette of his thin, uniformed figure. 'It was on the Home Service too,' the man added. 'It's not good news, is it?' he said, in a sympathetic tone. It was a statement rather than a question.

'No Paul. Not at all good news, I'm afraid.' Ben ran his hand through his hair while he tried to collect his thoughts. 'Anyway, come in, come in …' he added absently, his mind still reeling. 'I'll want to send a reply if you can give me a moment to think. Pour yourself a cup of tea if you want…' he said, waving his hand airily at the teapot sitting under its cosy on the table. A minute or two passed in silence as words were scribbled and tea was sipped. 'Got a notebook?' Ben said at last. 'Good man. Then, take this down.' He dictated his message as follows: 'To Tim at Backworth Colliery comma thank you stop message received stop tell my mother I'll be back as soon as possible stop.' He paused, wondering if he should say more, then added: 'Oh, and better finish with: 'Regards comma Ben end'

Ben retired early to his bed that evening, resolving to make an early start the following morning having devised a 'cunning plan' that might speed his journey northwards! Sleep was slow to come, however, with Ben's thoughts haunted by imagined scenes of his father and his brother trapped underground. His mind drifted dreamlike, from one cameo of his recollections of times spent with them to another. Some of these recollections were pleasant memories of his childhood, others not so comfortable. He recalled his last visit to the miners' welfare club in Backworth when he'd sat at a big table amongst his father's and his brother's comrades, their faces around the table so familiar, like members of his extended family – except that war and time had changed him (and them) in so many ways that he hadn't seemed to fit in anymore. He hadn't expected to be celebrated as a war hero, but to have been blanked and treated so coolly by those men that night had hurt and puzzled him. He had once been proud to earn his place amongst them, but he'd been made to feel that he'd somehow betrayed his own kind. As sleep began to take him, his thoughts drifted back to his childhood in that old mining community. In an instant, he was there again playing marbles in the gutters of its grimy streets, breathing the grey air amongst the rows of coal-blackened terraces with slag heaps looming darkly above the rooftops. He'd been unquestionably happy in his boyhood but had become seriously disaffected with it all in his adolescence. Uncomfortable recollections of working as a young miner underground soon entered his dreams too: dirty, heavy work in dark tunnels with the fear of being buried alive never far from his mind. It was these nightmarish thoughts that brought him back to wakefulness with a start and in a sweat, suddenly remembering that his father and his brother were now facing that very fate. He didn't get much sleep that night.

Chapter 29

De Havilland MkT3 Mosquito over Backworth Colliery

The following morning, Ben woke with the dawn, dressed quickly, and threw some things into a holdall, anticipating some days away. Descending to the kitchen, he bolted down his customary breakfast of toast and cereal, scribbled a note for the cleaner to add feeding the cat to her list of daily duties, and departed for Boscombe Down.

He'd acquired a second-hand Morris 8 for his daily commuting – a small red and black two-door saloon that while still probably roadworthy had seen much better days. He'd bought the vehicle from a used-car garage in Amesbury with a three-month guarantee but was beginning to doubt that it would last even that long. With his right foot pressed down hard on the accelerator, the little Morris could achieve an impressive fifty miles an hour (with the helpful following westerly wind), and in twenty-five minutes, Ben was arriving at 'A' Squadron's operations room just as the aircrew were beginning to assemble for their morning briefing. He made straight for the flight commander's office to find the current holder of that post, Squadron Leader Clive Rustin, already sitting at his desk. Ben had been working recently with Rustin on the performance trials of the Mosquito trainer, a two-pilot version of the single-pilot wartime fighter-bomber known for its high speed and long range. It was this aircraft and its capabilities that had given Ben his idea for rapid transportation northwards as he had pondered possibilities the night before. If he wanted to get to Newcastle quickly, going by Mosquito was the surest way to do it, for he doubted very much that his little Morris was up to such a mammoth journey.

On entering the senior test pilot's office, Ben was still out of breath from running up the stairs. He greeted his air force colleague with a curt nod absent of the customary pleasantries: 'I need your help my friend!' he said, plainly. 'I've got a problem.' Not wasting any time, Ben told Rustin about the pit collapse at the Backworth coalmine, about his father and brother being trapped below, and about his urgent need to get there quickly to comfort his mother and to assist in any way he could. His manner was steadier and more forthright than he felt. The solution to his problem was in his colleague's hands and he knew he was about to ask for something that would stretch the flight commander's authority to its limits.

'Cutting to the chase, Clive,' Ben concluded, coming at last to the point of his visit, 'how d'you fancy a long-range proving flight in the Mossie to Woolsington this morning?' (RAF Woolsington was a mere five miles from the Backworth colliery and thus the obvious destination).

'Woolsington!' Rustin exclaimed, rocking back in his chair. 'Blimey Ben, the round trip would take all morning!' he said, shaking his head. Ben grimaced. 'Maybe we could call it a test flight to collect range and endurance data?' he suggested, hopefully. Rustin swivelled in his chair, threw a glance at the blackboard on his wall where the flight programme for the day had been chalked up, studied his watch, then sucked his teeth. Ben half expected a flat refusal and steeled himself for disappointment. He cast a hopeful glance through the window to the concrete apron outside on which the aircraft in question sat with a fuel bowser at its side. It had been chalked up for a test flight later that morning. He and his test pilot colleague had already flown half a dozen trials flights together in the aircraft over the past few weeks and were programmed to fly the sortie planned for today. The two of them had formed a good working relationship, which felt to Ben more like a genuine friendship; he hoped that Rustin would feel the same way and be sympathetic to his unusual request. Rustin was known to have a somewhat cavalier attitude to rules and regulations, especially when they interfered with his relish for a challenge or a bit of fun. A former wartime Spitfire pilot, he had the looks and manner of a swash-buckling privateer, and Ben hoped that his swash-buckling might extend as far as an unofficial flight to Newcastle.

'Well Ben,' Rustin replied, as a crooked smile crept across his face and a glint came into his eye, '*you're* the trials officer, aren't you', he said with emphasis. Ben pursed his lips and nodded. 'Then you'd better write me a trials instruction!' With which the pilot pushed a foolscap notepad across his desk. Ben smirked, took out his pen, and scribbled out the most rudimentary trials instruction he'd ever written. If his section leader ever got to see it, he'd be in trouble, but by then its objective would have been achieved. He put his signature on the bottom and pushed the notepad back across the desk. 'That enough?' Ben asked. Rustin read Ben's brief and scribbled note:

'Mosquito T Mk.III two-seat trainer. Long range fuel consumption tests at various cruise airspeeds and altitudes. Conditions of tests to be directed by the accompanying trials officer.'

'Hmmm! Sounds clear enough to me,' he chuckled, throwing the notepad into his pending tray. 'It'll stay there until I get the bird back in one piece and then it'll go in the bin,' he added emphatically. 'You'd better go and get yourself kitted up! I'll check the weather and put in a flight plan.'

The T Mk III trainer, like the earlier single-pilot DeHavilland Mosquito marques, was powered by two Rolls Royce Merlin engines, essentially the same engines used in the Lancaster in which Ben had accumulated his five-hundred operational hours and fifty wartime missions. Its airframe was practically identical to the earlier Mosquito versions, but the cockpit had been re-designed to accommodate two pilots and two sets of flying controls – one for the instructor and one for his student. By 09.30 that morning, Ben was climbing into the right-hand seat of their Mosquito T Mk III as Rustin took the left. Both strapped in, pulled on their leather flying helmets, and plugged their telecoms leads into their respective sockets.

'You on?' A tinny version of Rustin's voice crackled over the intercom into Ben's earphones. Ben fastened his oxygen mask in place and switched on his microphone. 'Loud and clear,' was his reply.

'Right-ho Ben! Let's get the thing started! I've got a round trip of six-hundred miles in front of me, and I want to be back in time for lunch! Here's the checklist,' he said, handing it over. 'Engine start checks, please!'

As the crow flies, the distance between Boscombe Down and Newcastle Woolsington airfield was roughly two-hundred and fifty miles, but Rustin's route would take the aircraft around areas that are best avoided, and this would add a few more miles. The aircraft could achieve phenomenal performance from the nearly three-thousand horsepower generated by its two Merlin 21s and could cruise comfortably at upwards of three-hundred miles per hour. 'You have it, Ben,' said Rustin, handing over control once the aircraft had been established and trimmed into a fast cruise climb. 'Level her at fifteen thousand, then come back on boost and RPM to maintain two-hundred-and-fifty knots. The heading on our first leg is three-five-two degrees. I'll do the navigating and the radio; you can do the flying!'

Just over an hour and twenty minutes later, the grass airfield of RAF Woolsington was in sight as the descending Mosquito broke out of cloud and headed towards the landing pattern. Rustin gave directions for Ben to set the aircraft up on an extended left-hand base leg for a final approach to the westerly landing strip. 'OK Ben, I'll take it from here,' said Rustin, taking the yoke with his left hand and the throttles with his right. 'Well done. Couldn't have flown it much better myself!'

Ben sat back, feeling pleased with himself for the accuracy of his flying. He hadn't lost his touch.

Flying was like riding a bicycle, he thought, once learned, never forgotten. He surveyed the scene below, searching for familiar features in the landscape. He had never seen his home territory from the air before and it took a while to orientate. The air below the cloud was clear, but the stratocumulus layer through which they had just descended dimmed the daylight and Northumberland seemed washed out with no impression of its contours and no colour either. It looked as gloomy as Ben's mood. As his colleague banked the aircraft in the finals turn, Ben spotted his home village almost directly below. The four parallel terraces of miners' cottages, with their grey-slated roofs and their smoke-blackened walls, hardly stood out against the dismal backdrop of the mine works. Looking across the cockpit from his right-hand seat, the scene was oddly distorted by the curves in the glazing of the canopy. The colliery estate was a bleak and scarred landscape of black ground, slagheaps, and railway sidings Its ugly and disproportioned buildings stood out like tombstones in a battlefield obscured partly by drifting smoke. He could see a crowd of people clustered at the pithead gate – women in shawls and men in flat caps – some faces turned up towards the sky, attracted no doubt by the aircraft engine noise overhead. The winding wheels on the lift gantry were stationary, the little shunting engines, normally puffing about so busily, sat idle in their sidings, smoke billowed upwards from two tall chimney stacks – power for the pumps and ventilation, Ben thought. But the conveyor belts from the screening and washing plant lay idle. No coal was being shifted today. Rustin rolled the wings level as he straightened on his course towards the runway and Ben lost sight of his former workplace as it slid beneath the fuselage. As it disappeared, he was left with a hollow feeling in the pit of his stomach. Somewhere, trapped in the tunnels hundreds of feet below that blackened surface were his father and his brother. It was an uncomfortable thought.

Rustin lowered the undercarriage and flaps and brought the Mossie in for a perfect landing on the mown grass of the landing strip. 'OK Ben,' said he, as he taxied towards the control tower, throttled back the engines to a tick-over, and brought the aircraft to a halt just yards from the building. 'I'll let you out here and head straight back to Boscombe. I've radioed the control tower that you'll need transport to Backworth, so just head up to the ops room and they'll sort you out. I'll be thinking of you old chap and hoping that your dad and brother will get out OK. Anyway, good luck. Give me a call when you're ready to come back.'

Ben unstrapped, unplugged his telecoms, grabbed his holdall from behind his seat, and clambered out. As he strode towards the control tower, the Mosquito's Merlins opened up with a roar behind him. He turned to watch as the aircraft swung its tail around to head back towards the take-off point and raised a hand in farewell. Rustin responded with a grin and a wave of his hand from the cockpit, followed by a burst of his throttles that sent several hundred horsepower of propwash behind him that nearly blew Ben over.

Chapter 30

At Ben's request for urgency, a Land Rover from the MT section at RAF Woolsington hurried him directly to his mother's home. He found the front door unlocked and went straight in, calling out for his mother but not expecting to find her there. There was no sign of life at all in the house, nor was there any sign of life elsewhere in Walkworth Street. Indeed, an abandoned air hung over all four of the parallel, terraced streets that formed the Backworth mining community. Ben guessed where everyone must be.

Still wearing his flying overalls, his leather flying jacket and boots, he dumped his holdall in the parlour and set off immediately for the pithead. The alleyways between alternate houses in the street gave access to their back gardens and the colliery perimeter fence which lay immediately behind. The pit site's boundary was marked by a line of crumbling concrete posts and a sagging steel wire that was supposed to keep people out. It had never deterred Ben from crossing it in his mining days as a shortcut when he would otherwise have been late for his shift. Nor had it stopped Ben and his young brother from entering the site as children. It had been their adventure playground where, with other bare-kneed, tousle-haired miners' sons, they had used the compacted clinker as their football field – with rusty oil drums as its goal posts. Ben's rebel gang of boisterous youngsters had looked like urchins from the city slums when they came home for their tea as black-faced and filthy as their fathers from their shifts.

Ben made his way down the alleyway and stood at the wire boundary fence for a moment and surveyed the bleak landscape before him, remembering the carefree days of his youth. It did not seem so enticing now, and his recollections of those happy days of childhood were tainted with fears for his trapped brother and father preying on his mind. He pictured them huddled in the dark beneath the very ground he stood on, waiting, afraid, and hoping for rescue. He stepped across the sagging wire, crossed the railway tracks beyond, and strode out along a familiar winding path. His beacon in the hazy distance was the headgear gantry and chimneys that rose above the sundry buildings of the Backworth complex, all non-descript, equally ugly and run down. He skirted the murky pools of run-off, wound his way between the heaps of slag, turned left at the old allotment granary building and followed the shunting tracks – until at last he came upon the gathering at the colliery main gate. There must have been forty or fifty people standing there, he reckoned, some miners wearing mining gear amongst them, but mostly women, children, and old men, all clearly anxious and waiting for news. He approached them from the rear and, not wanting to announce his presence, he stood silently behind them all, scanning their backs for recognition. Some, he knew – former workmates and schoolfriends – all grown older now but still so familiar – and also some mothers of the boys he had once known well. If Ben's mother was there, however, she was lost amongst them.

He had not been standing there long when the winding wheels on the headgear gantry began to spin. A cage must be coming up, he thought, and wondered what news it would bring. Those in front of him must have seen the wheels turning too, for there was now some shuffling and some hopeful mutterings amongst the crowd, some lifting onto tiptoes and some craning of necks. The entrance to the shaft and the steel-mesh gates that guarded it until the rising cage completed its ascent, could be seen through the open double doorway of the pit head building. Inside, it was a dark and grimy place. Half a dozen rusty, cast-iron coal tubs stood ready to have their contents tipped into the screening plant below, but the rotating gear was idle. Men stood about in small groups looking disconsolate – mostly miners in helmets with gear on their belts, others wearing flat caps and grubby suits with hands in pockets. A broad tarmac pathway led from the building towards the main gate at which Ben and his companions waited anxiously. It would be along that pathway that any news from below would come, and this was where the crowd's attention was now directed. Being somewhat taller than many of those in front of him, Ben had a clear view. He could see the banksman, the controller of the lift mechanism, standing at the shaft gates watching the indicator dial that showed the cage's rapid ascent. Ben guessed its arrival was imminent.

A moment later, the cage appeared, and the gates were drawn back. Inside the cage, packed shoulder to shoulder, were upwards of twenty men in mining gear. Their helmet lamps flashed about like fireflies in the relative darkness of the lift top as they exited. The waiting crowd pressed forward as rescuers and rescued came along the pathway in a slow and steady procession, some faces so grimy with dust as to be hardly recognisable. A few of the men broke from the line and raced ahead, searching for their loved ones amongst the waiting crowd. Others ambled by, bent-shouldered, grim-faced, and looking exhausted. Finally, bringing up the rear, a casualty on a stretcher, his head swathed in a bandage and his arm in splints, his black face was nevertheless split from ear to ear with a toothy grin, so evidently overjoyed was he to be back in the daylight and breathing fresh air.

Searching the faces of the motley procession as it passed through the gates, many of those in the waiting crowd recognised their loved ones and broke from the throng with screams of delight to reclaim their men. More and more of them were re-united until eventually it was like a party in the street, a joyous scene of happy reunions, with wives, girlfriends and children clinging to men's necks, with laughter and tears of joy. But as those re-united souls moved noisily away in the direction of their homes, a depleted crowd still waited at the gate. These unhappy few soon fell quiet, realising that they faced a further anxious wait for news and now suffering a greater uncertainty than before. The frightened looks upon their faces revealed their states of mind, but while some undoubtedly feared the worst, most still clung to hope – as did Ben and Susannah Hardy too.

Ben spotted his mother in the thinning crowd and made his way forward. 'I'm here, Ma,' said he softly, whispering into her ear as he came up behind her. He took her shoulders gently in his hands, turned her around and embraced her.

'Oh, Ben! Ben, you dear boy. You came! You came!' she cried, her eyes searching his, communicating much more between them than any words could express. Ben felt her frailty and the slightness of her form. 'They're still down there, Ben: your Da and your brother,' she said, in a steady voice that belied the pallor and the strain of her facial features. 'They haven't come out.' She shook her head glumly and broke from his embrace to turn her gaze back to the pithead as if hoping that her men might belatedly appear. Ben's eyes followed hers. There seemed to be some kind of hiatus there, men in jackets and suits huddled in quiet conference. The gates to the shaft remained open with the empty cage visible inside the shaft.

'I know, Ma,' Ben said, calmly. 'But don't give up; they can't bring 'em all up in one go, you know. There'll be more to come up yet, you'll see.' These last words, he spoke out a little more loudly so that others standing nearby might hear, and he saw some heads turn towards him with hope in their eyes. Recognising many of their faces, he smiled with a confidence he did not fully feel.

'You're Levi Hardy's boy, aren't you?' asked one of the women standing nearby. 'The boy who went off to join the RAF before the war?' Ben nodded, and she came up to him and put her hand gently on his chest. 'It's good to see you back, son,' she said, gazing up into his eyes.

'I wish it could have been better circumstances,' said Ben. 'Your husband's still below too, I suppose?' Ben already knew the answer, and her nod confirmed it. At that moment one of the officials, wearing a suit and tie, broke from the cluster of men gathered at the pithead and made his way towards the gate. Ben guessed he'd been sent to report on the progress of the rescue. As the man neared, two young, fresh-faced men that Ben had noticed earlier moved forward, one producing a notebook, the other a camera – a rather bulky press camera with concertina bellows and a flash. They'd be hungry for information too.

The official cleared his throat as he came amongst the gathering. His face was flushed, and his manner was rather nervous as he silenced the clamour for answers by raising his hands. 'As you saw,' he began, as silence fell; and speaking in that artificial and stilted manner that officials sometimes adopt in the presence of the press, he continued: 'We've got fifteen men out already with only a few minor injuries recorded so far.' He cleared his throat again. 'It seems from the reports we've just received from the rescue team, however, that there may have been a number of roof falls in the same tunnel, and we don't yet know the full extent of it. This may mean that the remaining men are trapped behind other falls in the tunnel further on. We're trying to get a fuller picture now.'

Hearing this news prompted some anxious questions from his listeners. The official carried on regardless, his voice rising above theirs to recapture their attention. 'The fifteen men we've already pulled out were found behind the first of these falls, which was apparently relatively easily cleared. I'm told that the damaged section there has been shored up to allow further penetration of the tunnel, and that has allowed a small team to reach the site of the second fall and carry out a survey. With their report just back, we now know what's involved, and we're assembling a new rescue team and the items of equipment that will be required to tackle it. As soon as everything's ready, they'll get started. From what we now know, however, the second fall is more extensive than the first, so it's likely to take some time to break through.'

'Can you tell us how many men are still missing?' interrupted the reporter.

'We're not sure yet, the official replied. 'As soon as we've done a tally of the miner's discs and finished questioning those who've come up, we'll know more.'

'Surely you keep a head count?' persisted the reporter.

The official cleared his throat again, then raised his voice and his hand to quell the questioning mutterings that broke out amongst the crowd. 'Look, there would have been a hundred or more miners working in different parts of the mine at the time of the collapse,' the official said, beginning to go a little on the defensive, 'and there's often movement of men between one section and another depending on the work. So, it's not always possible to keep track of exactly who is where at any time.' There were some expressions of surprise at this. 'We keep a tally of the total number of men below, of course,' he asserted quickly, 'but we don't always know exactly where they are.' He paused for breath. 'Let me explain…every miner going down exchanges a numbered disk for a safety lamp, and both the disk and the lamp have the same number. When he comes back up, he hands his lamp in and retrieves his disk, so normally we'll know who's topside and who's below. In an accident situation like this, however, lamps can get lost or left underground or get mixed up, so it's not always possible to get an accurate picture straight away. That's why I can't be more precise right now, and that's what we're working on. Is that any clearer?'

Some muttering followed the official's explanation, but there were no specific questions.

'As I say, we're getting more information as we speak,' the official went on, 'and I don't think that there's any more I can say at this stage. But if I can take the names of the men you people here are waiting for,' he said, as his hands drew a notebook and pen from his pocket, 'it'll help us get a more complete picture.' Eight names were shouted out, including Levi and Frank Hardy's, all of which were noted in the official's notebook. 'Thank you,' he said at last. 'I suggest you all go home now. We'll sound the whistle when there's more to report. Until then, please be patient, we're doing the best we can.' With that, the man turned on his heel and strode off in the direction of the pithead.

Ben whispered into his mother's ear: 'Go home Ma. Being here in this cold wind's not doing you any good. I'm going to get more out of him if I can,' he said, flicking his glance to the official striding back along the path, 'and I'll come home when I've got any more information. In the meantime, try not to worry. Da and Frank are strong men, and I'm pretty sure they'll be OK.' He wrapped his arm around her shoulders, gave her a gentle squeeze, and then left to follow the retreating official.

'You're Tim's father, aren't you, sir?' called Ben, catching the man up at a run. 'I wasn't sure it was you at first. I'm Ben Hardy, Mr Wainwright. Tim and I worked together as putters for a while. We both started on the same day back in thirty-five, but he had the good sense to join you in the Admin office after a few weeks. I carried on working underground for a couple of years and then left to join the RAF. Tim let me put his name down as my line manager on my application form when I applied,' Ben admitted smilingly. 'I know he shouldn't have, but he actually wrote me a reference too!' Wainwright chuckled. 'Yes, I know all about that; he told me last night when your mother came round to ask about sending you a telegram,' he said.

'Anyway, how on earth did you get up here so quickly? You must have driven all night!' Mr Wainwright was a bluff, florid-faced character who had allowed himself to become portly in middle age. He had carried on walking as the pair talked, but now he stopped, turned, and looked Ben up and down, registering his flying jacket and overalls. 'Ah!' he uttered, as a look of understanding passed across his face.

'Yes, that was me arriving in that Mosquito earlier,' said Ben. 'I'm still in the flying game. It's useful when you want to get about!'

'Ah yes, we saw it passing overhead. Lovely looking machine! Your mother will be glad you've come.'

'Yes, sir,' Ben replied, and went on quickly, 'Sir, I realise that you can't know everything yet and perhaps didn't want to say too much in front of the press, but is there anything more you can tell me?'

Wainwright glanced back at the crowd at the gate, then took hold of Ben's arm and led him onwards towards the pithead. 'I wasn't ready to give them the full picture just yet,' he admitted. 'Didn't want to raise hopes unduly; but the tunnel's telephone cable's been reconnected, and contact's been made with the survivors. I haven't been given the full picture yet and didn't want to get into a guessing game about who and how many men had been accounted for, especially with the press there. It's your father who we're in contact with, Ben,' he added. 'He seems to be OK, but your brother's been injured. Not life threatening as I understand it, but bad enough to make things more complicated, especially if it takes a long time to get him out.' Wainwright didn't seem to want to dwell on this and hurried on. 'The good news is that we think everyone's accounted for – all of them are in that second chamber with your father – so we're pretty sure that there are no men trapped anywhere else in the tunnel. We'll be more confident of that once we've finished our head count.' He was still clutching his notebook in his hand, and he lifted it up for Ben to see. 'This list will probably help to speed things up.'

'Frank's injury, sir, how bad is it?'

Wainwright looked a bit shifty and hesitated. 'It's apparently pretty serious, Ben,' he said at last. 'Levi says he's going to be difficult to move and infection's a worry – a nasty break apparently – hit by falling timbers. The sooner we get him out of there and into a hospital bed the better his chances.'

Ben's tone became urgent: 'Mr Wainwright, you mentioned a fresh rescue team being assembled. When's it going down?'

'There're men shoring up the tunnel around the first roof collapse as we speak. Once it's safe, there's more rescue gear and timbers to go down for the new team to pick up when they get there. They'll be on their way as soon as all that's in place.'

'Well, I'm going to be joining them!' Ben's tone showed that he would brook no objection.

Wainwright visibly rocked on his heels. 'Sorry Ben, that won't be allowed, I'm afraid…' he stuttered. 'You're not employed, and…' He was clearly trying his hardest to find good reason to deny Ben's demand, but he was struggling.

Ben cut him off. 'Look, I spent two years working in those tunnels, sir.' he retorted. 'It was eleven years ago, I admit, but nothing much will have changed, and I'm as capable of shovelling as any man. They'll need all the hands they can get! Anyway, I can't just wait around up here like a hanger-on at a funeral while my father and my brother are trapped below! I *have* to help. They are my kin, after all!'

Ben's outburst stemmed Wainwright's protest before his steam could be got up. The two men stood face to face for several seconds, lips tight and brows furrowed, neither willing to back down – until Wainwright found a way out of the impasse. Glancing again at the pithead, he said: 'Alright, Ben, come along with me. The rescue team leader and the banksman there can make the decision. If they agree, I'll do whatever paperwork is needed to make it legal.'

Chapter 31

The rescue team leader was a square-jawed, thick-set Scot of about fifty years of age, with bushy eyebrows, ginger hair, and ginger facial stubble to match. He wore a knotted neckerchief around his neck and had rolled his shirtsleeves up tightly to his elbows to reveal thick, muscular arms and large hands. Ben recognised the man straight away as he and Wainwright made their way towards him. The veteran miner had been one of the overmen at the mine during the time that Ben had worked there in the thirties – a team-leader and overseer, one of the most experienced and well-respected miners at the colliery. He was in quiet conversation with a balding, middle-aged man dressed in suit and tie, probably one of the mine's managers, Ben guessed. Wainwright acknowledged the two men with a curt nod then introduced Ben as the son of Levi Hardy, whose name immediately captured the Scot's attention. 'He's volunteering for your rescue party, Scotty,' Wainwright said. The Scot ran his eyes over Ben's flying gear. 'Ah yes,' he said, cottoning on quickly. 'Levi's talked a lot about you. You used to work here before the war, didn't you?' Ben nodded. 'Yes, sir. It's a few years ago, I admit. But I think I still know the safety rules for working underground and I can wield a pick and shovel as good as any man. With my dad and my brother down there, I can't just hang around up here when I know I could be helpful.'

Scotty threw a questioning glance at the besuited companion at his side, and receiving a nod of approval, he turned back to Wainwright: 'Alright Ronnie,' he said. 'We'll take him with us; put him down on the list and sign him off.' Wainwright nodded, flashed a wink at Ben, and departed. 'Glad to have you aboard, Ben,' Scotty said, taking Ben's hand with a cast-iron grip. 'We need a few more lifters and shovellers. You'd better go and get yourself kitted up!' he said, nodding in the direction of the locker room.

Fifteen minutes later, Ben was back at the pithead suitably clothed and equipped with borrowed kit to join the twenty other volunteers already assembled. He acknowledged the looks he got from one or two familiar faces as he took his place amongst them, but the atmosphere was too strained for much intercourse. It felt strange to be back amongst these men, yet oddly also so completely normal. It was as if it had been weeks rather than years since he'd left the craft. He could see Scotty at the cage gate surrounded by a knot of senior miners. Their discussion seemed earnest, their expressions grave. They seemed to be engaged in a briefing of some kind, but it ended as Scotty broke away and came forward.

'Alright, everybody! Listen up!' he shouted, gaining the rescue team's attention instantly. 'For those who don't know already, we're going down to Level Four – that's the Bensham Tunnel at nine-hundred feet. It's got less than four-foot headroom in parts, so I want helmets on at all times please. We don't want any more casualties!' He swung his gaze around and seemed satisfied that his order had been understood. 'I've got some good and some bad news,' he continued. 'First, the bad news is that the rescue site is a good half mile from the tunnel entrance, which is where all our gear has been stacked up waiting for us. But the good news is that the conveyor belt and the tracks and pully system are back in operation now, so that'll help us get the stuff as far as the site of the first roof-fall without too much heavy lifting. I'm afraid that after that, we'll have to move everything by hand or sledge because the track from there on has been buried under rubble.' Scotty took a breath and paused for a moment in case of questions, but not getting any, he went on. 'We'll decide how we're going to organise ourselves once we've had a chance to assess the situation. I've been told that the tunnel's telephone cable's been reconnected, so we'll be able to talk to the men trapped on the other side of the fall. The senior man with them is Levi Hardy, an old hand. Having an experienced man on the other side of the fall will be helpful. We'll get a thorough update from him when we arrive.' He caught Ben's eye and beckoned him over. 'This young man here is Levi's son, Ben, who's volunteered to join us. Some of you may know him. He's a former putter here so knows the ropes.' Pausing now, as if mentally ticking off his list of things to say, Scotty then brought the briefing to a close with a brisk: 'OK gentlemen, when you're ready, let's load up.'

Ben received a few friendly pats on his shoulder as the team surged towards the cage. He'd hoped to remain anonymous and had been embarrassed by the attention. The pressure on him was building; he'd now have to do well to do justice to the Hardy name. Wearing his borrowed helmet, overalls, battery belt, steel-capped boots, and kneelers, he might otherwise have passed for a seasoned miner. He certainly looked like one. But for

Ben, descending again into the tight confines of a coal mine presented a real challenge. Though he'd worked underground before and had once taken it all in his stride, he weighed the risks more soberly now, and his stomach churned at the thought of what he was about to do. It had been a long time since his last descent, and the one he now faced was deeper than he'd ever been before. Worse, the tunnel he was about to enter had already suffered at least two roof-falls, and it was therefore quite possible that there could be more.

The Eccles shaft was the deepest and the most modern of the four pits in operation at the Backworth colliery at the time. It served seven coal seams at different levels from three hundred to fourteen-hundred feet below the surface, with tunnels extending from the shaft for several miles. Highly mechanised, the pit was equipped with mechanical cutters at the coal faces and conveyor belts and rope haulage systems to transport the coal to the lifts. It was these conveyances that the rescue party would be using to transport their gear. The main lift shaft was separated into two by brattice screens. This aided ventilation. The down-going cage in one half-shaft, counterbalanced by the up-coming cage in the other acted like two air pistons, drawing fresh air in and pumping stale out. There was also a smaller, separate ventilation shaft equipped with fans and filters to regulate air quality and remove smoke in the event of a fire. This shaft might have offered a possible emergency exit route (although with no lift), but it was the wrong side of the roof-fall and thus not an option for rescue on this occasion.

Each cage could carry about twenty-five men or six loaded coal tubs. During normal mine operations, these cages would be descending and ascending almost continuously twenty-four hours a day, moving miners, coal, and materials between the tunnels and the surface. Today they would only be used to support the rescue operation. The speed at which they travelled up and down the shaft depended upon the weight carried and the height dropped, but for the deepest tunnels, a speed of up to eighty-five miles per hour could be reached at the mid-point. The descent to the Bensham level would thus only take a minute or so. For Ben, it would feel much longer.

With the whole team standing shoulder to shoulder in the cage, it was as chummy as London's Northern Line at rush hour (but better ventilated). Moments later, the safety gates were slammed shut as a warning bell rang out and the cage was abruptly released of its constraint. Ben had forgotten what those first moments of near-zero gravity felt like. It was like stepping off a cliff or hitting an air pocket in his heavily loaded Lancaster, and the ride down was like freefall as the shaft walls hurtled past in a blur of reflected lamplight. The groans and screeches of flexing metal and the mighty uprush of forced air was dizzying. Ben's ears popped with the sudden increase of air pressure. Even Blackpool's Big Dipper wouldn't have caused such a rush of adrenalin. It was frightening and exhilarating at the same time. At the bottom of the drop, the cable brake was applied only just in time to arrest the fall. The rapid deceleration bent Ben's knees and caused the lift cable to stretch and recoil and stretch and recoil again, the cage bouncing up and down like a yo-yo before finally settling at the tunnel gate. If Ben hadn't had such a cast-iron stomach, the gymnastic finale would have finished him off. He reflected afterwards that the mining business was not for the faint-hearted.

Chapter 32

It took a further hour and a half for the rescue team and all its equipment to reach the site of the second roof-fall just short of a thousand yards along the tunnel. This was not a slick operation where everything went smoothly and with clinical precision. It was more an exercise of brute strength and improvisation with Ben not merely accompanying the team as a hanger-on but playing a full part, putting his full weight behind all the lifting and hefting that was necessary. For him, it was a sort of penance for the guilt that still lingered in his mind for leaving his community and abandoning his father's craft. The coolness that he had felt from his former workmates on his return home after the war had left him with that legacy, irrational as he knew it was. Here at last was an opportunity to prove to them that he was at heart a miner to his roots

The conveyor beltway and the rope-hauled coal tubs were loaded with the heavier gear – the jacks and cable winches, the timbers and the pit props – while other tools were carried by hand. Many of the men also carried short-stocked pick and shovel combination tools – a tool developed for infantrymen to dig trenches and now used by miners in tight spaces. The team had come fully prepared for any likely contingency.

The first few hundred yards of the tunnel's roadway from its entrance gate at level four was about three yards wide. Ben found it surprisingly spacious compared with the narrow tunnels he had worked before. Lamps had been rigged up at intervals along the tunnel by the first rescue team. They dotted the dim distance with pools of light like punctuation marks. It would make the going easier, but cap lamps would be kept switched on nevertheless – there were still large pockets of pitch blackness where a man could trip and fall on the uneven tunnel floors.

In the first section of the tunnel, the roof was supported by welded steel-girder arches placed every yard or so along the route, with the conveyor beltway and tub trackway running in parallel along the tunnel floor. It was possible for the shortest men to walk upright here, but others, Ben included, were already walking with a stoop. As the team penetrated further, the roof descended, and the steel arches gave way to wooden props and low horizontal lintels. Soon, everyone was walking hunch-backed, looking like beings from some primeval era. The final hundred yards or so were the most troublesome, made difficult by residual debris from the first cave-in. Only a short section of the tunnel roof had collapsed here, which had made its clearance by the first rescue team a relatively straight-forward task, but the trackway had been destroyed and the tunnel floor was littered with stone and rubble. Equipment and timbers now needed to be dragged and manhandled by the men, a task made more difficult yet as the tunnel narrowed to about four feet wide and only a little more in height. Temporary pit supports and cross-timbers had been put in place but between the timbers the roof was loose and craggy. The slightest knock by a helmet or the touch of a passing shoulder would bring down a hail of rocky debris. The rescuers soon had their neckerchiefs over mouths and noses to protect them from the dust.

Eventually, the team reached the site of the second roof collapse. The last of the temporary timber props and crossbeams stood before them like the entrance to a neolithic burial mound – except that that entrance was now blocked with a wall of rubble. This second fall appeared much more substantial than the first, and the clearance of such a tonnage presented a daunting task. Scotty signalled his team to gather round. Here, with only four feet of headroom, the men had to squat on their haunches. A field telephone lay in its leather pouch on the ground nearby, its connecting cable leading into a narrow vertical cavity at the side of the rubble mound. The cable was part of the mine's emergency telephone system. Miraculously, it had somehow remained intact in the roof collapse. Unearthed and reconnected to a mobile handset by the first rescue team, it had already been used to communicate with the men trapped on the other side of the fall. Scotty pulled the handset from its housing, gave the handle a few brisk winds, and pressed the earpiece to his ear. He listened intently for a moment in silence, then tried again several times. Eventually, he got a reply.

'That you, Levi?' he said, at last, a grin creasing his craggy face. 'Good man!'

Ben, squatting nearby, leant closer, attempting to listen in, but the faint metallic sound of his father's voice emanating from the handset was unintelligible.

'Scotty here, Levi,' the team leader went on, 'I've got the second rescue team with me and we're just preparing to make a start.' His voice was upbeat and confident. 'Yes, yes. We're on the other side of the fall,' he added after a short pause. The team were listening intently, but they could only hear Scotty's side of the conversation. 'What state are you all in?' Scotty continued. 'What does it look like on your side? Can you see any possible route out?' Scotty fell silent as he received Levi's report, examining the wall of rubble closely as he did so. 'Yes, yes, there's a bit of an opening at the top on this side too. You think it's possible that the strata above the fall might have held? Have you tried to get into it?' Scotty listened in silence for some more long moments, his face adopting a grave expression. 'Alright, understood,' he said, finally. 'OK Levi, don't worry, we'll try to push through from our side. We've got some heavy equipment that should do the trick. In the meantime, conserve your energy and your lamps. We'll keep in touch and report progress. Hang in there, old fella, we'll be with you as soon as we can.'

At this point, Ben caught Scotty's eye with a wave of his hand.

'Oh, just a sec, Levi! I've got someone here who wants to say hello,' said Scotty, beckoning Ben closer with a grin. He offered up the handset, which Ben grasped and pressed to his ear. 'Hello Da,' he yelled, excitedly, 'it's Ben.' He laughed. 'Yes! Ben! Flew up from Boscombe this morning. Thought you boys needed a hand.' He grinned. 'I'm a miner, remember? I can still wield a shovel as good as any of these reprobates! Yes, yes! I've been with Ma. She's making your tea!' He laughed again, but it was a show, an instinctive attempt to lighten the gravity of the situation and keep his father's hopes alive. 'Anyway, how are you? Good! And Frank?' A moment of silence passed while he listened to his father's report. 'Oh.' Ben's face suddenly became serious; the news about his brother was apparently not so good. 'Well, just tell him I'm here and to hang on. Remind him that he owes me a beer and we're coming to get him out,' he said. 'Just give us some time, Da. There's a mountain of rubble in the way, but we're going to get all of you out, so don't worry.' This pep talk was Squadron Leader Ben Hardy DFC speaking in his best RAF motivational tone as though rallying the crew of a stricken Lancaster.

Scotty raised a dubious eyebrow as Ben handed back the handset. 'Let's hope you're right, son,' he whispered gruffly, then fired off a few more questions down the line. Ben watched the team leader as the conversation continued, searching his face intently, attributing every inflexion in his voice as somehow reflecting his father's words. He noticed Scotty's gaze wandering across the rubble again as he listened, his eyes narrowing as if searching the furthest extremities of the fall. Something at the interface between the mountain of rubble and the roof strata seemed to be a special focus of his interest.

Scotty finished his conversation, placed the handset back in its pouch, and pushed the apparatus aside. 'Right, lads,' he said at last. 'Here's the situation: We've got one casualty – Ben's brother, Frank – cracked ribs and a broken leg by the sound of it – hit by falling timbers. They've lashed up a splint to immobilise it, but the bone is exposed, so there's a danger of infection, which is worrying. He's going to need a stretcher. Levi tells me that there are eight men in all behind the fall, all except Frank apparently fit enough to walk out. And everyone's accounted for, so there's no one else to go looking for once we've got them out. Air's not a problem – for the present at least – the tunnel behind them is clear all the way to the coal face apparently and no gas has been detected. Water leaking through the roof may become a problem though if we take too long because the pumps aren't working. I don't think that that's likely to become critical though. At least they'll have something to drink if they get desperate!'

Scotty paused here as if collecting his thoughts. He threw a glance to the top of the rubble pile again and pointed at the feature that had captured his earlier interest. 'That fissure there,' he said, pointing upwards, 'I'm hoping that it may offer us a way through. My guess – and hope – is that there's overlying rock strata holding things up above all the stuff that's come down. I think that what we're looking at here,' he said this waving his hand at the rubble, 'is the lower rock layer that was sitting on top of the coal seam before it was extracted. Taking out the coal could have fractured it to the point of giving way. Levi has come to the same conclusion because he can see a gap on his side too. Some of his men tried getting into it but weren't able to get very far – boulders and timbers in the way, apparently – too big for them to shift. I'm hoping that the two fissures connect. If they do, we may be able to find a way across the top of the fall – rather than through it – which will be a whole lot easier and quicker than trying to shift all this stuff out of the way!' He paused and took a breath. 'So that's what we'll try first. Everyone happy with that? Questions?'

There were no questions.

'Right, let's get started!' said Scotty. 'I'll climb up to have a closer look at that fissure and see how far it goes. Ben, you follow me up to give me a hand clearing the loose rock out of the way. The rest of you can start bringing the gear forward. I want everything laid out up here checked and ready for use when we need it. I'll do a recce first, then we'll reconvene and talk again. OK?'

Scotty and Ben clambered up the rubble pile and began levering out the larger lumps of rock from the lip of the fissure, rolling the boulders down the slope as they came away. Loose scree and fragments of stone followed in a steady cascade, all of which was quickly pushed or shovelled aside by a couple of the men at the bottom. The rest of the team busied themselves collecting the equipment and preparing it as instructed. For a while the scene was a hive of industry.

Chapter 33

Rescue in the Tunnel!

Half an hour later, the fissure had been made large enough for Scotty to climb in. Ben watched the Scot's feet disappearing then inched himself up to the opening to peer in, detaching his lamp from his helmet and holding it out in front of him on its cable like a torch. The sight that met his eyes astonished him. This was not a dead-end nor even the craggy, narrow passageway that he had expected, but a tall cavern that rose above the fallen rubble to a height of six to ten feet. As his eyes adjusted, Ben saw Scotty standing on top of the rockfall further in, illuminated in the pool of light thrown out by his own lamp. He looked as bemused as Ben felt.

'Blimey, Ben, look at this!' shouted Scotty incredulously as he swung his gaze about, his voice echoing in the emptiness. 'Come on in – and bring a few men with you if they've finished transporting gear. Not too many for the moment! We'll need the rest to bring the timbers and equipment in once we're sure that we can get all the way.' Ben relayed the message to his fellow rescuers who by then were waiting attentively at the base of the rubble slope behind him, then clambered into the opening himself. Once in, he got gingerly to his feet and tentatively raised a hand, expecting to feel a rocky roof just inches above his head. But there was nothing but thin air. For the last hour, he had been stooping, crawling, or crouching on his haunches, so it was such a relief to be able to stand upright and straighten his back. He moved carefully towards Scotty, picking his steps between the rocks and rubble, as men clambered through the opening behind him. In the increasing illumination provided by all their lamps, the extent of the cavern was revealed. The men came forward silently and stood almost in awe at what they surveyed.

'That's hard rock above us,' said Scotty, gazing up above his head, swinging the beam of his lamp to give the rocky contours depth in the shifting shadows. 'Igneous, probably,' he said. 'And this', he added, stooping to finger some of the rocky rubble on which the team now stood. 'This is mainly limestone.' he declared. 'What we're standing on here, is the sedimentary strata that was sandwiched between the coal seam and the harder rock that now forms that roof above us.' He lifted his lamp and gazed upwards again. 'Limestone's very brittle. It was probably fractured by the drilling and blasting at the coal face – then it finally gave way when the coal was taken out. Without the coal seam supporting it, it became too heavy for the timbers, hence the cave-in.'

He pondered for a moment then swept his eyes across the faces of the men gathered around him, his eyes settling on the last man of the group to arrive. 'Henry!' he said, 'Go back and tell the others what we've found. And tell one of them to call up Levi again and ask him to get up to the opening that he mentioned and shine a lamp into it. If it's what I hope it is, we may be able to see his light from this side.' Then, as an afterthought, he called out again to the retreating Henry: 'And get them to make a racket too. Metal on stone if they can! And make it loud.'

The pilot rescue group waited in silence for a while, then turned off their lamps and stood still as their eyes stared blindly into total blackness and their ears strained to pick up the slightest sound. In situations like this, in total darkness and absolute silence, the eyes and ears play tricks. But when the sound came, after several minutes of silent nothingness, with hopes fading as the minutes passed, there was no mistaking the distant clatter of metal tins and helmets on rock. And moments later, a faint loom of light was detected in the darkness straight ahead. At these most welcome signs, sighs and murmurs of relief came from the rescuers' mouths like a celebratory chorus. 'We've cracked it chaps,' said one, triumphantly. 'There's got to be a way through,' exclaimed Scotty.

With their lamps once more switched on and illuminating the rocky path ahead, the small team moved forward, and in less than twenty paces came upon the blockage that Levi Hardy had reported from his side. It was a large, irregular lump of limestone with some smaller rocks and boulders wedged in place around it like a dry-stone wall. There were a few gaps and fissures through which the dim light from Levi's side was visible, but none of these was big enough to get more than an arm through. Scotty moved up and examined the obstruction closely, running his hands over and around the stones, feeling for loose material.

'Levi?' he shouted, bringing his mouth closer to one of the larger gaps. 'Can you hear me?'

The voice of Levi Hardy came back immediately, muffled as if speaking through a pillow. 'We're still here, Scotty! We haven't gone away!' the old miner replied in a sardonic tone. He was probably only a few feet away.

'Just hang on, old fella,' shouted Scotty into the gap. 'We're just figuring out how to open the way through. Better get everyone back now; some of this loose rock'll come tumbling down when we move this big 'un. We'll tell you what we're doing by telephone once we've got things in place.' The team leader turned and addressed the men behind him. 'All right men let's get some props and timbers up here now. The last thing we want is another cave-in when we pull this lot out of the way.' He ran his hand over the boulder. 'And we should be able to get a cable round here, so, we'll need the winch, a sledge, and some long steel pins to use as anchors. Oh, and bring a stretcher up too,' he added, throwing a meaningful glance in Ben's direction – it was his brother, after all, who would be needing it. 'Ben, you, and…' he swung his eyes around the group, settling on a wiry and athletic-looking miner of about the same age. '…and you, Steve,' he said, fixing the young miner by eye. 'Both of you position yourselves at the entrance back there and help to carry the stuff in as it arrives. All you others, look sharp! Enoch, you take charge to make sure we've got everything we need,' he called to one of the older members of the group as the team moved back.

It took half an hour for the timbers and the specified items of equipment to be brought forward in relays to the site of the obstruction. By then Scotty had figured out exactly what he would do, and he directed his men with the kind of confident authority that Ben had only seen before exercised in a military setting. He was impressed. He realised that Scotty was no ordinary miner as he watched the team work so efficiently under his eagle eye. This was a team that had clearly worked together on rescues before – mature, muscular craftsmen of different specialities who knew what to do without much telling. Ben felt privileged to be amongst them and more and more confident that the rescue would succeed. Soon the props and timbers were hammered and wedged into place to stabilise the roof above the blocking boulder. Then the cable-winch apparatus was assembled and anchored with steel rods some fifteen paces back. Its steel hawser with its drop-forged hook was then run forward and secured around the obstructing boulder at its narrower top where purchase could be obtained. With everything set, Scotty now crouched some few feet away and ordered his men into their places like the captain of a cricket team: Ben and Steve were to remain with him near the obstruction ready to assist when the rock was loosened, while two other men of heavy build – weightlifters by appearance – would operate the cable-winch. Everyone else was to retreat outside the cavern entrance except for one man who would remain at the lip of the opening to relay messages if required. There was no sense, Scotty insisted, in having more men inside the cavern than necessary when there was a risk of a further fall.

'Take up the slack!' called Scotty. The two beefy winchmen positioned each side of the winch-housing with their legs braced, clamped their hands around the winch lever – a long steel pole standing about four feet high. At Scotty's call, they began to move the lever forwards and backwards in a slow, rhythmical pumping action, their biceps swelling with each stroke as if pumping iron at the gym. Most of the slack in the cable had already been pulled in by hand before the grippers in the winch mechanism had been engaged, so what little slack was left over disappeared quickly as the cable tightened. Soon it was as rigid as a steel rod: 'Slowly now!' shouted Scotty. The winch was capable of exerting up to ten tons of force, building up in small increments, one increment with each full stroke of the lever. At first, all the men's power went into building up tension in the cable, stroke by stroke. Ten, then fifteen, then twenty full strokes were thrown, yet still no movement of the boulder was observed. By the visible strain on their faces, the men were soon near the limit of their strength, and Scotty had begun to mutter that a more powerful winch might be required. But even as he grumbled, the sound of stone grinding on stone could be heard. 'Nearly there, boys!' he cried out. 'Just a few more strokes should do it.'

Scotty had secured the cable around the upper extent of the obstructing slab of limestone, so it was its top edge that first showed signs of movement. As it inched and ground its way outwards, its movement broke the geometric lock of the smaller rocks that had wedged it in place. These smaller rocks, loosened of their hold, now tumbled down in a miniature avalanche that sent Scotty, Ben, and Steve scrambling backwards. Suddenly freed from its constraint, the massive slab was now able to rotate more freely on its base, and with a final lurch, it fell flat on its front face with a monumental thump, filling the air with clouds of choking dust. For some minutes, the dust was like a thick fog – dirty, grey and impenetrable in the dim light of the miners' lamps; but as it slowly cleared, Scotty moved forward tentatively on his knees, wary of a further fall. He checked that the newly installed timbers and props were doing their job, and satisfied, he peered into the blackness of the opening ahead. As he did so, a distant and disembodied cheer rang out. Ben and Steve moved up behind the rescue leader holding their lamps before them, and in the combined light of all their lamps, a cluster of dirty, grinning faces appeared like ghostly apparitions in the dusty gloom.

Chapter 34

Word of the successful rescue must have been hurriedly transmitted around the village by word of mouth, because Susannah Hardy and the other wives and loved ones of the rescued miners were all waiting at the pithead gate as the first lift reached the top of its very fast ascent. First out, carried on a stretcher by the two burly winchmen and accompanied on either side by Levi and Ben Hardy, was the injured Frank. He was in much pain from his broken femur and cracked ribs but still conscious enough of his whereabouts to be happy that he had survived. Despite his discomfort, he had raised a smile on seeing his older brother come to his rescue in the tunnel nine-hundred feet below, and he was smiling again as his mother smothered him with her embrace – until the pressure of her weight upon his chest caused him momentarily to wince and cry out. Despite the best part of thirty hours trapped by the roof collapse in the Bensham tunnel with only what was left in their tins and flasks to sustain them, all the other rescued miners were able to walk out unsupported – if a little unsteady on their feet. With Frank speedily loaded into the waiting ambulance and whisked away under clanging bells and flashing blue lights, there followed much backslapping man to man, and many happy reunions at the pithead gate. The photograph that would appear in the Northumberland Journal the following morning would show two dozen sets of white teeth grinning broadly from a sea of coal-smudged faces, those of the rescuers and rescued all together, posing for the flash bulbs of the press. Levi Hardy and Scotty were at the centre of the picture and standing alongside his father with an arm around his shoulders, was Ben, who's grin was perhaps the widest of them all. A short article underneath the photograph, written with typical journalistic hyperbole, carried the headline '**WAR HERO SON IN BACKWORTH MINE RESCUE OF FATHER AND BROTHER**', much to Ben's embarrassment.

The following day, with the rescue successfully concluded, Ben felt that his duty was done. His mother had been reunited with his father (subbed with two days earnings from the Miners' Welfare fund to allow him time off to recover), and his brother was safely in the care of Newcastle's Royal Victoria Infirmary. But Ben's loyalties were split. He really should return to Boscombe Down, he thought. The Mosquito T Mk III flight trials for which he was the responsible trials officer, were not yet complete, and being a diligent young man, he was anxious not to be the cause of a delay in progress. A telephone call to his test pilot colleague, the 'A' Squadron flight commander, Clive Rustin (who it will be remembered had delivered him to RAF Woolsington only the day before), cleared his conscience. With the weekend approaching and no flying planned for the aircraft until the following week, nothing would be lost, assured Rustin, if Ben remained in Northumberland for a few days of leave. 'The 'Mossie' will be at Woolsington at ten o'clock on Monday morning,' the test pilot confidently asserted, 'Weather and serviceability permitting, of course. So, be ready to climb in and go,' he added sternly, 'because I shan't be stopping engines!'

No longer fretting about the need for a hurried return to Boscombe Down, and with four clear days of leave ahead, Ben took charge of his mother and father and arranged a taxi to visit the injured Frank in hospital. By all accounts he was already on the mend. The RVI had put Levi and Susannah Hardy's second son in a Nightingale ward amongst a dozen other orthopaedic patients in various states of re-construction and repair. When they entered the ward, Ben and his parents found Frank sitting up in bed with his left leg in a plaster cast hoisted up like a dockside derrick by a complicated arrangement of pulleys and weights. The ward sister informed the visitors that Frank's fractured femur had been satisfactorily reset. 'Although,' she added, in a cautionary tone, 'you must expect a lengthy period of convalescence even after the plaster comes off – and some physiotherapy sessions before we'll be able to release him – probably in three or four weeks. And he's unlikely to be able to do physical work for several months.' His ribs, she added, though undoubtedly going to be painful for a while, had been strapped up and would heal themselves in their own good time. 'But he's still woozy from the anaesthetic and needs to rest,' she said firmly, 'so I'm afraid I can't allow you to stay too long.' The good lady then turned on her heel and left the visitors standing at Frank's bedside. 'You can have ten minutes,' she called over her shoulder as she swept away with a swish of her starched skirt and apron. Frank was so 'woozy' indeed, that only a few words could be exchanged before those few short minutes had been spent.

With time on his hands the day after, therefore, Ben took a bus back to the hospital again in the hope that he would be able to spend a little longer with his brother. He was glad to find Frank's condition continuing to improve. Still immobilised by his elevated plaster cast, the invalid was hardly able to raise himself to greet his brother, but the smile on his face, though weak, was welcoming. He raised an arm as Ben approached and offered up his hand, which Ben took and squeezed in a brotherly fashion before seating himself in the bedside chair.

'It looks like I'm not going to get that beer, doesn't it?' said Ben wryly, glancing at his brother's leg and shaking his head hopelessly. 'Afraid not, big brother, at least not for a while. Anyway, how long are you staying up this time?' Frank asked, hopefully. 'Not long enough to see you back on your feet judging by the look of you.' Ben replied quickly. 'And I probably won't be coming up again for a bit, so you'll have time to save up for it!' This raised an involuntary chortle in Frank's throat, which ended in a furrowed brow and a gasp of pain. 'Ribs still hurting?' asked Ben. Frank nodded as his face relaxed. 'Food edible?' asked Ben. 'Survivable,' said Frank, 'I'll think I'll live despite it!'

Conversation between the two young men struggled on for a while – consisting mainly of clipped platitudes of the sort just related, which is sometimes the way that hospital bedside conversations go – especially between two men whose self-protective manliness inhibits expression of their inner feelings, and especially between two brothers whose relationship had become a little frosty. Their talk, therefore, had become somewhat thin on spontaneity and content, and despite some valiant efforts on both men's parts, topics of mutual interest were quickly exhausted and gazes soon began to wander. 'Oh well, better be on my way,' said Ben eventually, raising himself from his chair with a sigh. 'You've got a bus to catch, I expect?' suggested Frank.

And that was that. Except that as Ben took his brother's hand again in making his farewell, Frank turned earnest: 'Thanks for coming to get me, Ben – down the mine, I mean.' His face took on a solemn look. 'It meant a lot to Da and me to know that you were on the other side of that mountain of rubble and rock. We didn't think we were going to make it out at first, you know. It looked too much to shift. We thought it would take too long and we wouldn't last. But then Scotty and you arrived…and…well, suddenly things didn't look so bleak after all. You're still one of us at heart, aren't you?' He smiled.

Ben made to release his brother's hand, but Frank's grip tightened on his instead of letting go. 'One more thing, Ben, before you go,' he said. 'I know I've been a bit stand-offish and a bit cool towards you, haven't I? Ben shook his head in protest. 'No, let me say it,' Frank insisted. 'I've not been very friendly to you these last few times you've come home and I'm sorry for that. I had some time to think things through while we all sat in that tunnel hoping for rescue, frightened that it might not come. And truth is Ben, I've been a bit jealous of you – jealous of how much you've made of yourself – squadron leader, distinguished flying cross and all that.'

Ben shook his head dismissively, wondering why anyone would envy exposure to the wartime horrors that he himself had endured. He sat himself back down on the chair again as his brother went on.

'I didn't tell you, but I did apply to join the RAF, just like I said I would – as soon as I was old enough. But they wouldn't let me in. They said I had to stay at the mine.

Something about needing coal for the war effort. Understandable I suppose, but I resented it because I had had other ideas for myself. I guess I became jealous of you too, because I never got the chance to do what you did – never got the chance to do my bit...to be a war hero, like you, Ben.' His tone was as admiring as his expression.

Ben shook his head again. 'You were better out of it, Frank,' he said, wearily. 'War's not what it's made out to be in the pictures – it was endlessly grim, desperate, terrifying, and only barely endurable – nothing grand or heroic about putting up with being shit-scared night after night! We just did what we had to ... like you did in the mine. And God has let us both survive, hasn't He? Thousands didn't. We're the lucky ones, and we owe it to those who didn't make it to build a better future for us all. You and I both did our bit, Frank,' he said. 'And you should be proud of your part...just as I am proud of you for sticking it.' Ben gave his brother's hand another squeeze as he got to his feet. 'I'd better be on my way before I wax too lyrical,' he said, with another of his wry smiles. 'Anyway, I've got a bus to catch.'

The two brothers' eyes met briefly as Frank nodded his understanding but said nothing more until his brother reached the doorway where he turned to wave goodbye. 'And I still owe you that beer,' Frank shouted down the whole length of the long ward, turning the heads of other patients in their beds, 'so come back to see us again soon, you hear!'

Chapter 35

The recognition that Ben seemed to have earned within the Backworth mining community, even for the small part he had played in the successful rescue, buoyed his spirits. It was as if he had been readmitted into the clan, acknowledged as 'one of us' again by those he passed in the street – if perhaps only 'one-of-us' in an honorary capacity. He no longer felt their unspoken disdain when amongst them. He was no longer seen as someone who had 'jumped ship' for an easier ride on life's journey. His 'life's journey', if that was the name given to it, had hardly proved such an easy ride as things had turned out, but he had felt their censure all the same. When he left Backworth in 1937, he could not possibly have imagined what frightening times he was letting himself in for by joining the RAF, but his recent return to the coal tunnels had shown him that he had been right to seek a different path. His participation in the rescue, however, had given him a chance to show an empathy with his father's craft, a craft he still admired and respected. Working with old comrades again in the rescue mission had healed a rift. The success of it, moreover, had flushed away that uneasy feeling that, somehow, he had let his father down.

The day following Ben's second visit to the hospital was a Saturday, and Ben took the opportunity to lie in. He reached up from his pillow and pulled his curtains aside to see what the dawn had brought after the lashing his windowpanes had received throughout the night. The blustery cold front that had disturbed his sleep had passed, leaving behind a watery blue sky peppered with isolated cumuli above which wispy cirrus streaked the highest levels of the atmosphere. Ben knew this augured well for the day and resolved to make the best of it, thinking that he'd occupy his time with a walk around his old home territory. Despite his escape from Backworth when he joined the RAF, he still harboured fond memories of the years of his growing up, memories in which April also seemed to play an overly large part.

With none of the usual chores that a weekend in his Wiltshire cottage might have demanded, and nothing planned for the day, he was in no hurry to get up, and so he allowed his gaze to wander. His bedroom was the one that he and Frank had shared until he'd left home, and it had not changed in all the years since. The same old beds and chest of drawers sat on the same old worn linoleum floor, while the repeating pattern of cowboys on horseback still galloped up the same old wallpapered walls. All these things were so familiar that he might never have been away. A quiet knock at his door brought him back to the present, as a cup of tea came into the room, steered with great carefulness by the two thin hands of his mother. She viewed her son with fond eyes as she approached his bed. 'Your Da's already up and gone,' she said, 'but he'll be back by three this afternoon, and he said to remind you not to forget that you are joining him at the club tonight for a celebration.' Ben greeted his mother with a smile and thanked her for the tea as she placed it on the bedside table. 'And I hadn't forgotten about tonight,' he said. 'I'm looking forward to it.' His mother smiled affectionately and made to leave but added softly as she reached the door: 'It's good to have you back, son.' 'It's good to be back, Ma,' replied Ben, as he threw back his sheets, swung his legs out of bed, and rubbed the sleep from his eyes.

An hour or so later, breakfasted and dressed for his walk (having donned his leather flying jacket and flying boots again), he set off, intending to walk the footpath that followed the little burn that wound above the village towards the sea. Once a favourite of his, the path would leave the ugliness of the colliery behind and lead through open countryside towards the dunes and beaches of the North Sea coast. Revisiting old ground often triggers memories of old times, and Ben soon found himself thinking of April as he walked that familiar route. The winding creek was full after the night's downpour and the rapid flow swirled and burbled between grassy, reeded banks and overhanging willow trees. In the distance, a mile or so ahead, the stone clock tower of St Alban's church at Earsdon rose up on a low hill in a landscape that was otherwise fairly flat. It was in the graveyard of that church that the two-hundred-and-four men and boys who lost their lives in the Hartley pit disaster of 1862 were buried. It was in that same graveyard that his grandparents lay at rest, and on a whim, he set his mind to visiting their graves. He and April had visited the graveyard together many times in their young days as her grandparents had finished up there too. He reached the church within an hour having dawdled along the way, and trod the grassy path to his grandparents grave, where he stood remembering the two old folks fondly.

Entering the church a short while later, he seated himself in the nave to enjoy the peace and quiet while allowing his thoughts to wander through boyhood memories. He had not been there long when the cast-iron latch of the church door was lifted with a metallic clunk that echoed around the plain plastered walls. Ben resisted the urge to turn around to see who it was who entered and remained in his pew, letting his mind drift back lazily into reminiscences. At heart, he was a romantic and had come in such quiet moments as these to take some solace from this sort of introspection. Some minutes passed before he heard someone slip into the row of pews behind his. There was a creak of wooden floorboards and a rustle of clothing as the person was seated, and Ben soon became aware of the visitor's breathing. It irritated him to think that, of all the empty pews in the church that could have been chosen, the new arrival had come so close to where he sat as to spoil his peace by their presence. He brooded for some moments more, thinking that it might be time to leave, but then a familiar voice whispered softly not six inches from his ear: 'I thought I'd find you here.'

April's voice was as warm and gently resonant as it had ever been, and Ben could not but be moved by it. He felt his heart swell and his pulse race as he turned in his seat and found himself looking into the face that he had once so loved, more rounded now with the passing years, but still his April. She was wearing a navy-blue overcoat with the collar turned up so that it cradled her trim and wavy hair. Her sparkling blue eyes were brimming, and her lips trembled as if she were trying to hold back a smile, uncertain of the response she might receive from the man she had twice rejected. Ben raised himself from his seat as she did from hers, and he leant across the back of his pew awkwardly to embrace her, not romantically, but like a long-lost friend. 'April!' he exclaimed breathlessly, not quite believing that in his arms he held the woman who had occupied so much of his thoughts for so long. 'Is this coincidence or providence?' he asked incredulously, and released her gently, letting his hands run down her arms as he did so, as if reluctant to let her go. 'Come around!' he urged eagerly, 'Sit with me,' he said, indicating with a sweep of his hand that she should come forward into his row. She was smiling fulsomely as she took the few steps and sat herself so close to him that he could feel the warmth of her body.

'I saw the piece in the newspaper, Ben – about the mine rescue,' she said. 'And there you were on the front page! And grabbing the headline too!' she laughed. 'So, I thought I'd come down and try to find you. It was about time I saw my mum and dad anyway, so that's what I told my husband I was doing.' She gave Ben a sly look. 'I came down by car and called in at your mother's just now to see if you were there. She told me you'd gone off for a walk in this direction and I guessed that this was where you might come – one of our favourite places wasn't it?'

Sitting so close together that their knees touched, Ben was so full of joy to be with his old love again that he took her hands in his without thinking about the appropriateness of the gesture; but she didn't resist. She was wearing woollen gloves, the sort she'd worn at school – knitted by her mother then but now probably on a machine. The feel of them was nevertheless so familiar and so evocative of old times that he let his fingers caress them. Some moments passed like this with no words spoken, while both gazed intently into each other's eyes with such tender fondness – until Ben realised that he had stopped breathing. He drew in a sudden breath, shook off his reverie and burst into laughter as he pulled his hands from hers. 'What on earth have you done to me!' he exclaimed, reproving himself, though with little conviction.

'We're still fiends, then?' asked April, with a sparkle in her eyes.

'Forever yours, April,' he smiled. 'You know that don't you?' At which she nodded seriously. 'And you, April?' Ben then asked, his face and voice becoming earnest. 'Are you happy?'

'...Yes, Ben,' April answered, after the slightest hesitation that would not have been noticed by less sensitive ears. It was enough of a hesitation to make Ben wonder if she really was happy, but he checked himself from pressing the matter further. 'I've got two lovely children and a nice home in Alnwick,' she said quickly, as if wanting to ward off more probing of the subject. 'Robert's the bank manager there now, you know. We've settled in very well. It's a pleasant little town.'

Ben thought to himself that hers was probably a more settled existence than he could have offered her, but he said instead: 'I'm very happy for you, April.' And he took her hand again and held it gently. She didn't withdraw it.

The two old sweethearts sat together in the quiet of the nave for a good long hour not minding about nor even noticing the hardness of the pew. They spoke so openly and comfortably with each other that they might have grown up together (which, of course, they almost had) and never been apart. She told Ben the story of her life since their last meeting; and he told her of his. They each spoke about their moments of happiness, their sorrows, and regrets. She told him of her move to Alnwick, and about her lovely son and daughter, now eight and six years old.

He told her about Daisy and her tragic death, his rural home in Wiltshire, and his work at Boscombe Down. But of their feelings for each other, nothing at all was said or even hinted at. It seemed that these were still so tender that neither he nor she dared to open up their hearts for fear of what might be revealed. Both now knew that time had moved on and could not be rewound. Yet in her face and words and touch, Ben knew with certainty that she loved him still. Perhaps he was loved now only as a good old friend, but it was love, nevertheless – old love, lost love, but a love that was fondly remembered. Meanwhile the sun moved in its orbit, throwing its shifting beams through the six tall, stained-glass windows of the south-facing wall of St Alban's church, creating a sort of kaleidoscope of colour on everything within. The image of April's face lit up in those warm hues would stay with Ben forever.

They left the church arm in arm and slowly walked the gravel path towards April's little Austin, which she had parked in the lay-by outside the church gate. 'Can I give you a lift back?' she asked lightly, as Ben opened the car door for her to get in. He shook his head. 'No, thank you. I'll walk. I'll go back along our old path for old time's sake. It'll remind me of our good times together,' he said, smiling lamely. She nodded, her expression suddenly grave, a mask of self-control, her eyes fixed on his so rigidly that it seemed too great an effort for her to tear them away. If her thoughts could have been conveyed by such looks, who knows what might have followed, but restraint and propriety held her back just as much as his urge to take her in his arms was held back too. Moments passed with neither knowing what more to say, until the connection that they had both so much enjoyed that day was broken by a hapless look that passed between them. Their farewell embrace was quick and cursory, merely a light touch of cheek on cheek, as if to avoid prolonging the agony of their parting. She climbed into her car and pulled the door closed, started the engine, and drove off without looking back. Ben thought that he would never see her again and inwardly he wept for the love that he had lost.

Chapter 36

We must now move the timeline of Benjamin Hardy's life forward the best part of forty years to 1985, the year in which, approaching the age of sixty-five, he is shortly due to retire. Of his life during that long intervening time, we already know the general shape of his career and there is little more of relevance to be added to his story in that period. Professionally, he enjoyed success as a flight test engineer and eventually a division leader at Boscombe Down, and while he achieved nothing spectacular as far as rank or distinctions were concerned, he was highly regarded by the flight test aircrew he worked with and by his colleagues as someone who would get any job done without fuss, mishap or drama.

He never married, though in his thirties and forties, no doubt feeling the loneliness of bachelorhood in his isolated cottage, he had two relatively substantial relationships. His first lasted more than seven years (on and off); his second, rather less than four (also on and off). These two female companions of his were pleasant enough company: the first, a scientist working in the computer and instrumentation section at Boscombe Down, the widow of an air force bomber pilot killed during the war; the second, a divorcee he met in the local community choir, which he had joined in order to get out more. She was an alto and he a tenor, neither particularly accomplished singers but useful makeweights in a choir struggling to keep numbers up. Both ladies had probably been as lonely as Ben when their eyes first met and when a mutual recognition of need and compatibility flashed between them. Though bringing the comfort of companionship during the years of those associations, neither of these relationships came to anything of a permanent nature. He certainly enjoyed their company and the interests and the outings he had had with them, but he never felt passion in his heart. Perhaps unreasonably, he expected his heart to be moved and his eyes to be entranced when looking upon a potential lifetime partner, the feelings he had once felt when looking upon his first and only *true* love, April. He liked women and enjoyed their company, but when looking for a prospective lifetime partner, anything less than rapture led eventually to disappointment and disaffection – which is the way that both these two friendships ended. Perhaps he expected too much? Even a later dalliance with a dark-haired, black-eyed, beauty from the typing pool who threw everything she had at him, suffered the same fate in less than three months! By then, he had become a difficult man to please.

As Ben passed into his fifties, he became so set in his unencumbered and unregulated bachelor ways and habits that his inclination to seek new relationships with women began to falter – just as his resistance to the few advances made towards him stiffened. Then a frightening diagnosis of advanced prostate cancer and the subsequent radical surgery robbed him of both his potency and his sexual drive. Although he still loved the company of women, he resigned himself thereafter to singledom and made the best of what he had – which was still quite a lot really, taking everything else into account. To all who knew him he looked like a self-contained and happy man, though wives of married friends and colleagues could not resist attempts to pair him up with single ladies in their social circle. Even his old friend, Woody Green, who, had finally got round to marrying his Dorothy by then, had tried a few times unsuccessfully to play Cupid – before giving up and leaving Ben to his own devices.

With a handsome head of silvering hair and an athletic figure maintained by his walking and his cycling adventures, Benjamin Hardy would have made quite a catch. He thus found himself frequently sitting at friends' tables being very well fed. Though it was all to no avail, since a match seemed impossible to find. By then he had got used to his freedom to do what he liked and to go where he liked, with a salary and an anticipated index-linked pension with which he could indulge every whim. He would now not easily give up this free-wheeling independence, a state that was the envy of many married men of his acquaintance.

Yet hidden behind the outgoing and engaging persona that he liked to project, there was still an unfilled vacancy in his heart that yearned to be filled by a more permanent female companion – and not just any female companion either. He had tried to nurture two relationships as we have heard and had had his fingers burned with a third, and yet had not found what he sought (though it is doubtful that he knew what he was really seeking anyway). As age inched on inexorably into his sixties, this need of his began to prey more and more on his mind. It was as retirement became imminent, however, that his longing for companionship became more insistent. Work and colleagues had been his family of a sort until now, but life in retirement needed someone with whom to share the time, for it could become empty otherwise, not to say frighteningly lonely – a state that he began to recognise as his likely fate.

Whenever Ben's mind was not otherwise actively engaged, perhaps while out walking in the countryside or pottering in his garden, he might find himself daydreaming, conjuring an image of a loving presence at his side, someone who cared for him, someone he would enjoy pleasing and who liked to please him. His sexual impotence had not deprived him of the human need for a loving touch, nor of the warmth and comfort of loving arms around him. He yearned for these intimacies. This presence that he conjured was at first merely a memory of those sensations – feelings of warmth but without form or features. The flapping of shirts and sheets on the line might trigger memories of summer skirts and blouses; the rustle of leaves in the wind might remind him of soft whispering in his ear. Returning home from work to his dark cottage in the depths of winter along his long and unlit track, he yearned to find a warm kitchen waiting, imbued with smells of home cooking and with a welcome waiting at the door.

In such a way did his heart begin to pine for company, and in lonely times like these especially, that imagined presence would be felt again. Over time, it gradually took on more substance, until at last he recognised it as the lingering memory of his first love, April – the April of his younger days. It slowly dawned on him that she had probably been with him in spirit all along, never far from his conscious mind, watching over him like a kindly angel as he made his way through life. He recalled their last meeting in St Alban's church so many years before, remembering her lovely face, bathed as it then was in the rosy hues of sunlight streaming through the stained-glass windows. Her eyes had glistened with affection as they had sat together on that hard church pew, hand in hand; and he had wanted her so much that it had hurt. But both knew by then that it was too late for them, that any chance that they might have had to find happiness together had been lost. All that, of course, was now a long time ago, but Ben could not help thinking that if she had tender feelings for him then, she might well have them still. And suddenly he had an overwhelming desire to find out.

What held him back now from doing so, however, and what had held him back before (for this was not the first time he had thought of it), was the fear that his reappearance in April's life might cause upset in one way or another. Any feelings she might have for an old beau, if indeed she still had them, might be rekindled and her marriage of so many years as hers must now be, thus knocked askew. He could not be so irresponsible or so self-indulgent. A predatory male might know how to disturb a married woman's equilibrium with flattering advances that would re-awaken dormant passions and distract even the most steadfast of hearts. That way, he knew, could lead to untold turmoil and misery. But Ben saw himself as a decent and honourable man and he would not want to disturb April's life (or heart).

But what if she were free again, he wondered? What if she had held back from trying to re-connect with him with the very same concerns, thinking that he might now be happily married himself? With such contrary thoughts in his mind, he came to believe that he owed it to himself to find out the truth of the matter one way or the other – or live forever after regretting not doing so.

But how best and most discreetly to do it, he wondered

If Ben's life had changed in all the time that had passed since his last meeting with April, however, his home village, the colliery, and indeed the entire coal mining industry had changed a lot more. The Clean Air Acts of the late fifties and sixties had denigrated the use of coal as a source of energy. Middle Eastern oil, nuclear, and North Sea gas were cleaner sources, and coal's hitherto near monopoly soon disappeared. Even as we resume Ben's story in 1985, the last great battle between the government and the miners' unions was in full throw, with strikes and three-day-weeks bringing the country almost to a standstill. Many coal mines had already closed across the country, and many more would follow Mrs Thatcher's coming victory over Mr Scargill and his unions. The Eccles pit, the last of the working pits at Backworth, and the scene of Ben's celebrated participation in the rescue of his father, his brother, and six other trapped miners, had closed in 1980. The railway tracks and sidings had been ripped up, the chimneys felled, the buildings bulldozed, the rubble used as hardcore for a new bypass. The view of the abandoned colliery site from Ben's old bedroom window had the barren look of a post-industrial wasteland, but not for much longer. With the wreckers ball already swinging, the streets of his childhood would soon be knocked flat, and new development and nature would reclaim the land.

Ben's family and his old community had changed too. Levi Hardy, having retired in 1957, had not had to suffer the later pit closures and redundancies that would force many of his younger compatriots to move to other coalfields in search of work. Sadly, he had died in 1974 after several years of debilitating discomfort, finally giving up his fight against the fifty years of accumulated coal dust that clogged his lungs. Ben's mother, Susannah, had pre-deceased her husband by ten years, succumbing to an incurable genetic disorder that had slowly wasted her away. And Ben's brother, Frank, falling victim to the second round of redundancies at Backworth, had moved to a Nottinghamshire pit as an overman. His childless first marriage had not survived the upheaval of strikes, redundancy, and his forced migration south, but by marrying again and fathering two boys, the Hardy family name would live on.

Over the years, Ben had returned home now and then, though not recently and never more than for a few days at a time, his visits separated often by a year or more. He had therefore watched the changing faces of Backworth and its population in a series of short glimpses like the individual frames from a stop-frame camera. His view of the place and its people had, therefore, changed incrementally in discrete and noticeable steps, diminishing and dying frame by frame. On his last visit, when he came up to give the eulogy at his father's funeral, he found the few faces in the congregation unfamiliar and his old village practically unrecognisable from what it had been in his youth. If Ben returned there now on his new quest to find April, he would be returning practically as a stranger.

Chapter 37

Taking some leave, Ben Hardy's journey north was the inaugural outing of his newly acquired VW Campervan, an ex-demonstrator model from the Volkswagen distributor on the Churchfields trading estate in Salisbury. He'd bought it as a retirement gift to himself, in the expectation of exploring new territory and pursuing adventure – principally back-packing and cycling expeditions. He dreamt of simply taking off in his camper and going where the wind took him, bicycle on the back, seeking out-of-the-way places to walk and ride, independent of the hassle of finding accommodation, which he anyway disliked paying for. He broke his journey northwards with a night stop at a small camping site in the Vale of Pickering before continuing to Northumberland the following day.

Driving those three-hundred-and-fifty miles from Wiltshire to Northumberland gave Ben plenty of time to think about how he might begin his search. He soon realised that it would not be an easy task to find the woman he now sought, especially if he wanted to avoid setting the cat amongst the pigeons with his enquiries. His first difficulty was that he didn't know April's married surname. If he had ever been told it, which he doubted, he had forgotten it. Thus, simply leafing through telephone directories was not an option. In Ben's last encounter with April, he'd learned that she and her husband, Robert, had moved to Alnwick with the National Provincial Bank, but that was all he knew – no address had been given or asked for. Neither could he assume that the couple still lived in the town. After so many years, they might be living anywhere.

Some of his wilder ideas included knocking on likely Alnwick doors posing as a surveyor of political opinion or hanging about on the streets (disguised by floppy hat and upturned collar?) on the off chance of an encounter with the woman he sought. But he'd discarded these as very likely to get him marched in front of the magistrates and locked up. After a lot of dead-end thinking which produced no more sensible inspiration, Ben decided that a visit to Mr P's garage in Backworth might represent the best start. If the Palmers were still living in their old house or could be found at some new address and called upon, Ben knew he could trust their discretion. It was more than likely, however, that by now the couple would have sold up their business and moved on (or passed on?) – after all, they would now be well into their eighties.

Ben drove his van onto the Springfield Road garage forecourt and switched off his engine, remaining in his seat as his eyes surveyed the sad state of the place that had once played such an important part in his young life. The whole site was deserted. Weeds poked up through cracks in the crumbling concrete hardstanding and the old workshop and family home were boarded up. On the forecourt, the pump attendant's kiosk and the petrol pumps had been removed, the only evidence of their existence being the rusting iron stubs protruding from the stand on which they had once stood. Mr P had evidently quit his business and moved out, and it appeared that no one had thought it worth their while to take it over as a going concern. The place looked as run down and as uncared for as Backworth had appeared when Ben had driven through it on his way there.

It had been a depressing sight to see his old school and some of the old houses and shops abandoned, some already despoiled by graffiti on the walls. Walkworth Street and the adjacent rows of miners' terraces where Ben had done his growing up were in the process of being demolished to make way for new development. JCBs, dumper trucks, and workmen in donkey jackets roamed about the rubble in hard hats. A giant billboard announced the site's new future with an artist's illustration of a 'new vibrant community of two and three-bedroomed family homes' nestled in a sun-bathed rural landscape with pretty gardens and mature trees. He'd driven along some of the old Backworth streets where familiar buildings still stood, where old men hung about in ones and twos on corners looking bored, hands in pockets and smoking. Ben didn't recognise any of them and they eyed him suspiciously as he drove slowly by. He'd thought of winding down his window and announcing himself as an old local boy, to ask questions that might help him in his quest, but he thought better of it. They hadn't looked very friendly. The pit's closure had consigned his old community to sepia-coloured photographs in a local history book. Sadly, only total regeneration could save it now.

As far as his search for April was concerned, he now realised that he would have to think again. If Backworth would not offer any leads, perhaps he would have to knock on doors or stalk the streets of Alnwick after all? It was now early afternoon and a grey sky threatened rain.

Ben had stocked his fridge up well and so needed nothing by way of supplies for another night in his camper. With nothing now to keep him in Backworth, he resolved to drive on into the countryside and find a suitable field or site in which to park. As he started up his engine, however, he found himself looking squarely at St Alban's church in Earsdon, its tall clock tower standing prominently on rising ground about a mile directly ahead. Ben glanced at his watch – half past two – plenty of light left yet to find a suitable camping site and time enough to visit his parents' grave, he thought. The couple lay together in the gently sloping ground below the church, and since there were no longer any Hardys nearby to take care of their grave, it might need a bit of tidying up.

He parked his camper in the layby opposite the churchyard's gate, climbed out, walked past the church, and followed a descending earthen pathway that led to an extension of the graveyard where more recent occupants now lay at rest. It was a jungle of long grasses, cow parsley, stinging nettles and encroaching brambles. The area had clearly been untended for some time, and so Ben was taken by surprise to find his parents grave so relatively unmolested. Not only had the encroaching undergrowth been roughly swiped back, but someone had laid a small posy of wildflowers in front of the headstone. Puzzled, Ben squatted down on his haunches to examine the posy more closely. The flowers were in an advanced state of decay, but they could not have been much more than a few weeks old. Perhaps some good soul from the community had visited the grave recently, he wondered – perhaps a friend of Susannah's or one of Levi's former workmates? He rose and stood for a moment and ran his eyes along the inscriptions on the headstone. The mere act of reading his parents' names sparked such poignant memories. In his current frame of mind, feeling their loss more acutely standing so close to their remains, he suddenly felt very alone.

He must have stood there for several minutes in that mournful reverie until a few light spots of rain landing upon his forehead brought him back to the present. Casting an eye up to the threatening clouds, he started back along a different earthen path that promised a more direct route back, idly glancing at other graves along his way for names that he might recognise. He'd only gone a few yards, however, when something on one of the headstones must have caught his eye. It took a moment or two for his brain to process what his eyes had registered and in the meantime his legs continued to propel him. When his brain caught up, however, it brought him to an abrupt stop. Hoping that he'd been mistaken, he went back to look again, and his heart sank when he saw that his eyes had not been deceived. The names on the headstone were those of April's parents.

Ben read the inscriptions reluctantly, as if by not doing so (as for Schroeder's cat?) he might avoid sealing their fate. *'John (Jack) Palmer, beloved husband of Marcia, father of Susan and April',* and then, directly underneath those lines: *'Marcia, his beloved wife. Both greatly loved and sadly missed'.* Ben read that Jack had died five years previously and that Marcia had followed him into eternity only a year later. If he'd known of their passing, he would have attended their funerals and was intensely saddened not to have been there to pay his respects. His and now April's parents all dead! All lost and unreachable now, yet all still so vivid and alive in his memory that he could feel their presence. His heart wept to think that he would never again see these four good people who between them had shaped his young life. All four of them lying within yards of where he stood, yet all silent now when he needed them more than ever.

Despite the rainfall, he would not allow himself to scurry away for shelter. Instead, he stood determinedly in reverence for a good long while remembering those dear souls and accusing himself of neglect – thinking of things he should have said and of the visits he should have made – when instead he'd put his own preoccupations first. He'd lost the opportunity forever now and he hung his head in self-recrimination. As he stood there quietly meditating, the sky darkened and a cool wind came up from the East, and his heart told him that his quest to find April was suddenly more important now. She was his only link with his fondly remembered past.

Chapter 38

St Alban's Church, Earsdon

Ben arrived back at his campervan, just as the heavens opened, unleashing a downpour that hammered the vehicle's roof and lashed its windscreen as if he alone were the target of its frenzied assault. Only when he began to gather his thoughts after a headlong race for cover did he begin to reflect upon the state of the Palmers' grave. Surrounded by so many other graves beset by rampant undergrowth and creeping brambles, he thought it curious that the Palmers' grave, like his own parents' grave, stood out as being recently attended. The little posies of wildflowers on both had been so similar too, he now remembered, that they might have been arranged by the same hand. It was more than a coincidence, Ben thought.

The heavy downpour then stopped as abruptly as it had started, leaving only light drizzle in its wake as the sky took on a lighter shade of grey. Curious to look again at the graves, Ben decided to return to the graveyard, but as he stepped down from his vehicle, he noticed a cassocked individual scurrying through the church gate. Thinking that something useful might be learned from the man, Ben set off in pursuit, catching up with him in the church porch, where he was immediately recognised as the St Alban's vicar. Ben held out his hand. 'You probably don't recognise me, vicar; I'm Ben Hardy, Levi Hardy's son. You led the service at my father's funeral about ten years ago.' The cleric took Ben's hand and greeted his visitor but looked puzzled at the same time.

'Ah, yes of course,' he said eventually. 'It's been a long time.' The cleric was a tall, balding man of about fifty years old, with soft eyes and a kind, unassuming face. He smiled inquiringly, but his hesitant manner suggested that he really hadn't remembered Ben at all. Ten years was a long time and Ben's visit on that occasion, as usual, had been fleeting.

'I live in the south now, near Salisbury,' he went on, 'and haven't been back for a while, I'm afraid.'

The vicar nodded sagely but the little wrinkle between his eyebrows persisted.

'I've only come up this time to track down an old friend,' Ben went on, 'April – one of Jack and Marcia Palmer's daughters. I think you might have officiated at her parents' funerals too. I've just been down to their graves.'

At Ben's mention of the Palmer family, the reverend's face brightened. 'Ah yes, I did indeed. I knew them well. Nice people. Not regular attenders here but they came now and then – high days and holidays, you know.' The vicar smiled indulgently, 'Jack used to service my car, so I got to know him and Marcia quite well. He had a hard time of it when people started to move away after the colliery closed. He struggled on for a bit but eventually had to sell up, poor chap. He died not long afterwards. Probably the stress of it all. And Marcia didn't last much longer, sadly. I buried them both. Nice funerals. Good turnouts. They were both very well liked around here.'

'You met their daughters then, I suppose?' asked Ben, bringing the conversation back to the point of his enquiry.

'Yes, I did. Susan and April were at both funerals, of course. Very pleasant ladies. They read the lessons – and spoke very well too.'

'They'll probably have grandchildren by now. It's so long since I've seen them,' said Ben, fishing.

'Yes. Quite a crowd as I remember!'

'I expect you met their husbands too.' Ben made this sound like a statement, but it was just another fishing expedition.

The vicar frowned. 'Can't say that I did actually,' he said, after a moment's thought. 'At least, I can't remember them. The front row was taken up by Susan, April, their grown-up children and all their grandchildren. I remember that clearly because the youngsters were not particularly well behaved – one of the boys threw a tantrum and had to be taken out halfway through. There certainly wasn't enough room at the front for the spouses as well, so they'd probably have been sitting in the row behind. I went to the wake at the pub across the road after the service but didn't get to meet everyone. Anyway, these days it's better not to ask who's married to whom,' he added, raising an eyebrow.

'I know what you mean,' said Ben. 'Would you remember April's married name by any chance?' asked Ben. 'It'll be difficult for me to track her down without it.'

'Hmmm. You're asking a lot. I see so many people in my job, and there've been a lot of funerals since then...' he said, his voice reducing to a mutter as he rubbed his chin. 'But we do keep copies of the orders of service,' he added, brightening. 'Come on inside, and we'll see if we can find them – we'll probably get her name from one of those. The funerals weren't that long ago, so they shouldn't be too difficult to find.'

The vicar led Ben into his cluttered office, and after rummaging through his files, he pulled out a funeral booklet with a flourish and flipped quickly through its pages. 'Oh, here she is! Her reading in Jack's,' he said, 'April *Smith*!' he exclaimed, triumphantly. 'She read 'Crossing the Bar' by Alfred, Lord Tennyson.' He offered the booklet up for inspection. Ben took it and studied the page. 'Of all the men she might have married,' Ben said, despairingly shaking his head, 'why on earth did she have to choose someone with such a common name!' The vicar laughed. 'It won't make your job easy, will it?' he ventured.

Thanking the man for his help, Ben politely took his leave and retreated to his campervan. The light rain had continued, and it pattered gently on his roof as he sat mulling things over for a while. He had now got what he'd sought – April's married name – but the identity of the mysterious grave carer still puzzled him. His engineer's training had taught him not to jump to conclusions, but there was only one person he could think of who might have cared enough to leave a posy on *both* the Hardy *and* the Palmer graves – April. In coming to this conclusion, Ben was assigning to April the same kind thoughts for his parents as he had for hers. Coincidence could still not be entirely discounted, nor the attention of some other person who might have known both couples well enough to care. But the idea that it was April was compelling. And if she were the bringer of posies, it suggested that she still harboured affection for the Hardy name – and therefore for him too, which is what Ben chose to believe.

Any discerning study of Ben's past behaviour might suggest that he would now act on instinct. He would have to do something to move his search on – anything, rather than just sit and wait on the off-chance that April might pay another visit to her parents' grave. Besides, with her married name, there was a good chance that he would find her address in the pages of the Alnwick telephone directory – although what he would do with it if he found it, was not yet clear in his mind.

After a night stop in a free overnight car park in the dunes just south of Walkworth, Ben caught a morning bus to Alnwick. The buses ran every hour in both directions, and Ben thought it a less troublesome means of transport than driving into Alnwick where parking restrictions might apply. He remembered Alnwick as a pleasant market town with broad streets and attractive stone buildings. The old town centre lay largely in the lee of an imposing Norman castle occupied by the Duke of Northumberland whose ancestors went back to the Conquest. Ben's last visit there had been with April some four decades before on a day's outing from Backworth when he had had it in his mind to propose marriage if the circumstances proved right. As might be remembered from an earlier chapter, the circumstances never had been quite right for Ben to make his proposal and thus it was never made, which led to him heading down to Southampton instead.

Arriving at Alnwick's bus station and walking through the town brought back the memory of that unfruitful outing, and in a nostalgic frame of mind, he made for the same public house in Fenkle Street where he and April had had lunch on that fateful day. It was an eighteenth-century tavern with old oak furniture, bare-wood floors, and wooden beams. A coal fire was already well aflame even so early in the day. Entering the establishment, he found himself to be the only customer. A young man stood behind the bar busying himself with something unseen, which evidently required so much of the young man's concentration that he hadn't noticed Ben come in. Ben announced his presence with a polite cough and asked for a black coffee and the loan of a telephone directory. The coffee looked so murky in its jug and smelt so bitter when it was poured that Ben thought it must have been sitting on its hotplate since the night before. He was about to make a comment to that effect but withheld it when the directory was produced, not wanting to sound ungrateful.

'That's the only one we've got,' the young man said, sullenly. 'Morpeth to Berwick-on-Tweed.'

Ben gave the young man a tight smile. Covering such a vast area, the directory was a good two inches thick, and Ben carried it and the unappetising brew to a nearby table, where he pushed the cup aside after only one sip. To his consternation (but not surprise considering the common name), the directory contained twenty-three residential subscribers under the name of Smith, with R for Robert as a first or second initial. Even when whittled down to those with an Alnwick address or those in the villages nearby, the number still amounted to eight. Ben felt somewhat overwhelmed. Even if he called all the numbers on the list on some invented pretext that wouldn't raise the suspicions of any Robert Smiths who answered, he may still not find April, for it was quite possible that Robert Smith, the bank manager, would have gone ex-directory! It was also possible that Robert Smith the bank manager commuted from further afield, if indeed he was still working at the Alnwick branch at all! Ben sat back in his seat and wrinkled his brow: 'Anyway, what the hell am I thinking!' he thought, suddenly cross with himself. 'If April *is* still married to Robert Smith, I should beat a hasty retreat southward and give up the whole idea!' Only now was Ben beginning to realise that this simple (if hairbrained) scheme of his would never have worked.

Feeling frustrated, Ben headed for the town's central square in search of a decent cup of coffee to flush away the bitter taste still lining his mouth. He saw at once that it was market day in Alnwick, for laid out across a wide expanse of cobbles were so many covered stalls that he could hardly see from one side of the square to the other. Attracted by the bright sunshine lighting up the far corner, he made his way through the milling crowd. With the sun soon warming his back, Ben found himself a seat at the last empty table outside a patisserie that appeared to be a popular congregating point for mid-morning refreshment. He had not been seated there long when two ladies of similar age to himself politely asked if they could join him as all the other tables were fully occupied. Ben, of course, gracefully acquiesced, and soon found himself amicably engaging with his new acquaintances (as Ben would, of course). A waitress soon arrived, took orders, and disappeared, returning some minutes later with three cups of coffee and the three Danish pastries on which the threesome had conspired to indulge themselves. It was as they chatted amiably that it occurred to Ben that these two friendly ladies might provide a short-cut to solving his conundrum. His idea, moreover, would still ensure the discretion that he still hoped to maintain.

'Do either of you two ladies know a Robert Smith by any chance? Ben asked lightly. 'He was the manager of the National Provincial Bank here in Alnwick when I last heard of him.'

'Why yes, of course; we all know Robert,' replied the two ladies almost in unison as they exchanged glances with knowing twinkles in their eyes. 'He still *is* the manager there!' exclaimed one.

In observing the ladies' reaction, Ben suspected some secret confidence was being enjoyed between them. 'We were at school together in the thirties,' he went on, lying through his teeth. 'I'm trying to organise a fiftieth anniversary get-together for all those in our school year who still live in the area. I'd heard that he and his wife…er, April, I think her name was… had moved up here…er… in the middle forties, I think, and I'm trying to track them both down.'

The two ladies glanced at each other again with the same knowing glint in their eyes. 'Well, you'll find *him* at the bank today,' one said, 'being a market day, of course. But April's long gone. He's on his third wife now,' she said, her eyebrows rising at least half an inch into her forehead. 'He's been quite a busy boy with the ladies, has our Robert!' The two ladies laughed.

Ben joined in the laughter as much to share the humour as in relief that April was an 'ex-wife!' But then he checked himself, realising that she too may have re-married, which immediately sobered him up.

'I'll call by the bank later,' said Ben, lying again. 'He may not remember me after all these years, but it'll be good to make contact with him again. You wouldn't have any idea where I'd find his ex-wife, would you?'

The two women glanced at each other, then laughed out loud. 'Which one!' they shot back in almost perfect unison.

Chapter 39

Coffee in the Alnwick Market Square

From that fortuitous encounter with the two ladies in the Alnwick market square, Ben had discovered where April now lived, at least he had discovered in which village she now lived, assuming, of course, that their information had not been out of date. It appeared that April now lived in Craster, a small, former fishing village on the North Sea coast some ten miles to the northeast of Alnwick. Those two gregarious souls had saved Ben an awful lot of trouble and very likely they had saved him a lot of embarrassment too, for that could well have been the outcome had he tried to call all the numbers on his list.

He arrived in Craster the following morning having spent the night in the staff caravan park at nearby RAF Boulmer, gaining entry there with his MoD identity card. He'd left the base early, impatient, excited, and hopeful of a happy reunion, yet feeling just a little bit apprehensive about what he might find. Like him, April would be nearly sixty-five now, and time would have changed her as much as it had changed him, and he wondered if there would still be any empathy left between them after so long. His heart was in his mouth as he drove what he hoped would be the final leg of his long journey.

The old part of Craster is formed around a small bay semi-enclosed by two massive harbour walls once used as piers for shipping out the local stone. The old quarry, lying just outside the village, was now the visitors' car park, and this is where Ben parked his campervan. Putting on his anorak, he continued on foot the last quarter mile along a footpath that led to the harbour. When he arrived, he was taken aback by the sheer beauty of the scene that appeared before him. It was his first sight of the sea for a long time – a breathtaking seascape with colours set aflame in the early morning sunshine. A shimmering sea stretched to the distant horizon under a clear blue sky. A flock of oystercatchers caught his eye, their pure white breasts glinting in perfect harmony as they swooped and turned before settling to feed on the wet sand of the foreshore. Inside the harbour's protective walls, a few small crabbing boats and sailing craft sat askew on the mud as the last of the tide ebbed away. To Ben's left, far off on a craggy headland, he could see the ruins of Dunstanburgh Castle, its crumbling towers standing like sentinels on guard. To his right, stood a smokehouse, identified in painted letters on its high stone walls as 'Craster Kippers, built 1856'. Smoke rose lazily from its chimney and hung about the bay in the still air. The smell of curing haddock reached his nostrils and reminded him that he'd not yet had his breakfast.

Ben seated himself on a bench to enjoy the view for a while, feeling the warmth of the sun upon his face, certain now that April must be somewhere near. Behind him, a row of a terraced cottages shared his view. It crossed his mind that she might even be living in one of them. But would he recognise her, he wondered, if she were to emerge from one of those front doors? And would she recognise him? Perhaps too many years had passed? Even if she *were* free, perhaps she'd be so changed that they would no longer find each other amenable as companions? He began to question himself for sitting there so brazenly.

Feeling at a bit of a loss for what to do next, Ben's first thought was to start his search again with a telephone directory. This time, he would have a much easier task for he would be looking for a Miss April Palmer, the name to which he guessed (or hoped) she would have reverted having divorced the infamous Mr Smith. Ben passed the smokery and the Jolly Fisherman public house on his walk about the village before he spotted a telephone kiosk in the lane ahead. Entering it, he pulled out the directory, and leafed through its pages until his eyes were drawn to a Miss A.M. Palmer in the list of names as if it possessed some magnetic property. Just seeing it on the page was enough to make his heart race. There was no doubt now that this must be his April. He knew her initials so well. April Marcia Palmer, her middle name being her mother's Christian name. He'd etched A.M.P indelibly into the leather flap of his school satchel all those years ago when they had sat in adjacent desks in the senior classroom of the Backworth school. Coincidences like this did not happen. And when he read the address that lay alongside her name, he was amazed when he realised that she lived in one of the terraced cottages behind the very bench on which he'd sat!

With the prospect of an imminent reunion now almost certain, however, his mind went into a spin of indecision. Should he pick up the telephone and dial her number, or should he go straight to her door? Suddenly afraid that the outcome of his quest would, for one reason or another, be disappointment, he began to doubt the wisdom of his whole enterprise. He even began to question if a reunion was what he really wanted. All sorts of worries arose in his mind, and for a while he stood in the kiosk dithering. But then his old impetuosity took hold as a heady mixture of excitement and curiosity coursed through his veins and pressed him to act. He let himself be taken by it; he'd come too far to turn back now.

He made to leave the kiosk at once to set out for her door, but then stopped himself. Surely, it would be more polite to telephone first rather than simply turn up unannounced. It would also serve to sound out whether a meeting was wise or even appropriate, for he could not yet know her circumstances. Rummaging in his pocket, he brought out some ten-penny pieces and laid them on the shelf, fed a couple into the payment slot, and dialled her number. His breath shortened as the ringing tone sounded in his ear.

'Hello?' a female voice answered, questioningly.

'Is that April? April Palmer? Who used to live in Backworth and Alnwick?'

'Yes,' came the hesitant reply. 'Who's calling?'

'It's Ben, April. Ben Hardy.'

Ben heard an intake of breath but nothing more.

'April, it's me – Ben,' he repeated after several moments of silence.

'Ben! How extraordinary!' came the slightly breathless reply. 'I can hardly believe it. I thought of you this morning!

I was looking out of my front window at the harbour and for some strange reason you popped into my head.'

Ben smiled inwardly. She had probably seen his lonely figure sitting on the bench without realising who it was. She wouldn't have recognised him with his back to her, but maybe something about him had triggered her memory.

'Are you free to talk, April?' Ben did not want to assume that she would be alone.

'Yes, Ben. All by myself now, sadly,' she said. 'Goodness; it's so good to hear your voice again!' There was real warmth in her voice. 'It's been …oh gosh, nearly forty years, hasn't it? Since we met in St Alban's church after the pit rescue in '48 – when you flew up in that Mosquito of yours? And got your picture in the newspaper as a local hero!'

'Hmmm! Yes,' he said flatly. '…a bit embarrassed about that, I was! But it brought you to me, didn't it? Yes, it *is* the best part of forty years since that meeting in St Alban's, April!' He shook his head disbelievingly. 'Actually, I visited the church not long ago – to visit my folks' grave,' he said, not ready yet to say how recently it was or to reveal his present whereabouts. 'And did you know that your parents and mine are lying within yards of each other?'

'Yes, I know, Ben. I go down there to visit mine every now and then, and I keep an eye on yours too.'

'Hah! So, it *was* you who left the little bunch of wildflowers on my parents' grave? I sort of guessed it might be.'

'Well, just for old time's sake, Ben' she admitted. '…I mean, I couldn't ignore your parents' grave when I was looking after mine, could I?' She paused uncertainly. 'Anyway Ben, how on earth did you find me?'

'Bit of a long story, April! But here I am talking to you again. Difficult to believe, isn't it after so long? And you don't sound a bit different! You know, I've never really stopped thinking about you in all these years. We once meant so much to each other in our younger days, didn't we? I just thought that it would be nice to make contact with you again – being old friends and all that. We're both getting on a bit now, aren't we, and old friends become more and more important, don't they?'

'Oh, yes Ben, they do. And I'm so glad you *did* find me. I've thought a lot about finding you too, but I guessed you'd be happily married by now, so it wouldn't have been fair of me to try. Robert and I split up you know…the divorce finally came through…oh, only about five years ago, but we were separated for years before that. I moved to Craster to begin my new life once we went our different ways – I couldn't bear to stay in Alnwick with him still living in our old home with his lady friends. He's been married twice since we divorced. He's the manager of the bank there, you know. Anyway, I'm much happier by myself, and I'm here quite settled now.' she said.

Rather than admit that he'd already heard the Alnwick scuttlebutt of April's divorce and her former husband's racy reputation, Ben thought it wise to circumnavigate this point. 'Oh, I'm so sorry to hear that, April. I don't mean to pry, but I'm surprised that some handsome chap hasn't snapped you up yet?'

There was a bit of a derisive snort from April. 'I don't get to meet many handsome chaps up here on the North Sea coast – except some burly fishermen, and all the men around here are a bit too young for me!' she laughed. 'Perhaps I'm still waiting for my Prince Charming to turn up? Perhaps he just has?' she said, laughing again. '*You're* still happily married, I suppose?' This bit of mischief was added in a light and humorous tone, but Ben sensed some seriousness behind it.

'Never have been, April,' Ben answered plainly. 'I got close a couple of times, but never close enough.'

Ben could have said a lot more, but not then. There therefore followed another short and uncertain silence as he wondered if he should risk taking the next step. He fed another ten-penny piece into the apparatus early to keep his credit topped up. He wouldn't want beeps on the line to reveal that he was calling from a local telephone kiosk just yet – and so spoil the huge surprise that he was about to spring.

'Sounds as if we should meet, April. How about it?' said Ben at last, containing his amusement with some difficulty.

'Oh yes, Ben, that would be very nice. Are you likely to be coming up this way? You're still working at Boscombe Down, aren't you? Still flying?'

'Yes, still at Boscombe and still flying from time to time, although the old Mossie retired long ago – and so will I be next month. I was given a back seat ride in the Tornado as my send off a few weeks back. My goodness, how things have moved on since my Lancaster days!'

Ben was getting close to springing his surprise and was barely able to stop himself bursting into laughter at the thought of her likely reaction. 'Anyway, I'm fairly free these days, April, so I could make it up to see you any time. When would suit you?' He was milking the moment.

'I'm not planning to go anywhere for a while, Ben. You name the date and place and I'll be there.'

April could not have seen Ben's wide grin, but she may have sensed it in his voice. 'Then how about meeting at

The Jolly Fisherman in Craster, if that's where you are?' He was toying with her now, pretending that he didn't know exactly where she lived.

'Oh yes, that would be lovely, Ben! But when, Ben, how soon?' she replied, excitedly.

'How about eleven o'clock this morning, April? Today! I'm already here!'

Sitting in the lounge bar of the Jolly Fisherman over a coffee and croissant while waiting for April to arrive was too much for Ben. Not only was he impatient for the coming meeting, but it also reminded him too much of the time he had waited for Daisy in the pub in Salisbury, which brought back uneasy memories of her tragic death. He decided instead to walk back towards the harbour and found a low stone wall to sit on halfway down the hill that gave him a view across the harbour to the row of pretty cottages in which he now knew April lived. It was twenty minutes before he saw a female figure emerging from one of the front doors in the row of frontages that had formed the backdrop to where he had sat earlier. At first, Ben could not be sure that it was April, but as the figure made her way around the harbour and started up the slope towards him, there was no mistaking her. There was something unmistakable about her walk and the way she held her head that took his mind right back to the times he used to meet her walking home from work. She wore a hip-length Barbour jacket over a flowery shirt and a plain plaid skirt. Her figure seemed a little fuller than he remembered, and her fair hair had lost the wavy fullness it once had. But he liked the way she was not trying to hide the few grey wisps that were appearing (hating those artificial tints that some women use to disguise their aging), and she wore it neatly styled. As she came nearer, still apparently unaware that he was sitting patiently on the wall halfway up the slope, her features could be seen more clearly. The sun's bright rays brought colour to her cheeks, her face was kindly and pleasantly homely, and her clear blue eyes looked out above lips that held the enigmatic smile that Ben remembered from a distant past. Ben sat so still that she was within ten yards of him before she realised that her old beau was right in front of her, and the sudden sight of him stopped her in her tracks. Momentarily, she seemed to lose her balance and she reached out to steady herself on the same low wall on which Ben sat, the broad grin on his face now reflecting hers. Ben rose to his feet to greet her.

'Ben!' she exclaimed breathlessly, as her eyes sparkled with a look that showed that she was as excited to see him as he was to see her.

Epilogue

Ben and April spent the rest of that day together talking of old times and getting to know each other again. They strolled around the harbour, came back to the Jolly Fisherman for a mid-morning coffee and later for lunch, and they walked the coastal footpath to and from the ancient castle ruins. They then sat for a long time on Ben's wooden bench enjoying the warm afternoon sunshine while gazing at the sea, all that while unwinding the lost past in telling each other the stories of their lives. Conversation between the pair was so comfortable and spontaneous that they might have been a married couple who'd never been apart. Passers-by must have thought them just that, while April's neighbours smiled at her knowingly from their front gardens.

But, as individuals, their lives were now so different and so separate, that even if both had thought of it often, the prospect of marriage or living together seemed too big a step even to contemplate. With April's son's and daughter's families living nearby, her lovely grandchildren and her friends, neighbours, and activities also so much a part of her life, Craster had become a beloved home. Ben, similarly, was now a Wiltshire man with roots put down, and such a volume of friends, former colleagues and commitments to tie him there that he would not want to abandon everything and everyone to move away. The idea that either April or Ben should uproot and transplant themselves into the other's domain was just too unsettling. While it was obvious that love for each other had been rekindled, the flames of that love could no longer be fanned by sexual desire that might in their younger days have swept such sensible thinking aside. Instead, their love had matured into a true and caring friendship, founded in their childhood relationship as sweethearts and laced with nostalgia and the regrets of times lost. Ben would spend the following week with April in her home, enjoying their reunion, filling each quiet day with outings, domesticity, and walks by the sea – with the occasional evening on the Jolly Fisherman's sun deck with a glass of something in their hands while wistfully gazing at the sea.

Ben drove his campervan back to Wiltshire after an enchanting week with April in her cottage, feeling that he had finally found the friendship and companionship that he had sought. During that week, he and April had promised themselves to each other irrevocably for what was left of their existence on this earth, yet both would retain the independence of their settled lives. It was a bond that would span the distance and the time that sometimes separated them. They would telephone each other weekly, send gifts from time to time, write often, and meet several times a year – spending weeks at a time together here and there – in Northumberland, in Wiltshire, and sometimes in-between. And they would always be in each other's thoughts.

How things would develop as the pair aged into their seventies and beyond, we will have to wait and see, but for the time being, both were content with the understanding that had been built between them. They had resumed their friendship after four long decades apart, and they had now bound themselves together in a true and uncomplicated relationship that was undemandingly platonic yet intimately warm and comforting. It was also a relationship that left them both free to live their own lives.

It suited them both.

If you have enjoyed reading Finding April, you might like to read other books by Ron Burrows:

Fiction

An American Exile
Fortune's Hostage
The Road to Fort Duquesne

Non-fiction

Cold War Test Pilot
A personal memoir of the author's life as a fighter pilot and test pilot in the Royal Air Force.

About the Author

Ron Burrows was born in 1943 and grew up in the Vale of Evesham in the heart of England. He spent the first half of his professional life in the Royal Air Force. He was first a fighter pilot, then a flying instructor, and then a fast-jet test pilot testing many Cold War military aircraft including the Harrier 'jump-jet' and the supersonic, swing-wing Tornado. In twenty years of test flying, he rose to become the chief test pilot at the UK's experimental flight test centre at Boscombe Down. After leaving the RAF, he became in turn the principal of a post-graduate flight-test engineering school and the vice-principal of a city further education college. Since retiring from full-time employment in 2003, he has been a magistrate, a hospital director, a charity director in Tanzania, a health-service company chairman, and more recently a published author. 'Finding April' is his fourth novel.